ANIMAL INSTINCTS

"Please don't!" Margaret whispered, clutching at his shirt. "You haven't seen it like I have! It's gigantic! If it sees you, it'll do to you like it did to Pa."

"I can run fast when I have to." Grinning, Fargo patted her head. "Close the door after me, then bar it."

Fargo glided to the corral and along it to where the broken rails lay. He had sixty feet of open space to cross but first he removed his spurs. Their jingling might give him away. Placing each boot with care, he moved in a crouch, stopping every few yards to look and listen. Warily, he edged toward the opening.

Suddenly there was a sniffing sound, followed by a guttural grunt. Then silence. Fargo froze.

Tense moments passed. Then, abruptly, for no reason Fargo could fathom, he experienced an overwhelming premonition that he was in great peril. But the doorway was empty. The thing was still inside.

That was when the Ovaro whinnied. Fargo could just make the stallion out in the gloom. It was staring at him, he thought. Or was it? Looking closer, he realized, it was staring at something *behind* him. . . .

A GIANT
TRAILSMAN
ADVENTURE

MENAGERIE
OF MALICE

by

Jon Sharpe

A SIGNET BOOK

SIGNET
Published by New American Library, a division of
Penguin Group (USA) Inc., 375 Hudson Street,
New York, New York 10014, U.S.A.
Penguin Books Ltd, 80 Strand,
London WC2R 0RL, England
Penguin Books Australia Ltd, 250 Camberwell Road,
Camberwell, Victoria 3124, Australia
Penguin Books Canada Ltd, 10 Alcorn Avenue,
Toronto, Ontario, Canada M4V 3B2
Penguin Books (N.Z.) Ltd, Cnr Rosedale and Airborne Roads,
Albany, Auckland 1310, New Zealand

Penguin Books Ltd, Registered Offices:
80 Strand, London WC2R 0RL, England

First published by Signet, an imprint of New American Library,
a division of Penguin Group (USA) Inc.

First Printing, February 2004
10 9 8 7 6 5 4 3 2 1

PUBLISHER'S NOTE
This is a work of fiction. Names, characters, places, and incidents either are
the product of the author's imagination or are used fictitiously, and any resemblance to actual persons, living or dead, business establishments, events, or
locales is entirely coincidental.

The Trailsman

Beginnings . . . they bend the tree and they mark the man. Skye Fargo was born when he was eighteen. Terror was his midwife, vengeance his first cry. Killing spawned Skye Fargo, ruthless, cold-blooded murder. Out of the acrid smoke of gunpowder still hanging in the air, he rose, cried out a promise never forgotten.

The Trailsman they began to call him all across the West: searcher, scout, hunter, the man who could see where others only looked, his skills for hire but not his soul, the man who lived each day to the fullest, yet trailed each tomorrow. Skye Fargo, the Trailsman, the seeker who could take the wildness of a land and the wanting of a woman and make them his own.

Utah Territory, 1861—
Where nightmares come real
and the unknown is as deadly
as the bite of a rattler.

1

From a distance the homestead appeared to be deserted. There was a log cabin, a corral, and a barn, with no sign of life anywhere. It was typical of countless others Skye Fargo had come across in his travels, and he didn't give it a second glance as he wound along the trail that paralleled the Strawberry River.

Fargo was on his way west after treating himself to a few days of whiskey, poker, and friendly doves in Oro City. Every time he closed his eyes, he could still feel a certain lovely dove's warm arms around his neck and her soft red lips on his mouth. She had been the kind of gal who put zest in a man's step, and reminded him why he *was* a man to begin with.

Squinting skyward, Fargo pulled his hat brim low against the glare of the sun. His muscular frame was clothed in buckskins. Around his neck was a red bandanna, a gun belt around his waist. He was tanned so dark, he might be mistaken for an Indian if not for his lake-blue eyes. As he neared the homestead he noticed a few things he hadn't noticed before.

The place looked as if a tornado had hit it. Part of the cabin roof had been ripped off and lay in pieces on the ground. Several holes had been punched in the wall by the corral, and eight or nine corral rails lay

1

splintered in the dirt. The barn had suffered the worst. One of its wide double doors was torn half off, and there was a huge jagged hole where the east wall had been.

Fargo's eyes narrowed. From the way the planks were splayed outward, whatever made the hole had burst out of the barn from within. But that couldn't be. The hole was three or four times the size of a bull buffalo. Maybe a freak wind was to blame, he reckoned.

Life on the frontier was hard. Nature was a merciless mistress, as many green-as-grass settlers found out to their dismay. From every state they came, flocking west in the hopes of making a new start. Fertile land was theirs for the taking, but keeping it was another matter. Drought, floods, and tempests spoiled many a dream. Hostiles, wild beasts, and cutthroats ended many more.

Fargo never had any interest in homesteading, himself. He could never tie himself to one spot for that long. A streak of wanderlust as wide as the Mississippi River ran through him, forever spurring him to see what lay over the next horizon.

The settlers who chose this particular spot for their new home didn't choose wisely. The site was too near the river, for one thing; the buildings might be washed away with the next big flood. It was also too close to the woods, making it easy for hostile Indians to sneak in close.

The trail passed within fifty feet of the cabin, and Fargo was almost abreast of it when a strange sound caused him to rein up. He tilted his head, listening intently, unsure if he had heard what he thought he heard or if it was a trick of the breeze. Cupping a hand to his mouth, he called out, "Is anyone there?"

When he received no reply, Fargo clucked to the Ovaro and continued on his way. But he went only a dozen feet when he heard the strange sound again. This time there could be no mistake.

Placing his right hand on the butt of his Colt, Fargo reined toward the cabin. "What's wrong?" he hollered.

The door was shut but there were two windows and neither had curtains. Fargo plainly heard sniffling and low sobs. He halted about twenty feet out and tried again. "Do you need help?"

A flurry of whispers ensued, then a loud, "Hush!" The voices were thin and high-pitched and filled with fear. A wooden latch scraped and the door opened a crack.

"Go away, mister!"

Fargo saw a green eye peering at him about level with the latch. "Are your folks home, girl?"

The eye blinked. "How do you know I'm not a boy?"

"I have ears."

She responded in a rush, as if she could not get the words out fast enough. "Well, our folks are off chopping wood and we're not supposed to talk to people we don't know so you turn around and ride on because we don't need your help."

"Suit yourself," Fargo said. He lifted his reins to leave, then heard someone else whisper.

"Tell him the truth, Margaret!"

The eye at the crack disappeared. "You hush, Priscilla! I'm the oldest and I'm in charge and we'll do what I say!"

"Maybe he can help!"

"He's a stranger and you know what Ma always says about strangers."

3

A third voice chimed in, this time that of a small boy. "He's a grown-up and we need a grown-up bad."

"We don't need anyone, Timmy."

"But they might die," Timmy said, sounding on the verge of tears. "Please, Margaret. We need to do something."

Fargo had heard enough. Dismounting, he stepped to the door and knocked. Instantly, the bickering stopped. The door opened a few inches wider and, without warning, he found himself looking down the muzzle of a Sharps.

"Go away." At the other end of the barrel was a cherubic face streaked with grime and topped by a tangled mop of blond curls. The rifle was so heavy she couldn't hold it steady. "Go away right this second."

"Where are your parents?" Fargo asked.

"I told you. Off chopping wood. Now get on that paint of yours and skedaddle or I'll shoot you."

"You need to cock it first."

"What?"

"You have to pull back the hammer before you can fire," Fargo explained. "I should know. I owned a Sharps once."

The girl raised her cheek from the stock. "I guess I should have paid more attention when Pa shot game." She held the rifle nearly vertical, with the muzzle now pointing at the ceiling, and curled her thumb around the hammer. "It's awful nice of you to be so obliging."

"Think nothing of it," Fargo said. Grabbing the Sharps, he tore it from her grasp and shouldered the door open.

Margaret screeched and sprang back, planting herself protectively in front of a younger sister and brother, both of whom recoiled in fright at Fargo's abrupt entrance. Like her, they had straw-colored hair and were smudged with dirt from head to toe. "You tricked me!" Margaret howled.

"That I did," Fargo conceded, cradling the rifle. He guessed her age as twelve or thirteen. The other girl was a year or two younger, the boy not more than eight or nine. "I'm going to ask you one more time where your parents are. And I want you to tell me the truth."

"I've already told you!" Margaret blustered, clenching her small fists. She was so mad, she was livid. "Now get out! I won't let you harm us!"

Fargo stared at her brother. "Timmy, isn't it? What was that you said about someone dying?"

"Ma and Pa were hurt—" the boy began, but fell silent when Margaret spun and punched him on the arm.

"Quiet, darn you! How do we know we can trust him?"

The other girl, Priscilla, put her hand on Margaret's shoulder. "Maybe we should take the chance. We've done all we can and it's not enough."

"No!" Margaret stamped a foot.

Timmy gazed at the nearest window and said in a breathless whisper, *"But what if it comes back tonight?"*

"What if what comes back?" Fargo asked, and all three children swapped fearful glances. He was going to question them further but just then he heard a groan from a doorway to his right. He started toward it, only to stop when Margaret threw herself at him and wrapped her spindly arms around his left leg.

"Don't go in there! I want you to leave!"

Bending, Fargo carefully but forcefully pried her off. "Listen to me, girl. All I want to do is help. The next hombre who comes along might not be so obliging. Or it could be hostiles."

Uncertainty twisted Margaret's smooth features. "I don't know," she said softly, to herself more than to him. "I just don't know what to do."

Fargo held out the Sharps. "Here. If it will make you feel safer, take this." When she gasped in surprise, he shoved it into her hands and stepped to the doorway. It was a bedroom. A man and a woman lay on their backs on the quilt bedspread, the man's homespun clothes caked with dried blood, the woman's dress ripped and splattered with red drops.

"What in blazes happened?" Fargo went to the woman first. She groaned when he lightly touched her right leg, which was swollen to twice the size of the other. The reason was obvious—broken bone bulged against the skin, threatening to rip through her flesh.

The children followed him in, Timmy with tears in his eyes, Priscilla sniffling.

"They're both in an awful terrible way, mister. Pa is hurt the worst," Margaret said.

"It picked him up and threw him," Timmy mentioned.

"What did?" Fargo asked, shifting his attention to the father. The man's shoulder had been ripped open, accounting for all the blood, but his mouth was also flecked with scarlet, a possible sign of internal damage. He glanced at Margaret. "Put water on to boil." Then at Priscilla. "I need boards I can use to make splints." Then at the boy. "I also need an old shirt or a sheet or anything I can bind the splints with." When they stood there staring numbly at their parents, he smacked his hands together, startling them out of their daze. "Get a move on! You want your folks to get better, don't you?"

That did the trick. They rushed out, leaving him to gingerly probe the woman's leg to gauge the extent of the break. It appeared to be a clean one, midway down her shin. Setting it would not be hard.

Timmy returned first, with a towel.

Sliding his Arkansas Toothpick from its ankle sheath on his right ankle, Fargo cut the towel into three-inch strips. By the time he was done, Priscilla rushed in carrying several short, dusty boards.

"I took these from the woodshed. I didn't know which would be best so I brought all there was."

Fargo chose two and placed them on the bed, one on either side of the woman's broken leg. As soon as Margaret joined them, he had her climb on the bed and kneel on her mother's left leg to pin it to the bed. He had Priscilla apply her weight to the woman's left wrist, Timmy to the right. "It's important you hold her down," he cautioned them. "I can't set the bone if she moves around."

He had to work swiftly. First, he removed the woman's shoe, which took some doing, her foot was so swollen. Then, grasping it firmly, he braced himself and slowly pulled. The bone shifted, the bulge disappeared. He clamped his hands around the break and had Priscilla hand him the two boards. Once they were flush on either side, he tightly wrapped the strips around the splints to hold them in place. He wasn't a doctor and he didn't do the best job in the world but it would suffice.

As Fargo was tying the last knot, the mother stirred. She mumbled something and her eyelids fluttered. Suddenly they opened wide and she cried out, "It's coming right at us!" She tried to sit up, then looked around in confusion. "What's going on?" She glanced at Fargo, then at the splint. "Oh."

7

"You can get off her now," Fargo told the kids. He sat on the edge of the bed and introduced himself. "How did you and your husband get so busted up?"

"We were attacked." The woman turned toward her husband. "George! How is he? That thing had hold of him."

"What thing?"

She went as pale as a sheet of paper. "I'm not rightly sure what it was, mister. About ten o'clock last night we heard noises out at the barn and went to see what was making the racket." She stopped and trembled, then regained enough composure to offer her hand. "Where are my manners? I'm Rebecca Hagen. I can't thank you enough for stopping to help."

"Tell me more about the thing that did this."

"After it tossed George, I went running around the corral to help and it came right through the side of the barn and bowled me over."

Fargo recalled the huge hole with the boards splayed outward. "Are you saying a bear or a buffalo was to blame?"

"They couldn't throw my husband like that thing did. Or make the hideous sounds it did. When he went running into the barn, I would have sworn that all the demons of the pits had been unleashed. The next thing I knew, George came sailing out of there like he'd been slung from a catapult. Thirty feet or better, I reckon. He hit the ground so hard, I was afraid every bone in his body had been busted."

Fargo was trying to make sense of her account. "You had to see what did it."

"I'm not quite sure what I saw," Rebecca said. "It was pitch-dark, and it all happened so fast. The creature was there one second, gone the next. I was lucky it didn't step on me or I'd be smashed to a pulp." She opened her arms wide and her children eagerly snuggled close. "I was able to help drag George in here, then I must have passed out."

"We've been so scared, Ma," Timmy said. "We were afraid Pa and you would die and we'd be all alone."

"Tell us what to do and we'll do it," Margaret volunteered.

Fargo turned to the father. Internal wounds required a physician's care, and to the best of his knowledge, there wasn't a sawbones within hundreds of miles. "I was fixing to get your husband out of those blood-soaked clothes but maybe I shouldn't." Moving him could make the injuries worse than they already were.

"What we need is a doctor," Rebecca echoed his sentiments. "They have a couple in Salt Lake City, I hear tell."

"I can bring one," Fargo proposed. At gunpoint, if necessary. "I'll light a shuck right this minute."

Margaret uncurled. "But we'd be all alone. And the sun goes down in a couple of hours."

Priscilla nodded. "Whatever is out there might come back. It could break in here without half trying and kill us before we made it out the door."

"Please don't go," Timmy begged.

Fargo had no hankering to play nursemaid to a bunch of settlers, but he couldn't bring himself to ride off and leave them. Besides, this whole business had piqued his curiosity. He'd like to see the cause of all the destruction for himself. If it was a buffalo, it was the biggest damn buff since the dawn of creation. And if it was a grizzly, it had to be stopped before attacking humans became a habit. "I suppose I can stick around

9

a while." He slid off the bed. "But first I have to tend to my horse. And I'd like to see the tracks this thing made." That, alone, would settle the issue.

"I'll show you." Timmy was off the bed before anyone could stop him and held the front door open. "After you."

"Did you get a look at what attacked your parents?" Fargo asked as he led the Ovaro toward the barn.

"I saw something," the boy said. "It was as big as our cabin, with legs like tree trunks, and had a snake for a nose."

No creature on the continent fit that description but Fargo kept his skepticism to himself. He was a few yards past the corral when he saw the first of the strange prints. They brought him up short in amazement. "Are these the thing's tracks?"

"Yes, sir," Timmy confirmed. "My pa takes me hunting with him a lot, but I've never seen anything like them."

Neither had Fargo. They were as round as pie plates, and just as big. Judging by how deeply they sank into the hard-packed soil, whatever made them had to weigh tons. The imprint of the soles reminded him of leathery skin. He saw what appeared to be toe marks, but if so, they were the strangest toes he ever saw.

"Any idea what it was?"

Shaking his head, Fargo entered the barn. Evidently the Hagens had left the double doors open and their nocturnal visitor had helped itself to some oats in the feed bin. Along about then George Hagen had come rushing in and had been sent flying. Then, instead of barreling out the front, the thing had crashed right through the wall. He examined the planks, each half an inch thick. The strength the feat had taken was prodigious.

"You should have heard it, mister," Timmy remarked. "I almost wet myself, I was so scared."

Fargo scanned the rippling sea of grass beyond the homestead and wondered if the thing would come back to finish its interrupted meal.

"I wish Pa had killed it when he shot at it."

"No one mentioned that before," Fargo said.

"He had his Sharps with him. We all heard one shot but I can't say for sure whether he hit the thing."

"Did you look for blood?" Fargo asked, doing so himself.

"We were too worried about Ma and Pa to bother," the boy said. "And we've been inside ever since."

A thorough search turned up no evidence the thing had been hurt. In a way Fargo was glad. Wounded animals were always doubly dangerous, and much more prone to attack.

Timmy looked westward. "The sun will set in an hour or so. What do you think we should do?"

"For now let's go back inside." Fargo had decided against leaving the Ovaro in the barn. Whatever made the strange tracks could kill it without half trying. Instead, he took the stallion to the front of the cabin. Before going in, he shucked his Henry rifle from its saddle scabbard.

Rebecca Hagen had sat up and was applying a compress to her husband's forehead. "George has a fever." Beside her, holding a bucket, was Margaret. Priscilla had several wet cloths. They had been used to clean blood from George's face and shoulder, and were stained crimson.

"Any idea what it was?" Rebecca asked.

"None," Fargo admitted. But he would like to find out. "If you don't mind, I'll stay over until morning."

"Mind?" Rebecca's laugh was brittle. "You might be the only hope we have of making it through the night. If that horrid monstrosity comes back, there's no telling what it will do."

"Was there any sign of that thing before last night?"

"No. None. We've had a few problems with coyotes and raccoons, but that's all." Rebecca reflected a moment. "Oh. And a black bear about six months ago. It tried to get at our horses one night."

"Where are your horses now?"

"Two ran off when that beast broke down the corral. They must be halfway to Denver. The other two are tied out behind the woodshed."

Gritting her teeth, Rebecca slid her good leg over the edge of the bed.

"What do you think you're doing, Ma?" Margaret wanted to know.

The mother placed her hands flat on the bed. "What does it look like, daughter? I've been in bed nearly all day. It's high time I made myself useful. I'm sure all of you must be famished. Fetch me the broom so I can use it as a crutch."

Margaret put down the bucket. "You should rest, Ma. I'm old enough to make supper on my own."

Rebecca bunched her shoulders to try to stand anyway.

"Your daughter is right," Fargo said, coming over and placing a hand on her shoulder. "That busted bone won't set if you're hobbling all over the place." The glance she cast at him mirrored uncertainty. Here she was, entrusting her family's welfare to a total stranger. She was taking a great gamble and it naturally troubled her. "I won't let anything happen to your family." He sought to ease her worries.

Frowning, Rebecca sat back and tried to revive her husband. But although she gently shook him again and again, he didn't stir. "If anything happens to him," she said forlornly, "I don't know what I'll do."

Fargo understood. A woman alone, with children to support, had few options, none of them attractive. Jobs were few and paid little. "I'll go see how Margaret is doing."

It turned out the Hagens had a root cellar, and an amply stocked one, at that. Soon the cabin was fragrant with the tantalizing aroma of roast venison and sweet potato pie. Margaret was a fine cook, which didn't surprise Fargo any. Frontier girls learned early how to do all the things their mothers did, and to do them well, since one day they would be called on to do them for families of their own.

The meal perked everyone's spirits. Rebecca was fed in bed. She tried to get some food down her husband's throat but he wouldn't swallow.

While the kids did the dishes, Fargo claimed his rifle and went outside. The sun was about to relinquish its rule of the sky to budding stars. He made a circuit of the barn and the house but the only wildlife he saw were a few sparrows flitting among the trees and several deer slaking their thirst on the far side of the river.

That reminded him. Fargo took the Ovaro to a water trough by the corral. By then the sun was a golden sliver. The wind picked up, as it invariably did at that time of the day, rustling the nearby cottonwoods and oaks. Somewhere close by, a jay squawked.

Fargo tied the Ovaro in front of the cabin and stepped to the door. It opened before he could touch it.

"There you are!" Margaret exclaimed. "My ma was starting to worry and sent me to find you." She gazed past him at the gathering twilight. "You shouldn't be out here. What if that thing comes?"

"Maybe it won't," Fargo said. "Maybe it's miles away by now, and you'll never see it again."

As if to prove him wrong, from the northwest wafted a faint cry unlike any Fargo ever heard, a cry that could not come from the throat of any animal he knew. A cry so eerie and chilling that Fargo felt his breath catch in his own throat, and the skin at the nape of his neck prickle.

Margaret went as stiff as a lodge pole. "So much for your hunch," she whispered, as if afraid the thing could hear her. "Whatever that critter is, it's still out there."

2

The hours crawled by. The younger children stayed in the bedroom with their mother and their still-unconscious father, but Margaret hovered near Fargo as he stood at the window that gave him the best view of the barn. Girls her age were intensely curious, and she bubbled with questions. Fargo made it clear in his answers to her first few questions that he would not talk much about his past, so she asked about other things.

"I've never met a scout before," Margaret mentioned after he had revealed that he often scouted for the army. "Isn't it dangerous with all the hostiles there are all over the place?"

"There are just as many friendly Indians," Fargo said, "but you never hear much about them." Newspapers would rather publish lurid accounts of massacres. "I should know. I've lived with the Sioux and a few other tribes."

"Really?" Margaret's eyes grew as wide as walnuts. Seating herself in a chair, she urged, "Tell me about them. Which tribe did you like living with the best?"

"I don't have a favorite," Fargo answered. "They're all pretty much the same, even if they are all different."

"How can that be?"

Fargo turned from the window. "Take the Sioux and the Apaches. They have different customs. They have different languages. They dress differently. But they're people, like you and me. There are good ones and not-so-good ones. There are some you would be proud to call a friend and others who would stab you in the back if you gave them half the chance."

In the frank manner of those her age, Margaret asked, "Did you ever take an Indian wife?"

"I've been fond of a few Indian ladies," Fargo said, and let it go at that.

"What are they like? Polly Stanton told me that they never take baths and their hair is infested with lice and they eat animal guts raw."

Despite himself, Fargo laughed. "Stupid talk like that makes it hard for the red man and the white man to get along." Sighing, he shook his head. "Indian ladies are just as fussy as you are about their hair and the clothes they wear. They like nice dresses and to have their hair combed just right. And they like their food cooked. The only time I've seen Indians eat meat raw was when they were half-starved. I've done the same."

Margaret was more interested in the women. "Why do the ladies only wear buckskin? Why not clothes like we wear?"

"Buckskin dresses last a long time. It holds up a lot better than cotton or wool and—" Fargo stopped. He thought he'd heard a sound from over near the barn. He peered into the darkness but all was still.

"What is it?" Margaret anxiously asked.

Fargo shrugged. "Nothing, I reckon." He closed his eyes and rubbed them. It had been a long day and he needed sleep but he wasn't about to turn in with that thing out there somewhere. He glanced at the hole in the ceiling. Through it the Big Dipper and the North Star were visible.

"I've only seen a few Indians," Margaret mentioned. "Some Pawnees once, in Saint Louis. They wore their hair spiked down the middle, and they never smiled."

"It takes courage for them to visit a white man's city," Fargo noted. "They know what happened to the Mandans."

"The who?"

"A tribe that lived on the Missouri River. They were friendly as could be, and always welcomed whites to their villages. That's how they came down with smallpox and were nearly wiped out."

"Even the women and children?"

Fargo nodded. "Thousands died. And the Mandans aren't the only ones. Disease has killed more Indians than all the bullets ever made." He faced the window again. Once more he heard a sound hard to identify. Either it was his imagination, or there was a suggestion of movement near the barn doors.

"Did you see something?" Margaret quizzed him.

"I'm not sure." Fargo glanced at the Ovaro. It, too, was staring at the barn, its head high, its ears pricked. So something *was* out there. Snatching up his rifle, he reached for the latch.

"You're not going out there?"

"How else will I find out what it is?" With a little luck, Fargo thought he could reach the barn undetected.

"Please don't!" Margaret whispered, clutching at his shirt. "You haven't seen it like I have! It's gigantic! If it sees you, it'll do to you like it did to Pa."

"I can run fast when I have to." Grinning, Fargo

17

patted her head. "Close the door after me, then bar it." To keep her from arguing, he slipped out, and with his back to the wall, he crept to the corner. From the vicinity of the barn came crunching noises. The thing was eating the oats.

Fargo glided to the corral and along it to where the broken rails lay. He had sixty feet of open space to cross but first he removed his spurs. Their jingling might give him away. Placing each boot with care, he moved in a crouch, stopping every few yards to look and listen. The crunching stopped once but resumed after a few seconds. Soon he was in inky shadow to the right of the open doors. Warily, he edged toward the opening.

Suddenly there was a sniffing sound, followed by a guttural grunt. Then silence. Fargo froze. He wondered if the thing had caught his scent. He couldn't see how, when it was inside the barn and the wind was blowing the other way. He waited for the crunching to continue.

Tense moments passed. Then, abruptly, for no reason Fargo could fathom, he experienced an overwhelming premonition that he was in great peril. But the doorway was empty. The thing was still inside.

That was when the Ovaro whinnied. Fargo could just make the stallion out in the gloom. It was staring at him, he thought. Or was it? Looking closer, he realized it was staring at something *behind* him.

Belatedly, Fargo remembered the hole in the barn wall. His mouth went dry as, being careful not to make any sudden movements, he slowly twisted his head around.

It was enormous. So tall it blotted out stars. So wide it blocked part of the corral and cabin from view. Fargo had a fleeting sense of tremendous bulk and of something snakelike waving in the air. Then the thing unleashed a trumpetlike blast and bore down on him like a living avalanche.

In a burst of speed Fargo ducked inside. He couldn't begin to guess how something so huge had sneaked so close to him without him realizing it. The thing was as quiet as a ghost. A glance showed him it was framed in the doorway, and another trumpeting blast shook the walls. Then it put on a burst of speed of its own, and it was incredibly swift. Another second and it loomed above him.

Taking one more bound, Fargo dived into a horse stall. He heard a swish, then a crash and the rending of wood. Debris rained down. He covered his head with his arms and felt a sharp pain in his left shoulder and another in his right thigh.

A louder trumpeting blast sounded. Fargo still had the Henry but he was half covered by pieces of shattered stall. He kicked out with both legs to free them, and the next moment felt something wrap around his left ankle, and tighten. He reached down to free himself but whatever had hold of him gave a powerful wrench and he was swung high into the air.

The floor and the ceiling swapped places. Warm, fetid breath fanned his face as Fargo hung upside down, suspended like bait dangling from the end of a fishing line. He beheld a glittering eye fixed on him. His shoulder brushed what seemed to be a horn in the shape of a crescent moon.

The creature rumbled deep in its chest. A giant ear flapped like a bat's wing.

Recognition flooded through Fargo. On its heels came amazement. His mind refused to believe what he was seeing. He was given no time to ponder how it was possible, because the very next moment he was flung like a sack of grain toward the far wall. Certain he would suffer the same fate as George Hagen, he tried to shift in midair so his back absorbed the impact.

He hit on his side. Something soft enfolded him, something that rustled and clung to his skin and his clothes. Instead of crashing against the wall he rolled a dozen feet and wound up on his stomach, buried in whatever had cushioned the impact. Dust swirled into his eyes and nose and he suppressed an urge to sneeze. He heard another trumpeting cry, then the drum of heavy feet, rapidly receding.

Fargo slowly raised his head and looked around. He was in the hayloft, buried to his chest in hay. Sitting up, he brushed bits and pieces from his face and hair. Locating his hat took some doing. He had to grope about in the dark for minutes. Then he moved to the ladder.

The thing was gone.

Climbing down, Fargo searched for his rifle. He had dropped it when the thing swept him up off the ground and it lay amid the shattered stall.

The cool breeze was invigorating. Fargo mopped his sweaty brow and cautiously hurried to the corral to retrieve his spurs. He was only a few feet from the front door of the cabin when it opened and out hobbled Rebecca Hagen, a broom propped under her right arm. Behind her were her children, armed with knives and an ax. "What do you think you're doing?"

"We were coming to help," Rebecca said.

Fargo was touched. He ushered them inside and insisted the mother get back into bed.

The suspense was too much for the children. "Did you see it?" Margaret asked as he leaned the broom against the bedpost. "Do you know what hurt our folks?"

"Yes, on both counts." All were eyes on him as Fargo moved to the foot of the bed. "It's an elephant."

Rebecca's mouth dropped open. "That can't be! I've read about them. They're found in Africa or some such, aren't they? There aren't any elephants in the wilds of Utah Territory."

"There is one now." It defied logic, but Fargo couldn't deny the evidence of his own eyes or the bruises and scrapes on his body.

"What's an elephant?" Timmy piped up.

"A big animal with no hair and floppy ears and teeth as long as a pitchfork," Margaret answered.

"They call those tusks," Fargo said. "They're made of ivory." And ivory was extremely valuable, as valuable in its way as gold.

Rebecca couldn't get over it. "But what is an elephant doing *here*? This is the last place on earth one should be."

Fargo couldn't dispute that. "There has to be an explanation. Maybe we'll learn more when I find it."

"You're going after that brute?"

"In the morning." Fargo would never forgive himself if he didn't unravel the mystery. Margaret wasn't the only one with a strong sense of curiosity. "Tracking it shouldn't be hard." Although what he would do when he *found* it, he couldn't say.

Timmy, Priscilla, and Margaret all started talking at once but hushed up when George Hagen uttered a low gasp and raised his head off the bed. "The monster!" he cried, then caught himself. "Where am I? What happened?"

His wife leaned close and placed a hand on his cheek. "You're safe, George. It's all right. We got you inside." She pressed her palm to his forehead. "You still have a fever. How do you feel?"

Hagen ignored her momentarily. He had seen Fargo, and he reacted as would most any husband and father at finding a stranger in his house. "Wait a minute. Who are you, mister? Where did you come from?"

"Calm down, George," Rebecca soothed. "He's a friend."

"I never saw him before," George truculently responded. He tried to rise but his outburst had cost him in energy and effort, and he sank onto his back, saying, "I hurt inside something awful."

"We should see about getting some food into you," Rebecca said, and instructed the children to bring some venison and a cup of tea.

Fargo was left on his own. He stripped his saddle and saddle blanket from the Ovaro and deposited them in the front room. Moving a rocking chair to one side, he spread out his bedroll in a corner where he would be out of the way, and stretched out. He wanted to get an early start so it was best he turn in.

Sleep, though, proved elusive. Fargo could not stop thinking about the elephant, and how close he had come to being killed by it. He marveled at how quiet it had been, as quiet as a mountain lion, yet it was as big as a mountain. An exaggeration, but there was no denying it was the largest animal he had ever encountered, yet it could move as silently as the smallest.

Fargo had to admit to feeling a certain amount of excitement at the prospect of tracking a creature he had never tracked before. Grizzlies, black bears, wolverines, wolves—he had tracked them all at one time or another. Buffalo, moose, mountain sheep—he could read their signs with the same ease most men read books. But an elephant! Here was something new. A unique challenge, the likes of which would never come again. He could hardly wait.

Slumber claimed him, and once he drifted off, Fargo slept undisturbed until the crack of dawn, when, as was his habit, he invariably woke up. The stove had gone out but it did not take long to rekindle the flames and reheat what was left of the coffee. The Hagens were sound asleep, the parents in their bedroom, the children bundled in blankets near the fireplace.

Fargo tried not to wake anyone. He was at the table, sipping his second cup, when Margaret padded over, wrapped from curly head to bare toes in a blanket.

"You're still fixing to go after that critter?"

"Someone has to." Fargo left unsaid the fact that the elephant might keep returning to their homestead, with dire consequences.

"What will you do when you catch up to it? Ma says you can't shoot something that big."

She had a point. Fargo's Henry was all right for dropping most game, including deer and an occasional elk. It could drop a buffalo or a grizzly if he had to, although he would prefer to avoid putting it to the test. An elephant, on the other hand, was so enormous, and so massive, he would need a cannon to bring it down. "I'll cross that bridge when I come to it."

"Will we ever see you again?"

Fargo hadn't given it any thought. He was bound for Seattle and couldn't afford to dally too long in any one place.

"Please say yes. We don't get many visitors. Ma was

hoping you would make it back for supper tonight so we can thank you good and proper for all you've done for us." Margaret paused. "We'll have other company, too. Later this morning I'm to ride to our nearest neighbors, the Stantons, and invite them over. Pa wants to tell them all about the elephant."

"You should stick close to home with that thing on the loose," Fargo said.

"Shucks. Belle can outrun any critter that lives," the girl boasted. "I'm not worried."

"Belle?"

"Our mare. I've ridden her since I was knee-high to a cricket. Our sorrel, Clyde, is almost as fast, but he ran off, the coward."

"I'll keep my eyes skinned for sign of him," Fargo promised, and gulped the last of his coffee. He had already rolled up his bedroll and tied his saddlebags so all he had to do was throw them and his saddle over his shoulder, and with his rifle and the saddle blanket in his other hand, he went out. Dawn was always one of his favorite times of the day, a time when the world seemed fresh and new, and the river and woods were awash in its rosy glow.

Margaret followed and watched while he saddled up. "Be careful. I'd hate for that monster to stomp you flatter than a flapjack."

"That makes two of us." Fargo gigged the Ovaro past the corral and on around the barn. The elephant had left signs the girl could follow. Its tracks led straight to the trees bordering the river where it had barreled into the vegetation like a steam engine gone amok, crushing everything and anything in its path, leaving a swath of destruction yards wide.

From there the trail led west for several miles. Flat-tened grass showed where it slid down the bank to a gravel bar. From there it waded a deep pool. More flattened grass on the other side marked the spot where it had climbed out. Apparently its fury was spent because from then on it barely disturbed a twig. Several times over the next hour Fargo had to dismount and search for spoor. He would not have thought an animal that size could leave so little evidence of its passing. Had he not known better, he would think he was after a will-o'-the-wisp.

Midmorning came and went. Fargo expected to find where the elephant had stopped to rest but it never slackened its pace. It had somewhere it wanted to be and was in a hurry to get there.

By noon Fargo accepted he was in for a long chase. Twice he came on droppings that dwarfed a buffalo's, and at one point discovered where his quarry had fed on succulent shoots and stripped bark from some saplings.

By three Fargo had a decision to make. He could push on or he could turn back and take the Hagens up on their supper invitation. Hoping Margaret wouldn't be too disappointed, he pushed on.

By six that evening the elephant was still miles ahead and showed no indication of tiring. Fargo began to scout about for a spot to make camp and shortly before dark settled on a clearing close to the river. He didn't bother gathering firewood. Campfires could be seen a long way off, and while he had no idea how good an elephant's eyesight was, he didn't care to risk it spotting him.

His saddle for a pillow, Fargo chewed on a piece of jerky and contemplated his options when he caught up with the beast. He didn't want to kill it but that begged the question: What else *could* he do? It wasn't a longhorn to be roped and corralled. It wasn't a buffalo, to be skinned and eaten. But clearly something had to be done to prevent a repetition of the calamity at the Hagen homestead.

Dreamland claimed Fargo with the issue unresolved, and his first thought on awakening at the crack of the new day was the same as when he fell asleep. What should he do? Since he had no fire and couldn't make coffee, he dropped onto his belly and plunged his head into the river to get his blood flowing. The cold water did the trick.

Day two was no different from day one. The elephant had not slowed all night and now was twice as far ahead. Fargo brought the pinto to a trot every so often to lessen the gap but by the middle of the day he was faced with the likelihood of not being able to overtake it. And after all he had been through, that wouldn't do. That wouldn't do at all.

Then an idea struck him. Fargo had been through the territory before. Eventually the river meandered to the northwest, through a series of hills, in the general direction of Salt Lake City. Maybe, just maybe, he could strike off overland and reach the hills ahead of his oversized quarry. He had to make up his mind soon, though, or there would not be enough time.

Immersed in deep thought, Fargo came to a bend in the river and skirted wide to avoid a thicket, just as the elephant had done. But once past the thicket, the tracks disappeared. He was accustomed to losing the trail now and then, and he climbed down to find it again. But this time, although he looked long and hard, he couldn't find so much as a bent blade of grass.

"This can't be," Fargo said aloud, leading the Ovaro by the reins. For some reason he was reminded of an incident years ago when he had gone after a marauding grizzly and tracked the man-killer into the high country only to lose its trail in a talus strewn canyon. He spent half a day trying to find the bear's tracks again, without success, and finally headed down the mountain in defeat. He had his rifle across his saddle, and it was a good thing he did, because as he came to the mouth of the canyon, the bear rushed him. It had circled around behind and waited in ambush for just the right moment.

Circled around behind him. Fargo halted dead in his tracks. He pretended to study the ground while probing the undergrowth from under the brim of his hat. Other than a few birds cavorting in a tree and a butterfly fluttering from flower to flower, the woods were as still as a cemetery. He told himself he was being silly, that the elephant had no way of knowing he was after it. He was wasting time better spent on the go.

Fargo reached for his saddle horn and hiked his boot to slide it into the stirrup His gaze drifted beyond the saddle to thick brush cloaked in what he took to be a patch of dark shadow. But something about the shadow struck him as out of place. He couldn't quite say exactly why until one of the shadow's ears moved.

In a heartbeat Fargo was on the Ovaro and spurring it westward, but even as he vaulted into the saddle, the forest rocked to the trumpeting cry of a behemoth from another continent, and the elephant hurtled into the open. Its trunk high, its ears wide, it was faster than a charging griz.

For a few harrowing seconds Fargo's life hung in the balance. He raked his spurs and the Ovaro gained enough ground to spare him from imminent death but not enough to place them safely out of harm's way.

The elephant never slowed, never slackened. If Fargo had been on foot, he would be dead. Spying a thick low limb ahead, he smiled. He could duck underneath it but his pursuer was much too big and must go around. Bending low, he galloped past the tree and shifted in the saddle just as the creature's broad skull made contact. The limb exploded in a shower of fragments, and the elephant never broke stride.

With all the twists and turns the river made, Fargo couldn't gain the lead he needed. He palmed his Colt. Gunshots often drove off other animals, why not the elephant? He fired three times into the ground in front of it. Either the elephant didn't care or it was deaf because the shots had no effect. He had to try something else.

An idea presented itself when Fargo galloped around the next bend. The river narrowed, and on the near side was a strip of mud seven or eight feet wide. The mud wouldn't slow the Ovaro, but what about an animal that weighed ten times as much? Reining sharply, Fargo flew to the edge of the bank and left the rest up to the stallion. The jump was worthy of a thoroughbred, a high, arcing vault that cleared the mud with space to spare. Then they were splashing through knee-deep water, and Fargo looked back, hoping to find the elephant floundering in the mud. Instead, it was almost on top of him.

Fargo faced around to ride for his life. Too late, he saw another low limb, this one jutting out over the water. He tried to duck but it caught him flush across the chest, and the next thing he knew, he tumbled into the river directly in the path of the onrushing colossus.

Skye Fargo came up sputtering and coughing. Water had rushed into his mouth and nose and it was several seconds before he could breathe. He saw the Ovaro on the opposite bank and started toward it but froze when a shadow fell across him. His skin crawling, he looked over his shoulder.

The elephant reared over him, its eyes boring into him with blazing intensity. Its giant ears were thrust out wide from its broad head and its trunk was poised like a rattlesnake about to strike. It uttered no sound but its breaths were like the rasps of a blacksmith's bellows. Sunlight gleamed off its ivory tusks. The tusk on the left was flawless and intact; the end of the tusk on the right had broken off, leaving a jagged tip. Fargo flinched when the trunk descended. He was sure the beast would lift him into the air as it had done at the barn, then smash him to a pulp on the rocks. But all it did was wave its trunk in front of his face and neck, all the while sniffing like a hound reading scent. He was at a loss as to what to do, whether it was best to stand stock still and hope it let him live or whether he should say or do something.

Any other animal, Fargo would know how to react. Bears, mountain lions, wolverines, buffalo—he had dealt with them all. But an elephant was something entirely new. Or was it? Animals were animals, he reasoned, and the sound of a stern human voice was all it took sometimes to make them back down. But it might not be wise to be stern in this instance, so he settled for smiling and saying, "Nice elephant."

The trunk paused in its aerial gyrations and the elephant made a sound that was a cross between a grunt and a chirp. Its head dipped lower, its eyes that much nearer. And such eyes! There was something about them, a near-human quality Fargo found disquieting. They mirrored intelligence to rival his own—intelligence, and something more. He had the notion the thing was taking his measure just as he would take the measure of another man. Forcing another smile, he remarked, "I've never met one of your kind before. You're a long way from home."

A gurgling snort issued from the giant beast and it slowly rose to its full height. Its trunk curled across his shoulder.

This is it, Fargo thought. He would try to get off two or three shots before it killed him. He inched his right hand to his Colt but didn't draw. The elephant wasn't picking him up. It was playing with his ear. He could feel the tip of its trunk brushing back and forth across his earlobe. "Does this mean we're friends?"

Suddenly the behemoth turned its head, its ears flapping.

Fargo had heard it, too. A peculiar musical trilling, from out of the depths of the woods. The only sound he could compare it to was a flute. The effect on the elephant was remarkable. Voicing a plaintive whine, it wheeled and raced across the river, up the other side, and off into the undergrowth.

Fargo would be damned if he would lose it again. He waded to the bank, snatched the pinto's reins, and swung up. Plunging back across the river, he rose in the stirrups and was dismayed to find the elephant had vanished. He brought the pinto to a gallop, confident he would catch up quickly but several minutes went by and he didn't come across a trace of it.

Baffled, Fargo slowed to a walk and rounded another bend. Shock brought him to a stop.

Coming out of cottonwoods to the south was an apparition the likes of which no one had seen in those parts before. It was a rider, a portly man clothed in a yellow shirt with frills at the throat, bright blue pants and black boots, and a red jacket adorned with large brass buttons. He wore a brown bowler and held a pink parasol over his head to protect him from the sun. He was in his fifties, at least, and sported a bushy mustache and bushy sideburns. A spectacle in himself, the rider was nonetheless matched by his mount. He was bareback astride an animal that reminded Fargo of a fat pony in that it had a thick barrel of a body, short legs, and a bristly mane. What made the animal so amazing was its striking white coat covered with long black stripes of varying widths.

Fargo could not help gawking. Or saying the first thing that popped into his head. "If I was drunk all this would make a lot more sense."

The apparition beamed and kneed his bizarre mount closer. "A friendly and sincere greeting to you, sir," he said, doffing his bowler. "Permit me to introduce myself. Thaddeus T. Thimbletree, at your service." He tried to give a courtly bow but his ample belly prevented him from bending. "Impresario extraordinaire, showman supreme, founding genius and proprietor of the eighth wonder of the world, wined and dined by kings and queens and a close personal friend of the pope."

"Maybe you're the one who's drunk," Fargo responded.

Thimbletree cocked his head. "Forsooth, sir, your powers of perception are the equal of mythical Zeus. I confess to being unduly fond of the fruit of the vine, to say nothing of harder spirits, but at this particular moment, alas, I am as sober as your horse."

Fargo chuckled. "Do you always talk like this?"

"Is that an aspersion on my admittedly grandiose vocabulary?" Thimbletree straightened. "For your information, I am widely renowned for my poetical eloquence. Why, the queen of England, herself, complimented me for my entertaining conversation. And if anyone should be in a position to appreciate sterling English, sir, it would be that illustrious if opinionated lady." He lowered the pink parasol. "But that's neither here nor there. In truth, I've spent laborious hours scouring this formidable wilderness hither and yon, seeking that which I seem to have misplaced."

"You've lost something?"

"Isn't that what I just stated?" Thimbletree's bushy eyebrows arched. "Verily, sir, I begin to suspect one of us does not have his wits about him this fine day. Now, can you help me or not?"

"What did you lose?"

"An elephant."

Fargo couldn't help himself. He laughed until his sides hurt. When he finally stopped, Thimbletree was red in the face.

"I daresay, sir, that was unspeakably rude. How

would you like it if you lost your elephant and I made a mockery of you?"

Fargo had to ask. "How can you lose an elephant?"

"Ah. I see. You base your ridicule on its size. Well, be advised, my good fellow, there is no more devious creature in all existence than the wily pachyderm. Their intellect is second to none, and when they put their minds to something, there is no denying them." Thimbletree stopped, then sighed. "It wandered off a week ago when no one was watching. We've been searching for it ever since."

"We?"

"Why, the members of my troupe, sir. Haven't I made myself plain? I am the owner of the most spectacular assortment of animals and oddities known to mortal man." Thimbletree said it with immense pride.

"You run a circus?" Fargo guessed. He had seen a poster advertising one when he visited New York City some time back.

Thimbletree frowned. "Why do you persist in repeating everything I say? Yes, I am the fount of inspiration behind our illustrious enterprise. Now, have you seen Tembo or not?"

"Your elephant has a name?"

"This is becoming tiresome, sir. We name canines, don't we? We name felines, yes? Why, I even knew a fellow once who named his fish. What is so outlandish about bestowing a cognomen on a pachyderm?"

The man knew more big words than Noah Webster, Fargo decided. "Your Tembo, as you call it, attacked a homesteader and his wife and nearly killed them."

"Oh, my." Thimbletree appeared genuinely mortified. "I was afraid something like that might transpire. But I assure you Tembo would never deliberately harm a living soul. She is much too sweet-natured."

"The elephant is female?"

Thaddeus T. Thimbletree shook his head in mild disgust. "Honestly, sir. Consider having your ears checked by a competent physician." He grew somber. "Where is Tembo now? Did they fire at her? Lord, I hope she hasn't been harmed."

"Is that all you care about? The settler's wife has a broken leg and the settler might be bedridden for weeks."

"I sympathize. I truly do. And I shall attend to them at my earliest convenience. But at the moment, my paramount concern is finding Tembo before another calamity happens." Thimbletree reined his striped mount around. "Come with me, if you please. The others will want to hear this."

Fargo brought the Ovaro up alongside him. "What's that you're riding?"

Thimbletree snickered. "Your ignorance is abominable, young man. Surely you've heard of zebras? I obtained this one from a farmer on the plains of Serengeti. He raised it from a foal and taught it to do the most marvelous tricks. Remind me to show you later how it can count to five by stamping a hoof."

"You've been to Africa, I take it?"

"Africa, India, China, Malaya, South America, you name a country or a continent, and I've visited it in my unending quest for marvels with which to dazzle and delight," Thimbletree boasted. "I have stared down a charging water buffalo, been spit at by cobras, nearly entrapped in the coils of an odious anaconda. I have seen cheetahs run faster than the wind, heard the demonic cackle of hyenas in the dead of night."

If it was true, Fargo envied him. But the circus

owner struck him as the kind who spewed more hot air than a volcano. "What brought you out here?"

"What takes me anywhere?" Thimbletree rejoined. "Do you realize the American frontier is a vast untapped cornucopia of potential patrons of my enterprise? To say nothing of the untapped potential in terms of wildlife."

"Can you say that again in words even my horse would understand?"

The older man chortled. "Very well. I confess that sometimes I tend to get carried away. The answer, plain and simple, is money. I am on a grand tour of the United States, and I saw no reason to stop at the Mississippi. Not when there are cities like Denver, Santa Fe, and Salt Lake City where people are starved for entertainment and will pay top dollar to view an extravaganza like mine."

"You've been to Denver and Santa Fe already?" Fargo surmised, since they were to the east and south.

"That we have, my boy, that we have. And I tell you, the crowds turned out in droves! Why, we had a four-week run in Denver alone, and I would have stayed longer only I hope to arrive in San Francisco before winter."

Fargo had never heard anything so insane. "Have you any idea how far California is? And of the rough country you have to go through to get there?"

"Posh, sir, and double posh. My troupe and I are inured to hardship. We thrive on it as other men thrive on lives of ease and plenty." Thimbletree puffed out his chest. "If you learn nothing else about me, learn this. Thaddeus T. Thimbletree does not do things in small measures. I paint the tapestry of my life on a grand scale, in all the vivid hues of the rainbow."

"There you go again," Fargo said.

"My apologies. Habits are hard to break." Thimbletree grinned. "But to go on with my answer, my other reason for being here involves adding to my menagerie. I intend to add one of the most fierce predators alive to my collection."

"Which one?"

"Why, *ursus arctos,* of course. The legendary grizzly."

Fargo looked at him. "You're loco if you think you can put a grizzly in a cage and treat it like you do your pet elephant. Grizzlies are killers."

"So are lions and tigers but I have one of each. All told, I possess over a dozen exotic and dangerous creatures. In Europe they train bears to do all sorts of things. I fail to see why I can't do the same with the American variety."

"A black bear, maybe," Fargo allowed, "but never a griz. To them, all you are is food." The proposition was pure insanity. Even if by some miracle they caught one, taming it was impossible.

"You are speaking, sir, to someone whose indomitable spirit has conquered the king of beasts and the lord of the Indian jungle. To someone who has had elephants eating peanuts out of the palms of his hands, and who has netted the elusive hairy man of Sumatra. I will not be deterred."

Fargo shrugged. "It's your life."

Ahead, the forest bordering the river thinned, and Fargo caught sight of a long row of gaily colored wagons and vans. Some were big, others small. Some had bars inset into their sides. Others were fully enclosed. On many, painted in bold letters, were the words, THIMBLETREE'S TRAVELING MENAGERIE AND MYSTIC ARCANUM. "That's quite a name you came up with."

"Showmanship, my good fellow, is everything. Appearance matters more than reality in my business."

Fargo saw people moving about, men, women, and a few children, some in outlandish costumes. He heard strange cries, too; hoots and wails and the throaty cough of a big cat. "How many in your party?"

"Thirty-seven, counting myself. Some of the best performers on the planet, including the Great Gandolpho and the Flying Fleetwoods."

"Never heard of them," Fargo mentioned.

Thimbletree's eyebrows arched again. "Where have you been keeping yourself the past five years? On Mars? Why, my circus has been written up in every major newspaper from New York City to Zanzibar. We put on an exclusive performance for the president of these United States and it made headlines all across the country."

Someone had noticed them and shouted to bring others. Fargo found himself ringed by an amazing assortment of people. They were all shapes, sizes, and colors, from a white beanpole who had to stand seven feet tall, to a dusky black in a loincloth who wasn't four feet high. There was a woman who must weigh four hundred pounds, another covered in tattoos. There was a bearded man in a turban and a husky gent with some sort of metal cap on his head. There was also a pair of twins, stunning redheads in tight sequined outfits.

Several began talking at once but Thimbletree silenced them by raising his hand. "One at a time, my children. One at a time."

"Did you find any trace of Tembo?" asked the tattooed woman.

"Not yet, my dear Juliette, although this gentleman

informs me that she attacked a homestead a couple of nights ago."

"Oh no!" declared one of the redheads. Like her sister, she had vivid blue eyes and full red lips.

"Who is that with you?" her sibling inquired. The only difference between them was that she wore a purple ribbon in her hair while the other wore an orange ribbon.

Thimbletree turned. "Say, that's right. You never did introduce yourself. A deplorable lack of manners, if I must say so myself."

As Fargo remedied his oversight, he noticed a lean hombre in buckskins who stood apart from the rest, leaning on a rifle. The man's face was familiar.

"Mr. Fargo, is it?" the one in the metal cap said. "Perhaps you will be so kind as to take us to where you last saw Tembo? You can't appreciate how important she is to our livelihood."

"This is the Great Gandolpho," Thimbletree said. "One of only three men alive who make their living by being shot from a cannon." He pointed at a large contraption attached to the rear of a wagon.

"And the twins?" Fargo asked.

"Why, the Flying Fleetwoods, who else? The most amazing trapeze artists to ever defy gravity. Cyrena is the one with the purple ribbon, Dacia the orange. I insist they wear them so I can tell them apart. Otherwise, it's hopeless."

Fargo would like to get to know them better, but, before he had the chance, shouting broke out and everyone began pointing and running. He reined around and beheld Tembo striding ponderously from the woods. Walking by her side with a hand on her leg was a skinny black man in a loose-fitting beige shift and leather sandals. Around his neck he wore a silver chain from which hung a slender wooden instrument.

"Walikali!" Thumbletree gleefully cried. Sliding off of the zebra, he ran over and clapped the man on the arms. "You did it! You've brought our main attraction back safe and sound."

Fargo reined the Ovaro over near a van where it was out of the way, and dismounted. He strolled to the next wagon in line and peered through the bars. All he saw was a mound of reddish-brown hair. Whatever it was, it was asleep. Or so he assumed until he turned to watch the elephant's welcome and a hairy hand thrust between the bars, gripped him by the shoulder, and, with surprising strength, spun him around. He instantly stabbed for his Colt but stopped with it half-drawn. The thing had removed its hand and was studying him. "What in the world are you?"

It was almost as tall as a man but wider and bulkier, with loose folds of sagging flesh hanging in front and thick matted hair on its back, arms and legs. The face was as close to human as any animal Fargo had ever seen, with small, dark eyes that registered as much curiosity as a man's might. It had baggy jowls and droopy cheeks and yellow teeth it flashed in what Fargo took to be a smile. "Friendly cuss, aren't you?"

"I see you've met Prince Maylay," said a soft feminine voice.

"He's our orangutan," said another. "Thad picked him up in Sumatra about three years ago."

Fargo turned. Up close, the Flying Fleetwoods were even more stunning. Their lustrous hair, creamy complexions, and full figures were enough to stir a hunger in any man, and Fargo was famished. "Ladies," he said, touching his hat brim. "I don't see how Thimbletree can say the elephant is his main attraction when he has you two."

The twins glanced at one another, and laughed. "Why, listen to you," Cyrena said playfully. "Aren't you the flatterer?"

"Such delightfully broad shoulders," Dacia said, running her gaze over Fargo's whipcord frame. "I'll bet you have plenty of muscles to go with them, don't you, handsome?"

Fargo grinned. "Any time you want to take a peek and find out, let me know."

Cyrena nudged her sister. "This one could prove interesting."

"I hope so," Dacia responded. "It's been so long I could scream."

About to ask what she meant, Fargo saw the lean man in buckskins try to slink nearer without being noticed. "Well, well. If it isn't Judson Richter. Scalped any defenseless Arapahos lately, Jud?"

Richter's rodent features screwed into a scowl. "If it ain't the high and mighty Trailsman. Be careful, ladies. He has a reputation for beddin' down everything in a dress."

"He does?" Dacia's smile was radiant.

Cyrena winked at Fargo. "Now that's the kind of reputation I like. I do so hope you won't leave without putting it to the test."

Giggling merrily, the pair waltzed off arm in arm.

Richter stared after them, grumbling, "Tramps. The both of 'em. They throw themselves at anything in pants."

Fargo had never much liked Judson Richter. They were both experienced frontiersmen and they both frequently worked as scouts for the army, but there the resemblance ended. Richter was a notorious back-shooter and Indian hater who once took part in the slaughter of an Arapaho family whose only crime was being in the wrong place at the wrong time when a bunch of drunken whites rode by. "Did they throw themselves at you, too? Or do they have better taste?"

Richter flushed from his collar to his hairline. "Still the same smug bastard, I see."

"And you're still the same jackass." Fargo had let Richter sit in on a card game once at Fort Laramie. A poor loser, Richter had accused a friend of Fargo's of cheating and pulled a knife. To calm him down, Fargo had hit him over the head with a nearly full whiskey bottle.

"Now that the pleasantries are over with," Richter said sourly, "mind tellin' me what the hell you're doing here?"

"The elephant brought me," Fargo said with a grin.

"Fine. Don't say if you don't want to. But don't think for a minute that I've forgotten the twelve stitches I needed after you bashed me that time."

"It didn't knock any sense into you, though, did it?"

"You're one funny jasper." Richter smiled thinly.

Fargo saw Thimbletree and the black man in the shift coming toward them. At their heels, lumbering along like an oversized dog, was Tembo. "What about you?"

"I'm their guide. The fat one hired me in Saint Louis to see them all the way through to California." Richter patted his poke. "Paid in gold coins, if you can believe it. He has a chest full stashed somewhere. Told me so himself." Richter's eyes glittered greedily.

It wasn't smart of Thimbletree to let a coyote like Richter know he was carrying around a lot of money. Fargo didn't trust him any farther than he could throw the elephant.

Thimbletree waddled like a duck when he walked, the result of his legs being much too short for his ample body. "There you are, Mr. Fargo! Walikali and I would like to hear more about those settlers you mentioned."

The black man folded his hands and dipped his chin in cordial respect. "I am most pleased to meet you, bwana." He had a distinctly British accent. "I am told you have met my daughter."

"Your daughter?" Fargo repeated, puzzled.

"He means Tembo," Thimbletree explained. "You see, Walikali's people are famed as great elephant men. His parents died when he was young and he was sent to a British missionary's school."

"What's the name of his tribe?" Fargo had heard of one once, famed lion hunters whose name eluded him.

"Walikali."

"But that's what you call him."

"To be honest, I couldn't pronounce his real name if my life depended on it," Thimbletree said. "So I call him by the name of his people. It's easier on the tongue and he doesn't mind." Thimbletree patted Walikali on the back. "If it weren't for him, we wouldn't have Tembo. He's the only one who can keep her in line when she's in one of her moods."

"Elephants have moods?"

"Indeed, bwana," Walikali said, and winked. "Especially the female elephants. They are much like us in many respects."

Fargo was learning more every minute. He glanced at Tembo and smiled, and she suddenly craned her huge head forward, wrapped her trunk around his waist, and jerked him off the ground.

4

For a few anxious moments Skye Fargo thought Tembo intended to harm him. He thought she would toss him or maybe dash him to earth. But all she did was hold him at eye level and stare at him in that intense way of hers.

Walikali stepped in front of her and addressed her in a forceful tone in his native dialect. At the same time, he motioned with his arms, as if lowering something to the ground.

From Tembo came a surprisingly soft sound and she slowly set Fargo down on his feet. Her trunk slid up over his chest and neck and once again the tip brushed his ear.

"What the deuce was that all about?" Thaddeus T. Thimbletree demanded. "I've never seen her grab anyone before. We can't have her doing that at a performance or there will be the devil to pay."

The African patted Tembo's trunk and grinned at Fargo. "Not to fear, bwana. My daughter is not turning wild. She has found someone who touches her deep in her being."

It was hard to say who was more flabbergasted, Fargo or Thimbletree. "What the hell are you talking about?" Fargo snapped. The elephant was still staring at him.

Walikali's grin widened. "Tembo likes you, sir. To her you are special. Ask anything of her and she will do it."

"All I want is for her not to do *that* again," Fargo said gruffly.

"She cannot help herself. Elephants live by their hearts. And now you are in hers."

That had to be about the stupidest thing Fargo ever heard but he didn't insult Walikali by saying so. "She's just like a great big dog, is that it?"

"Far more than any dog could ever be, bwana. Her emotions are a lot like yours and mine." Walikali patted her, his affection undeniable. "I am jealous, sir. To her I am a friend. To her you are more."

"Just when I thought I'd heard everything," Fargo muttered, and was glad when Thimbletree changed the subject.

"About those settlers. Do you suppose we can reach their homestead and get back before nightfall?"

"It would take an entire day," Fargo said. And at that, they would have to ride like the wind. Tembo had covered a lot of ground.

"Then it's best to wait until morning," Thimbletree said. "I trust you'll do the courtesy of taking me? I must make amends. Financial restitution is in order. And an apology, although they brought it on themselves by scaring poor Tembo like they did."

"*They* scared *her*?"

"Indisputably. You've seen firsthand how sweet her disposition is. More than likely they made a loud noise or a sudden movement. She wouldn't have harmed them otherwise."

Fargo elected not to tell them that the Hagens had

taken a shot at her. "We can head out first thing in the morning. Mind if I bed down in your camp tonight?"

"Not at all. You're most cordially welcome. The same old company day after day can become tiresome after a while, even a company as varied and worldly as ours." Thimbletree took Fargo by the elbow. "Come along. I'll introduce you to everyone and show you our menagerie. I'll warrant you'll be impressed."

Fargo was. The circus people were friendly and cheerful, and the animals fascinated him. He had never seen an African lion close up, or stood a few feet from a dozing tiger, or had a zebra eat from his hand. The only animal he didn't like was one that even Thimbletree admitted gave him goose bumps.

"We call him Burma, which is where I obtained him. He's one of the largest specimens of his kind ever known, although the natives claim even larger exist far in the interior."

Fargo had to bend close to the bars to see the coiled shape in the shadows. "What kind is it?"

"A python. Twenty-four and a half feet of inde-structible, elemental death. I make it a point not to be biased against the Almighty's handiwork but snakes are at the top of my list of creatures we could do without."

Fargo would add mosquitoes, ticks, lice, and politi-cians. "What do you feed the thing?"

"Any small animals we can catch. Fortunately he doesn't need to eat often. Just don't touch the bars. He's too big to squeeze through but he can inflict a nasty bite."

In the next wagon a peacock was standing with its tail spread wide to dazzle the hens, and uttered a piercing cry.

"Typical male," Dacia Fleetwood said as she and

45

her twin came to the cage. "All strut and brag but not much between the ears."

Cyrena laughed and nodded in agreement. "If men were half as great as they like to think they are, women would swoon at their feet."

"Now, now, my dears," Thimbletree said with a twinkle in his eyes. "To hear you talk, a person would think you weren't fond of the masculine gender. But we know the truth is quite the opposite."

Dacia put a hand to her throat in sham shock. "Why, Thaddeus, we're positively scandalized."

"Everyone has their passions," Cyrena said. "With you, Thad, it's collecting things. With Alice, it's tattoos. With Gandolpho, it's being blown out of a cannon. With us—" She glanced at her sister and they both looked at Fargo and smiled seductively.

"You are incorrigible, ladies," Thimbletree pretended to rebuke them. "And before I forget, you are also taking a ride with me tomorrow. Our darling Tembo attacked some locals and we must make amends."

"Why take us along?" Dacia asked.

"Because according to Mr. Fargo there's a woman and children involved, and they will take more kindly to your presence than they will to mine."

"You old faker," Cyrena said. "You're just afraid they'll file charges or take the circus to court."

"Or demand that Tembo be put down," Thimbletree voiced his true fear. "Would either of you want that?"

"Goodness, no," Dacia assured him. "We like her, too."

"Well then." Smiling, Thimbletree excused himself. "I have work to attend to so I'll leave our guest in your capable hands."

Dacia took one arm, Cyrena the other, and led Fargo to the river. He sat on a log while they perched at the water's edge and idly dipped their hands in.

"Tell us about yourself," Cyrena urged. "Do you have a wife somewhere? Are you wanted by the law? Have you ever killed anyone?"

"Cyrena!" Dacia scolded.

"No, no, and yes," Fargo answered. "Out here it's survival of the quickest, and I don't aim to die before my time."

"We heard so many stories about how violent the West is," Cyrena said, "but you wouldn't know it from our journey so far. Why, the only Indians we've seen were tame ones in Saint Louis and Denver. And we never once saw buffalo the whole time we were crossing the plains."

"Nor have we seen a bear or cougar or any of the other savage creatures everyone always talks about," Dacia elaborated. "Why, as far as we're concerned, your so-called frontier is as peaceful as the Maine countryside where we were born and raised."

"You've been lucky," Fargo told them. Left unsaid was the implication that no one's luck lasted forever. "I hope it continues that way."

"Not me," Cyrena declared. "I'd give anything for a little excitement. We didn't join the circus to spend our days bored to death."

"Which reminds me," Dacia said. "We should set up and practice later. We haven't in days and we can't afford mistakes."

"You always were a worrywart." Cyrena grinned at Fargo. "You wouldn't know it to look at us but we're as different as night from day. She's always so serious about things. Me, I take life as it comes. My men, too."

"Has Judson Richter wanted to be one of them?"

Cyrena's grin evaporated. "That slug. You should see how he hovers around us, ogling us all the time. For a while there, after we started out from Saint Louis, neither of us could turn around without bumping into him."

"Finally he took the hint and has left us alone," Dacia went on. "Although I still catch him staring." She shuddered. "There's something about him that scares me a little. The same with those friends of his."

"Friends?" Fargo said.

Dacia nodded. "Some men he met in Denver. Eight or nine, as I recall. He brought them to meet Thad and Thad showed them around. Then they went off drinking and that was the last we were supposed to see of them."

Fargo gazed toward their camp. Richter was nowhere in sight. "How do you mean, supposed?"

"It's probably nothing," Cyrena said, "but twice now some riders have been spotted shadowing us. Once it was Lecter, our Human Flagpole, who saw them. Another time it was Walikali."

"They reported it to Thad and Thad asked Richter to go have a look. Each time he came back and said it must be a mistake because he couldn't find any sign." Dacia's lovely lips pinched together. "Once I could understand, but twice? How likely is that?"

Not likely at all, Fargo thought. "How many guns does the circus have?"

Dacia chuckled. "What would we want with firearms? We're performers, not roughnecks."

"Richter does all our hunting for us," Cyrena said. "And I must admit, he's good at it."

"He told me Thimbletree has a chest of gold. Is that true?"

The twins grew guarded. "Thad wouldn't appreciate us talking about the circus's finances," Cyrena responded. "To be honest, he doesn't tell us a whole lot about the money and we don't pry."

"If he does have a chest, we've never seen it," Dacia said, but her tone wasn't quite convincing.

Fargo figured they were protecting Thimbletree by keeping silent, but he wasn't the one they had to worry about. It was Judson Richter. "When were those riders spotted last?"

"Oh, a couple of weeks ago," Dacia answered.

Maybe it was nothing, Fargo told himself. The circus had traveled more than halfway between Denver and Salt Lake City. Surely Richter wouldn't have waited this long if he intended to rob Thimbletree.

"I wouldn't worry too much," Cyrena was saying. "We could always sic Tembo or Leo on anyone who causes us trouble."

Fargo didn't share her confidence. A few shots from a buffalo gun might bring the elephant down. And Leo the lion was so old, half his teeth were missing.

"Nothing will happen," Dacia predicted. "All those horrible stories about the West are nothing but tall tales."

Fargo knew better but he didn't say anything. He could talk himself blue trying to convince them and they wouldn't believe him. Some lessons in life were only learned the hard way.

They spent an idle half an hour, the twins talking about their childhood in Maine, and how they learned their profession from an aunt who had spent a decade touring Europe with a French production.

"Our parents had fits when we told them what we wanted to do," Dacia said. "Our mother regarded it as unfit for a lady. So we pointed out that her own sister was an aerialist, and a lady through and through."

"It's sad how few people get to do what they want to do in life," Cyrena commented. "Sis and I decided early on that we wouldn't fall into the same rut most everyone else does. We would follow our dream wherever it led."

"I wouldn't trade our lives for anything," Dacia declared. "We've been places and done things most women would give their eyeteeth to do. We gave a command performance for the king of Austria. Another time we spent a week at a duke's castle in Germany. And in India, we stayed at the palace of a rajah, one of the wealthiest men alive."

Fargo found that extremely interesting.

"Personally, I can't wait until we reach Salt Lake City," Cyrena said. "We'll be the first circus to ever pay them a visit. Think how many people will turn out! We'll be packed every night for a month."

"Two months," Dacia crowed. "San Francisco will be even better. Thad says we should have a good four month run there."

Just then Judson Richter stepped from the undergrowth, his rifle in the crook of an arm.

Cyrena put her hands on her hips and glared. "What do *you* want? Didn't we make it clear that we don't want you hanging around?"

"Don't flatter yourselves," Richter replied. "I have to rustle up meat for supper and your friend can lend a hand if he wants."

Fargo was instantly suspicious. "Why do you need me?"

"I don't," Richter said testily. "But Thimbletree wants to throw a sumptuous feast, as he called it, so we'll need extra. He's the one who suggested you might be willin' to help."

That was different. "I'll fetch my horse," Fargo said.

The twins went along, one on either arm.

"We don't want to be left alone with that cur," Dacia whispered, since Richter wasn't far behind.

"Did you notice how he looked at us?" Cyrena complained. "He's a born lecher, if ever there was one."

On one side of the clearing the Great Gandolpho's cannon had been set up and was being primed. A net was being erected sixty feet away. Much closer, a juggler had tossed four wooden bottles into the air and was keeping them constantly in motion with deft flips of his hands. The tiger was preening itself, while Prince Maylay clung to the bars of his cage, docilely watching the goings-on.

Thimbletree intercepted them, saying to Fargo, "I take it Mr. Richter found you? Do you mind, terribly, adding to our larder? Our meals have been sparse of late, but between the two of you we should end up with enough to gorge ourselves."

Detaching himself from the twins, Fargo forked leather. "We'll be back before sunset."

Cyrena rested a hand on his leg. "Don't let anything happen to you, big man. My sister and I are looking forward to getting to know you better."

Judson Richter was on a bay and had a packhorse at the end of a lead rope, waiting. "How do you want to do this? Together or alone?"

Fargo hunted best by his lonesome and said so. "I'll drift south. You take any other direction you want." He flicked his reins and rode into the trees. When he glanced back after a minute Richter had melted into the vegetation. He shut the other scout from his mind and concentrated on the chore at hand.

Thimbletree's remark about their sparse meals made no sense. Signs of wildlife were everywhere; deer tracks, elk tracks, rabbit, squirrel, and a lot more. A seasoned hunter like Richter should have no problem keeping their cooking pots full.

It was elk Fargo was interested in. They were huge in their own right. A bull stood five feet at the shoulders and weighed close to a thousand pounds. Just one would feed the circus for days.

At that time of year elk were usually higher up but occasionally a few strayed down to the river to graze on the lush greenery that grew so profusely along its banks. Riding in an S pattern, his eyes glued to the ground, Fargo traveled three-quarters of a mile without finding what he wanted.

It didn't help that Fargo's thoughts kept straying. Visions of Dacia and Cyrena filled his head, of their form-fitting outfits that left little to the imagination, of the luxurious sheen to their hair and the raspberry tint to their full red lips. Their superbly conditioned bodies were as shapely as shapely could be, their arms and legs toned by sleek muscle, their bosoms as full as the ripest melons. They were the kind of women that made a man's mouth water just to think of them, and his mouth did a lot of watering that afternoon.

Fargo never made any secret of the fact he liked the fairer sex. Maybe that was why women liked him so much. From the Atlantic to the Pacific, he had bedded and been bedded by more women than he would ever be foolish enough to try to count. It was a need in him, an urge as strong as his wanderlust, a constant craving for which he made no apologies. He was as he was, and that was that.

Fargo amused himself by trying to think of how to tell the twins apart without relying on the ribbons in their hair. Most twins were not identical. Some were close but no two were ever exactly alike. Yet try as he might, he couldn't think of a single difference between Dacia and Cyrena. Maybe the secret was under their outfits. But the only way to find out was to see them bare.

So preoccupied was Fargo with his daydreaming that he rode right past a set of elk tracks before he realized what they were. Drawing rein, he climbed down and hunkered. There were four elk altogether. Fine particles of dust layering the prints were a sign they had been made that morning, probably right before sunrise. If so, the elk were lying low somewhere nearby. All he had to do was flush them out.

Forking leather, Fargo backtracked the quartet. Their heart-shaped prints were a lot larger than those of the largest deer, the hind prints partially overlapping the front as they walked. Their dewclaws didn't register but that was normal. The only time they usually showed was in mud and snow.

He came across droppings but didn't dismount to examine them. Most people did not know, or care to know, that elk droppings changed with their diet. In the high country, where most of the forage was dry, elk pellets were like those of deer, only larger. But at lower elevations their diet consisted of moist succulents, and their droppings more closely resembled that of cattle.

Bending, Fargo shucked the Henry from its saddle scabbard and worked the lever to feed a round into the chamber. He had to be ready. If he spooked the elk before he spotted them, they would be gone in a flash. He'd have time for one shot, two at the most, and each must count.

Fargo was one of those who believed in a one-shot kill whenever possible. He never let game suffer if he could avoid it. Nor did he shoot an animal for the sheer hell of it, as some frontiersmen were wont to do. He saw no more sport in that than he would in shooting an animal in a cage.

The tracks led toward a low rise choked with vegetation. Fargo slowed so as not to give the elk cause for alarm, and as he lifted his gaze from their tracks, he spied other prints off to his right. Only these were oval, not heart-shaped, which meant they were horse tracks, and the hooves that made them were shod, which meant the men riding the horses were white.

The elk had to wait. Fargo reined over to read what he could of the new sign. Bent blades of grass already uncurling were proof the riders had passed by not more than an hour ago. Two men had come down from the rise and headed northwest, toward the river. Since there wasn't a town within a hundred miles and the last homestead belonged to the Hagens, it was a safe bet they weren't from around those parts. Perhaps they, too, were on their way to Salt Lake City and were seeking game, the same as he was. There was one way to find out.

Fargo trailed them. They had taken their sweet time, and he caught up to them a lot sooner than he figured. The scent of wood smoke warned him a campfire was near, and presently he glimpsed a clearing in which two horses were picketed and two men were lounging and drinking coffee.

Their faces bore the cruel stamp of hard cases. Both

wore revolvers, which wasn't unusual, except that theirs were tied down. Water hadn't touched their skin or their clothes in ages, and their boots were scuffed and caked with dirt.

Anxious to sneak close enough to hear what they were talking about, Fargo left the Ovaro well hidden and had crept to within forty yards when another rider materialized out of the woodland to the east. Instantly, Fargo flattened. The rider hadn't noticed him but had seen the pair in the clearing.

It was Judson Richter, a dead duck slung over his pack horse. Raising an arm, he waved.

One of the men returned the gesture.

Fargo crawled closer but he was not quite near enough to overhear when Richter reached the clearing and exchanged a few words with the twosome. Then Richter tugged on the lead rope to bring the pack horse up next to his mount, drew a Green River knife from a sheath on his left hip, and cut the rope that tied the buck to the pack horse. The dead deer raised puffs of dust when it hit the ground. Sheathing his knife, Richter nodded at the pair, reined back the way he had come, and casually departed.

Fargo would have a talk with Richter later. Right now he continued crawling, careful not to snap twigs or rustle the brush.

"—mighty tired of coolin' our heels," the gun shark who had waved to Richter remarked. "How much longer do we put up with this, anyhow?"

"We wait as long as it takes. You agreed, just like everyone else, so I don't want any more of your bellyachin'."

"I just hope it's worth it," groused the first man. "If this has been a waste of our time, there'll be hell to pay."

"What did I just say about your damn bellyachin'?"

"Are you going to sit there and tell me you're not as fed up as I am? That you don't want to get this over with?"

"When it comes to havin' more money than I've seen my whole life long, I reckon I can afford to be patient. You'd do well to do the same."

Removing his hat, Fargo raised his head for a better look. A sudden noise caused them to glance in his direction, a noise he didn't make. Ducking, he twisted and saw two more riders approaching from the southwest. Two more curly wolves cut from the same coarse cloth—and they were coming right toward him.

5

Skye Fargo crawled into a patch of high weeds and lay flat. Parting the stems, he watched the newcomers. He had his suspicions what these men were up to, but until he could prove it, it wouldn't do to confront them. They would only deny it.

Then there was the little matter of those who were unaccounted for. Dacia had told him Richter had eight or nine "friends," which meant four or five were missing. He would rather have them all in one place when the showdown came.

The two riders were not paying much attention to their surroundings. Talking and joking, they passed within twenty-five yards of the Ovaro's hiding place without spotting the stallion. Nor did their mounts catch its scent.

In a few moments the pair lounging by the fire jumped to their feet. "About time you got here, Proctor!" the grumpy one declared.

"We saw Injun sign, Stewart," responded the lead rider. His clothes were shabby and he was slovenly in appearance but there was nothing shabby or slovenly about the ivory-handled Colt riding high on his right hip. "Twenty or more redskins passed through this stretch of woods a couple of days ago."

"What kind?" Stewart asked.

"Utes, most likely."

Fargo had his cheek to the ground and his trigger finger on the Henry's trigger as the two riders filed past.

"Are the Utes friendly?" Stewart asked. His ignorance hinted he was new to the frontier.

"Not to our kind, no," Proctor responded. "Although they tend to leave whites alone unless they're provoked."

"They're not as fearsome as the Blackfeet or the Sioux," commented the other rider, "but we don't want to tangle with them if we can help it."

Nor did the circus, Fargo mused. He must warn Thimbletree and have them take precautions until they were clear of Ute country.

Proctor had reined up and was staring at the deer. "Jud was here, I gather?"

Stewart nodded. "He says he still hasn't learned where it is but that doesn't change the plan any."

"If we had to depend on him, we'd have white hair and be in rockin' chairs before we see a lick," Proctor complained. "We agreed on how to go about this when we jawed last, and I aim to hold him to it, whether he likes it or not."

"You've got my vote," Stewart said.

Proctor and the other rider hadn't climbed down. "Put out the fire, throw the deer over your horse, and mount up. The others are as hungry as we are."

Fargo wasted no time in turning and crawling to the Ovaro. He was in the saddle, hunched low, when the foursome rode southwest. He waited until they were out of sight, then followed. It wouldn't be long, he reckoned, before he set eyes on the whole outfit. Short of killing them, there were various ways to discourage them from causing trouble for the circus.

People like Thaddeus T. Thimbletree were too trusting for their own good. Thimbletree should have asked around about Judson Richter before hiring him. The circus had put their lives in Richter's hands without any notion of the kind of man he was.

Hard experience had taught Fargo never to trust anyone until they proved worthy, and even then to always keep his gun hand free. He would live longer that way. Not that he expected to live to old age. Violence was as much a part of life on the frontier as breathing. It came with living on the raw edge of existence, where the only law was the survival of the swiftest and strongest. He had kept his hide intact so far but the odds were bound to catch up with him eventually.

Fargo wasn't about to change, though. He refused to spend the rest of his days cooped up in a town or city. Trading his freedom for a few extra years of life was like trading gold for paper money. Cities were gilded cages where all a person's needs were met so long as they stuck to the rules, and he never had liked having others tell him how he ought to live.

In due course Fargo came to where Proctor and the others had left the belt of vegetation and struck off across open country. They were a quarter of a mile out, making for hills in the distance. Fargo dared not leave cover until there was no likelihood of their spotting him, which would be a while. But there was only an hour of daylight left, and the circus people were counting on having their grand feast.

Fargo mulled it over and decided to head back. Since Richter's friends weren't an immediate threat, they could wait.

It took half the remaining daylight to find the elk tracks, another fifteen minutes to follow them to a tree-lined gully where the elk had spent the afternoon. They were still there, four juvenile bulls who had banded together after striking off on their own. From behind a boulder Fargo watched as several stirred and stood. As soon as the sun went down, they would venture to the river to drink.

Fargo took aim at the nearest. He went for a heart shot. At the crack of his Henry all four bolted. Elk could move as fast as a horse when they wanted to, and he was only able to put one more slug into the young bull before it disappeared into the undergrowth.

Vaulting onto the Ovaro, Fargo gave chase. He had to rely on his eyes instead of his ears since elk made little noise when they were on the move. Bright red streaks were proof he had inflicted a grave wound. Soon he spied a yellowish-brown rump.

The bull had slowed considerably, and by its sluggish gait, was rapidly weakening. Pink froth flecked its lips and it wheezed with every breath.

Fargo raised the Henry to put it out of its misery but at that exact moment the elk's legs buckled and with a loud snort it collapsed and rolled onto its side. Its legs thrashed, its tongue lolled, and then it was still. About to climb down, Fargo heard the crackle of underbrush and swiveled to find Judson Richter trotting toward him.

"I heard your shots," the other scout declared. He nodded at the bull. "Nice animal you brought down. Thimbletree will jump for joy."

"Did you have any luck?"

"Not a lick. I reckon it just wasn't my day." Richter

grinned as he lied. "We'll need another pack horse or two to tote all that meat back."

"Not if we rig a travois and haul it," Fargo suggested.

The moon had been up quite a while when they arrived at the camp. Four fires were blazing and a man in a white apron was tending a large cooking pot. Tembo was over by the river, staked to a chain so she couldn't wander off. Leo and the tiger were both restlessly pacing their cages, the tiger growling and snarling at everyone and everything. Prince Maylay had his forehead pressed against the bars of his cage and was gazing longingly at the benighted foliage.

Thimbletree and a dozen others rushed to greet them. "It took you long enough! We were debating whether to send out a search party." His craggy face lit like a candle when he saw the elk. "I say! Is this your doing, Mr. Fargo? Well done. Mr. Richter practically had us believing the local wildlife had migrated south for the summer."

"I never said any such thing, you old coot," Richter snapped, but no one was listening.

"Otto! Otto!" Thimbletree shouted at the man in the white apron. "Get your Bavarian backside over here! We are in for a treat tonight!"

Fargo relaxed with a cup of coffee and let them do all the work. They prepared several spits and soon had haunches and large chunks of meat sizzling over the flames. The delectable scent made his stomach growl. He had not seen the twins since his return but that was soon remedied when they emerged from a van looking as lovely as two roses in bloom. They had bathed and done womanly things with their hair and switched from their trapeze outfits into identical dresses. All smiles, they sashayed over and stood in front of him, grinning coquettishly.

"Like what you see?" the beauty on the right asked.

Fargo glanced at their hair to tell which was which but they had removed their ribbons. "Are you Dacia or Cyrena?"

The twin on the right giggled. "We'll never tell."

"We do this from time to time," said the other. "It confuses everyone to no end and amuses us greatly."

"I'll bet." Fargo honestly tried but he couldn't tell them apart. He thought that maybe Dacia's lips were slightly fuller than Cyrena's, but if so, it was a whisker's difference.

"Mind if we join you?" asked the lovely on the right.

"Do I strike you as loco?" Fargo rejoined, and patted the ground on either side of him.

Curling their legs under them, the twins eased down, sitting so close, their shoulders brushed his. Dacia—or was it Cyrena?—placed a warm hand on his arm, and grinned. "Play your cards right, handsome, and you're in for a night you'll remember fondly the rest of your days."

Cyrena—or was it Dacia?—nodded. "We came to an understanding about you while you were off hunting. It isn't often both of us are smitten by the same gentleman, but there's something about you. Something we can't quite put our painted fingernails on."

"Even Tembo thinks so," the other said. "And if anyone is an excellent judge of character, it's her." Both women laughed.

So did Fargo. He could do with a nice, relaxing night. The next couple of days promised to be busy, what with Thimbletree wanting to visit the Hagens, and Richter's outfit to deal with. "Do I get to draw straws out of a hat? Or is it two for the price of one?"

Tittering, the twin on his left whispered in his ear, "Let's just say we have a treat in store for you and let it go at that, shall we?"

Soon they were joined by Thimbletree, the Great Gandolpho, Juliette, and Walikali. The circus owner brought a bottle of expensive whiskey, which Fargo was more than happy to help him empty. Two hours later he was willing to swear that the tattooed lady's tattoos were moving.

Thimbletree was talking about an incident in London. "Prince Maylay broke loose and led us a merry chase over the rooftops. You wouldn't think it to look at him, but when he wants to, he can move frightfully fast. He had been gone for hours and I had about given him up for lost when someone found him hiding in a chimney."

Gandolpho bobbed his helmeted head. "I remember. The orang was so dirty, you were washing soot out of its hair for weeks."

"*His* hair," Thimbletree amended. "How many times must I tell you that animals have feelings and thoughts just as we do, and should not be referred to as 'it'?"

"Not that again," the Great Gandolpho said, and glanced at Fargo. "Thaddeus and I have gone around and around about this since I joined his circus. He thinks animals are just as much people as we are, and should be treated as such. I say animals are animals, and that's all they'll ever be."

"What do you say, Mr. Fargo?" Thimbletree asked. "Someone with your vast wilderness experience must have an opinion on the matter."

Fargo had been admiring a unicorn tattooed on Juliette's neck; whenever she bent toward the fire, it seemed to gallop toward her cleavage. "A bear is a bear, a buffalo is a buffalo. That's all there is to it."

"Come now," Thimbletree said. "Surely you can't sit there and say you've never met an animal that wasn't almost as human as we are? A dog, say? Or how about that pinto you're so fond of?"

"I'd die for that pinto," Fargo stated, and he meant it. The Ovaro had saved his life more times than there were stars in the sky. "But the last I looked, it has four legs, not two."

The whiskey had turned Thimbletree's ruddy cheeks even redder. Wagging the bottle, he declared, "Humanity, sir, is not predicated on the number of appendages a creature has, but on the soul that animates those appendages."

"Uh oh," the Great Gandolpho said. "Here he goes with the big words. I swear, half the time I don't have any idea what he's saying."

"Then permit me to spell it out for you in words of one and two syllables." Thimbletree was well under the influence and had to try twice to sit straighter. "If you prick a so-called beast, does it not bleed? If you treat it kindly, does it not respond in kind? Proof, I maintain, that animals have hearts and souls just as we do and should be treated with the same respect."

Fargo chimed in with, "Being kind to a coiled rattler won't stop it from biting you. Or a hungry griz from chewing you down to the bone."

"Ah. But if you fed that bear, then it wouldn't need to eat you, would it? And what a bear doesn't need to eat, it doesn't need to chew. So all you need do is always have some steak handy."

Fargo looked at his tin cup, then at the Great Gandolpho. "Is it me or was that just plain ridiculous?"

The twins rocked with mirth.

"It's him," Gandolpho said. "Thad couldn't hold his liquor if his life depended on it. Two drinks or more under his belt, and he spouts the most incredible nonsense you've ever heard. Why, one time he spent an entire evening trying to convince us that if the world were covered by water, people would look like octopuses."

"That's *octopi*," Thimbletree corrected him. "Clearly, I am a thinker ahead of his time. My worldly travels have imbued me with wisdom far beyond that of normal mortals."

"And humility," Gandolpho said. "Don't forget that."

"Cast all the aspersions you want. They roll off me like water off an aquatic fowl's back." Swallowing more whiskey, Thimbletree smacked his lips. "But we have yet to hear from our African friend, who has lived among wild creatures all his life. What say you, Walikali? Are animals merely animals?"

"Yes."

Thimbletree stared, apparently expecting more, and when Walikali merely kept gazing into the fire, Thimbletree muttered, "I expected a slightly more profound insight from you, my friend. Why, you call Tembo your daughter."

"She is," Walikali replied soberly. "She is also an elephant. Elephants have hearts, yes, but their hearts are not our hearts. They feel and think like elephants, not like people."

The Great Gandolpho raised his glass. "I'll drink to that!"

"I am appalled, Walikali," Thimbletree said indignantly. "You have stung me to the quick. It's enough to compel me to rethink my entire personal philosophy on the relationship between natural man and nature." He rose, swaying like an aspen in a chinook. "Now if you'll forgive me, we must arise early to pay our respects to the settlers Tembo visited, and I need a good night's sleep." Holding his head high, he waddled off, staggering every third or fourth step.

The Great Gandolpho also rose. "I hate to say it but I'm bushed, too. I think I'll turn in."

Most of the other performers had already retired. Among those still up was Judson Richter. Richter wasn't all that popular and had spent most of the evening by himself near the peacock cage, sucking on a flask.

Now Walikali rose and bowed. "I bid you good night as well, bwana. I will check on Tembo and retire. Tomorrow she will apologize for the terror she caused, and all will be well again."

Fargo was going to ask him how an elephant could say it was sorry, but the African had faded into the darkness. "Looks like it's just the three of us, ladies," he told the twins.

"Minus one," the twin on the right said.

The one on the left playfully pinched him, then they stood and walked off a short way and stood with their backs to him, whispering. Fargo polished off the last of his whiskey and sat back to await developments. They didn't keep him waiting long.

Grinning from ear to ear, one of the twins sauntered over and held out her hand for him to take. "We flipped a coin earlier and you're my prize."

"Dacia, isn't it?" Without the other twin to compare her to, Fargo couldn't tell if her lips were slightly fuller.

"You'll have to guess." Smirking, she pulled him

erect, then looped her arm in his and turned toward the woods. "Are you up for a moonlit stroll?"

The moon was no more than a sliver but Fargo wasn't about to quibble. "I'm up for a lot more than that."

"I do so hope you're not one of those who talks big but leaves a girl panting for more."

"I've never had any complaints."

As they strolled from the circle of firelight, she rimmed her lips with the tip of her tongue in enticing invitation. "I should warn you, handsome. I can be quite demanding. I always expect the best of myself when I perform." Her hip rubbed his leg. "And of everyone else."

"Then I guess it's only fair I warn you," Fargo said, and pinched her bottom. "It's been a spell since I was with a woman. I'll eat you alive."

"Promises, promises."

They were not quite out of sight of the camp but that did not stop Fargo from wrapping his arms around her slim waist, molding her lush body flush against his, and hungrily fusing his mouth to hers. She uttered a tiny gasp, then hooked her hands behind his head and ground herself against him with an ardor to match his own. He tasted her sweet lips and felt the velvet sheen of her tongue as it entwined with his. When they parted for breath she was panting and her skin was hot to the touch.

"Where did you learn to kiss like that?"

"Beginner's luck."

Hand in hand they walked deeper into the woods. Fargo moved toward the river, seeking a secluded spot, and found it on a grassy bank beside a pool. Mirrored on the pool's surface were the stars and the crescent moon, lending the illusion that the sky had come down to earth. He sat with his back to a tree and reached for her. "Right here will do."

She sank into his lap and snuggled against his chest, her luxuriant hair spilling over her shoulders. "It's beautiful," she whispered.

Tilting her head, Fargo kissed her a second time. His tongue met hers while his hands explored her shapely form from her shoulders to her knees. She returned the favor, her fingers sculpting the contours of his broad shoulders and chest and slowly delving lower until they were at his belt.

Drawing back, she breathed deep of the crisp night air and remarked, "You turn me into a furnace inside."

"Isn't that the general idea?" Fargo responded, and lightly nipped at her ear and earlobe.

"Yes," she throatily conceded. "But I've never met anyone who excited me so much, so fast."

"It's the whiskey."

"I hardly had any." Taking hold of his fingers, she studied him a few moments. "Maybe Walikali is right. There *is* something special about you. So special even an elephant can sense it."

Fargo chuckled.

"I'm serious."

"You sound as crazy as Thimbletree."

"Make fun all you want, but a woman knows what she knows."

Fargo had learned long ago never to try to fathom female logic. "If you say so," he said, and covered her mouth with his. Roving his hands to her backside, he molded her cheeks as if they were clay.

She squirmed deliciously, her breasts against his chest. With one hand she removed his hat while the other tugged at his shirt until she loosened it enough to slide her palm up across his stomach.

"My goodness. So many muscles," she complimented him.

Fargo could say the same of her. Her long hours of exercise and practice had toned her body until it was firm and hard. Her arms were smooth yet sinewy, her thighs as perfect as thighs could be. But it was her stomach at which he marveled; she was the first woman of his acquaintance whose stomach was as well-muscled as his. He had to undo a lot of stays and buttons to gain access, and once he did, he massaged steadily upward until he came in contact with her breasts. At the touch of his fingers to a nipple, she shivered and clung to him, her breath fanning his neck.

"Mmmmm. I'm tingling all over."

Fargo was just getting started. He opened her dress to expose her bosom and inhaled her left nipple. He tweaked it between his teeth. He rolled it with his tongue. Her fingernails dug into the nape of his neck and she rubbed herself against him down low, where it would excite him most. His skin tingled and he felt his manhood swell.

Shifting his weight, Fargo laid her in the grass and reclined next to her. The play of moonlight on her upturned face painted a living portrait of carnal craving; her eyes were hooded with lust, her mouth a delightful O. She was a ravishing vision no man could resist.

Their mouths met yet again in molten hunger.

"Ohhhhhhhhh," the twin cooed.

Fargo cupped a breast and her nipple became as rigid as a tack. He pinched it, eliciting a drawn-out moan, then gave the other the same treatment. She responded by arching her back and thrusting herself against his member. He was content to lavish her heaving globes with the attention they deserved. Only when she gripped him by the shoulders, bored her eyes into his, and whispered "Please!" did he hike at the hem of her dress and position himself between her legs.

"Finally!" she exclaimed, reaching for his buckle.

Moving her hand, Fargo started to slide down her body.

"What are you?—" she began. Her eyes widened and she stifled an outcry. The upper half of her body came up off the grass but sank right back down again. Seizing him by the hair, she husked, "Yes! Yes! Oh, yes!"

Fargo's jaw was sore when he eventually rose onto his knees, freed his pole, and rubbed it along her moist opening. She trembled and bit her lower lip so fiercely, she drew a drop of blood. Placing his hands on her hips to hold her still, he slowly fed his throbbing sword into her wet sheath. When he was all the way in, he paused to savor the sensation.

"Don't rush," she requested.

He had no intention of hurrying things. Sliding his hands higher, he was about to commence rocking on his knees when the snap of a twig warned him they were no longer alone.

6

Skye Fargo bent to his right to find his holster, which had slid down around his knees. His hand on the butt of his Colt, he peered into the inky woods in the direction the sound had come from.

"Is something the matter?" his companion breathlessly whispered.

"Shhhhh," Fargo cautioned. "There might be someone or something out there." He felt her tense, then she turned her head and scanned the trees as he was doing.

"I don't see anything."

"Quiet, damn it." Fargo strained his ears for the stealthy pad of man or beast but heard only the sigh of the wind and the gurgle of the river. A minute went by. Two minutes. But there was nothing to indicate they were being spied on; no movement, no telltale sounds.

The twin's breathing had calmed and her chest no longer heaved. "Maybe we should just go," she whispered.

"Like hell." Not when Fargo was buried inside of her, his manhood as rigid as a ramrod. "Not until I'm good and ready." So saying, Fargo placed the Colt where it was within easy reach, gripped her hips in both hands, and thrust into her with renewed vigor.

"Oh!" Her mouth went wide and her nails raked his arms. "You fill me so nicely."

Fargo nearly lifted her off the ground with his next stroke. She cried out, then bit her lower lip and leaned her forehead against his chest. A groan escaped her, long and low and ripe with the promise of rising release. Her hips met each thrust with a counterthrust, her body moving in synchrony with his. She was breathing faster and harder by the moment.

The twig faded from Fargo's mind. So did Richter and the Hagens and the circus performers and everything except the exquisite sensations rippling through his body, sensations of pure and total bliss. For a short span he had the illusion he was adrift in a sea of pleasure. It filled his every pore, filled him to his core, and as always, he could not get enough. As usual, he craved more, more, more. To that end, he tried to last as long as he could, postponing the inevitable for the sake of that added minute, that added second, of sensual ambrosia.

Then the twin gushed. She moaned and mewed and tossed her head from side to side, her bottom slapping against him with the driving beat of a steam engine piston. She drenched him, so powerful was her release.

Fargo could feel his own explosion build. He was at the brink but he did not want to lose control yet. His body had other ideas. He almost cried out as the world around them blurred. Again and again he pounded into her, until he was so spent he couldn't muster the energy to stay on his knees. Sagging onto her bosom, he nuzzled her neck and pecked her ear.

She was panting as if she had run five miles.

"You're magnificent!" she praised his performance. "The best ever!"

"I try," Fargo said, and went to roll off.

"Not yet you don't." She hugged him close. "I like a tender interlude afterward. Just lie still."

Fargo let her have her way. "Care to tell me which one you are?"

Giggling, she kissed his cheek. "And spoil the mystery? The allure? My sister and I think it's more fun this way." She nipped at his chin. "Will she ever be jealous when I tell her what she missed!"

"There's always tomorrow night," Fargo said.

"Tomorrow night we will either be at the homesteaders' or on the trail." She curled a finger in his hair and twirled it. "You did say, did you not, that it will take us the better part of a day to get there?"

"At least." Fargo had tried to convince Thimbletree to wait a couple of days, which would give him time to pay Richter's friends a visit, but the circus owner was a stubborn cuss.

"Thaddeus will set things right with them. You'll see. He's the kindest person you would ever want to meet."

Kindness wouldn't stop a bullet, Fargo reflected. Men like Richter were prone to see it as a weakness, not a strength. A weakness they would gladly exploit to line their own pockets.

He and the twin were still for a while, until she shivered and pushed on his shoulders.

"I'm getting cold. Do you mind if we head back?"

The camp lay quiet under the canopy of stars. Everyone else had turned in and all the animals had bedded down except for the tiger, which tirelessly paced its cage and every so often vented savage growls.

"That's Lord Sydney for you," the twin said, grinning. "You can take the tiger out of the jungle but you can't take the jungle out of the tiger. He will never be as tame as Leo or Prince Maylay."

"Why call a tiger Sydney?" Fargo wondered.

"After Lord Sydney, an Englishman. He was the last of the unfortunates the tiger ate before he was captured."

It took a few seconds for the full implication to hit him. Fargo stopped and looked at her. "This tiger is a man-eater?"

She nodded. "Thaddeus felt it would have more appeal that way. Help bring more people to see the show." She stared at the pacing cat. "Our feline friend, there, killed seven people, maybe more, before he was trapped in a pit, and netted. The real Lord Sydney was a noted British hunter who tried to put a stop to the slaughter. One night he tied a goat out as bait and sat up in a platform in a tree waiting for the tiger to show."

"What happened?" As if Fargo couldn't guess.

"The tiger came, all right, but it caught Lord Sydney's scent and stalked him instead of the goat. It jumped up on the platform and killed him, then dragged his body into the jungle and ate him. Thad thought it fitting that we honor the lord's memory by giving the tiger his name. Wasn't that sweet?"

Fargo glanced at the man-eater. It was at least nine feet long and had to weigh upward of four hundred pounds. It would dwarf a mountain lion, and as a proven man-killer, was as dangerous as a rabid wolf.

"You don't approve?"

"Why didn't Thimbletree capture a different tiger and claim it's a man-eater? It would be a lot safer, and no one would know the difference."

"It would also be telling a lie, and Thaddeus doesn't have a dishonest bone in his pudgy body. He's not one of those promoters who exaggerate to line their pockets." She put a hand on one of the bars and nearly lost it when the tiger suddenly lunged and snapped at her. Recoiling, she shook a finger at it as if it were a frisky pet. "Behave, Sydney! How many times must we tell you?"

Its fangs glistening, its tail twitching, Lord Sydney snarled in defiance.

Fargo walked the twin to her wagon and bid her goodnight. He still suspected it was Dacia but when he said her name, she laughed merrily, and before ducking inside, teased him with, "Admit it, handsome. It's more fun this way, isn't it? You'll spend the rest of your life wondering."

A flash of her pearly teeth and she was gone.

"Women," Fargo said under his breath. Sighing, he walked to where he had left the Ovaro. His saddle and bedroll were on the ground beside a log. Unrolling his blankets, he lay down and tried to get to sleep. His body was tired but his mind was racing like an antelope. He liked these circus people, liked some of them a lot, and he didn't want them to come to harm. Which they were bound to do unless someone could talk some sense into the lunkhead who ran things.

He was up before sunrise to do just that. After rolling up his bedroll and saddling the Ovaro, he went to Thimbletree's wagon and leaned against it, marking the gradual spread of pink and yellow in the eastern sky and the slow brightening of the shadows under the trees. The scrape of a latch preceded a loud cough and the tromp of boots on the short flight of folding steps. "Sleep well?" he asked.

Thimbletree drew up so abruptly, he nearly tripped

over his own feet. "Mr. Fargo! My word, you gave me a start! I didn't see you standing there." He smiled and ran a finger across his mustache. "An early riser, I see. Most admirable. It's long been my opinion that we are not put on this earth to squander the time allotted us." He inhaled the brisk air and raised his arms to the golden halo to the east. "Ahhhhh. Glorious. Simply glorious. Mornings are nature's crowning achievement. I find them more stimulating than anything else life has to offer. How about you?"

Fargo could think of a few things that excited him more but he hadn't come to talk about the splendor of the new dawn. "Are you still set on paying the Hagens a visit today?"

"I certainly am. They must be recompensed for any and all hardships they have suffered as a result of our carelessness in allowing Tembo to wander off." Thimbletree pursed his lips. "Why do you inquire?"

Motioning, Fargo led him out of earshot of the wagons. "I saw something yesterday," he said, and detailed his encounter with the riders and the part Richter had played.

"The devil you say!" Thimbletree bristled. "We'll go find him and demand an accounting of his actions or know the reason why!" He turned to march off.

"No," Fargo said, gripping his arm.

"No?" Thimbletree scratched his head. "But surely it behooves us to get to the bottom of this before Richter and his secretive allies can carry out whatever nefarious scheme they've concocted?"

"Richter will deny he's up to no good. What then?" Fargo asked.

"Why, I'll demand he leave and warn him never to come anywhere near my circus again!"

"And you honestly think he'll listen?" Fargo sighed.

"Richter and his friends won't rest until they get their hands on the chest of gold they think you have. The only way to stop them is to kill them."

"Isn't that a tad severe? There must be some other way to discourage them. Perhaps if I threaten to go to the authorities, that will suffice."

"The nearest law is in Salt Lake City."

"Then how about the military? Richter mentioned there are army posts scattered throughout the frontier."

"Fort Bridger is closest but you would have to turn back and it would take weeks to reach it." Fargo paused. "And when you got there, what would you say? That you suspect Richter wants to steal from you? The army doesn't have jurisdiction in civilian matters. The best they can do is escort you to Salt Lake, provided they have the men to spare."

"You present a bleak outlook," Thimbletree said. "It sounds to me as if you're saying we must deal with this ourselves, and our only recourse is violence." Thimbletree gestured. "I refuse to accept that. Violence is the last resort of the uncivilized. There has to be a better alternative."

"If there is, I don't know it," Fargo told him.

"With all due respect, sir, by your own admission you have spent most of your life in the wild. Violence is in your nature. Your solution to every problem is to exterminate it. I, on the other hand, am a firm believer in the rule of reason over brawn, in the triumph of the human brain over brute force. I refuse to lift a finger against Mr. Richter until and if he lifts a finger against me."

"And then what?"

"I seldom fret over a problem until it has arisen." Thimbletree smiled. "Since for the moment there is nothing we can do, suppose you see if Dacia and Cyrena will be ready to leave soon while I check on Walikali? He insists on going along so he can apologize in person, and to show the Hagen family Tembo isn't to be feared."

"We're taking the elephant?"

"Of course. She's the cause of the misfortune that befell them, is she not?" Thimbletree smoothed his jacket. "This works out nicely. While we're away, my performers can practice for Salt Lake City. We'll be at the top of our form when we put on our show there." He waddled off.

As much as Fargo liked the man, Thimbletree was a fish out of water when it came to the frontier. The man judged everyone by his own high standards and could not seem to grasp that there were people in this world who would as soon kill him as look at him.

Fargo had another decision to make. Should he refuse to take Thimbletree to the Hagens and go after Richter's gang instead? And take care of Richter while he was at it? As if in answer, who should come ambling toward him at that very moment but Judson Richter, himself.

"Mornin'. I hear tell you and the big man and some of the others are fixin' to pay those homesteaders a visit?"

"You heard right," Fargo confirmed.

"Any chance I could tag along? I hate sittin' around twiddlin' my thumbs. Which is about all I've been doing since the stupid elephant wandered off."

The last thing Fargo wanted was Richter tagging along. He was about to say no when it occurred to him that the best way to keep from being bitten by a rattler was to never let it out of your sight. And Richter's partners weren't likely to strike at the circus while Richter was away. "If it's fine by Thimbletree, it's fine by me."

Within the hour they were set to leave. Thimbletree was once again astride the zebra. Walikali rode Tembo.

Dacia and Cyrena had ribbons in their hair again, but neither gave Fargo a clue as to which one had lain with him the night before. They weren't particularly pleased that Richter was included, and Fargo couldn't blame them.

All went well until late in the afternoon. Fargo held to a brisk pace in the hope of reaching the homestead before nightfall. But Tembo had a mind of her own. Although Walikali did his utmost to hurry her along, she fell behind, and Thimbletree insisted on suiting their pace to hers.

Ironically, it was Judson Richter who summed up Fargo's attitude by saying, "Isn't this just about the silliest thing you ever heard of? Traipsin' over the countryside with a damn elephant."

That evening they made camp beside the river. Fargo shot a doe and Richter roasted it. After they ate, they sat around the fire, no one saying much. It was obvious to Fargo the twins were uncomfortable with Richter there. They made it a point to stake out a spot to sleep on the other side of the fire from where Richter had his bedding, and were the first to retire.

Fargo was the last. He stayed up sipping coffee until long after the rest crawled under their blankets. Gradually the flames burned low. They were on the verge of extinction when Judson Richter intruded on the quiet by sawing logs loud enough to be heard in Boston.

Draining the last of his coffee, Fargo stepped to his bedroll. He could use some sleep after the long day on the trail, but no sooner had he cupped his hands behind his head and closed his eyes than fingers plucked at his sleeve. One of the twins was bent over him, beckoning, a finger to her lips to enjoin secrecy. She had removed her ribbon and he couldn't tell which one it was.

Fargo followed her into the forest. They were a hundred yards from the flickering embers of their campfire when she halted and faced him. "What was so important you had to drag me out here this late?" he demanded.

"Sharing," she said.

Not quite sure she meant what he thought she meant, Fargo asked, "What is it you want to share?"

"What do you think?" She brushed against him. "My sister and I share *everything*, and after her glowing account of your lovemaking ability, I won't be left in suspense."

"You want to do it *now*?" As Fargo had learned, for all their modesty, women were as aggressive as men when their mood was right.

"Why not? The rest are out to the world. It's just the two of us, free to do as we please. And I, for one, want to find out if my sister was telling the truth. She's been known to trick me for the fun of it."

"What if one of the others wakes up and finds us missing?" Fargo was thinking specifically of Judson Richter.

"We're adults. We can do as we damn well please." She stepped so close, her breasts were against his chest. A seductive smile curled her luscious lips as she rose onto the tips of her toes to kiss him on the bridge of his nose. Next she kissed his cheeks, his chin, and finally his mouth.

Fargo's fatigue melted like butter under a hot sun.

His member twitched as she licked his ear and traced a wet path down his neck to his shirt. Without warning she cupped him between his legs and his pole surged against his pants as if attempting to burst free.

She grinned impishly. "Look at this. You want me as much as I want you. Don't deny it."

The only thing Fargo wouldn't deny was that she had kindled a hunger he could no more control than he could control the weather. Embracing her, he ground his hips against hers and roughly smothered her mouth with his. She melted in his arms, her left hand hooked around his neck, her right busy below his belt. For long minutes they stayed locked in intimate caress, her breathing growing more rapid, her fingers more and more brazen. She was different from her twin in one respect; she was much more bold. In no time she had his pants undone and was fondling his manhood.

"Ohhhhhh. She didn't say how big you are."

Fargo noticed a nearby tree and backed her against it. He worked at her dress and when he had it partly undone he hiked the lower half high enough to bunch it about her waist. Exposing her breasts, he glued his mouth to her right nipple while simultaneously stroking her inner thighs. A groan was his reward. He flicked her nipple with his tongue, then nipped it between his teeth and stretched it by pulling back. She groaned louder and ran her knee up and down his leg.

Fargo's face was red-hot, his groin on fire. He stroked every part of her he could reach; her soft neck, her firm, full breasts, her muscular stomach, and her long legs. She was particulary sensitive above the knees, and when he ran a hand to within an inch of her nether lips, she threw back her head and opened her mouth wide but did not cry out.

Fargo heard a roaring in his ears. It was his own blood, coursing like lava through his veins. He sucked on her tongue and she sucked on his. He licked her chin, her cheek, her ear. She did the same to him. Suddenly sinking to his knees, he pressed his cheeks to her thighs and she gripped his hair so hard, it was in danger of being yanked out by the roots.

To heighten her anticipation, Fargo slowly kissed and nibbled his way to the fount of her womanhood. He nuzzled her crevice and she opened her legs to grant him access. Reaching up, he cupped both breasts. She gasped when he fastened his mouth to her swollen knob, gasped louder when he sucked. In a display of raw abandon, she thrust her bottom against his face.

"Oh my! So soon! So soon!"

Fargo inhaled the sweet scent of her and tasted the nectar of her release. She came with violent intensity, nearly knocking him over, so forceful were her gyrations. In order to stay on his knees he had to hold on to the tree.

When her upheaval subsided, she sagged against him, momentarily spent. Rising, Fargo looped one arm around her waist and slid his other hand between her legs. His forefinger penetrated her tunnel to the knuckle. It sparked a low whine. Raining a deluge of burning kisses on his throat, she tried to push his pants down.

"I want you! I want you *now*!"

Maybe so, but Fargo was setting the pace, not her, and he was not ready to grant her wish. He lathered her other nipple while down below he inserted a second finger. She was liquid satin inside, her inner walls contracting and rippling. He rubbed his fingers together and her bottom dipped as if she were trying to impale herself.

"My sister was right. You do things to me no man has ever done. I've gone over the edge twice already."

"That's more than Dacia did, Cyrena." Fargo gambled that in the excitement of the moment, his ruse might work.

"Is that what she told you? Dacia lied. She told me that she—," Cyrena stopped. "Damn you. She'll scratch out my eyes for spoiling our fun."

"Not if we don't tell her."

Cyrena grinned. "I would be forever in your debt, kind sir. I only hope you can think of a way I can repay you."

"You already are." Bending at the knees, Fargo guided his rigid shaft to the source of her soaked thighs.

"You are one in a million, Skye Fargo," Cyrena said huskily. "Any chance we can entice you to stick with the circus a while? I'm sure Thad can find work for you."

"Shoveling zebra shit?" Fargo shook his head. "No thanks." She opened her mouth to say something but he silenced her with a kiss. Covering her breasts with his palms, he massaged them, taking his sweet time about it. She was squirming with impatience when he slid his arms behind her and down to the small of her back. "Think you're ready?"

"Was that a challenge?"

In a swift, deft movement, Fargo speared his redwood up and in. Cyrena threw her arms around him and buried her face in his shoulder. Her winsome legs rose to his waist and locked. Stepping away from the tree so she wouldn't scrape her back, he levered upward on the balls of his feet, driving into her again and again, each thrust heightening their mutual delight. Her mouth glided to his ear.

"Harder, handsome. I like it harder."

Fargo obliged. He squeezed one of her breasts until she cried out. He kneaded her bottom until she pleaded for him to quit. He tugged on her hair until her head was bent back as far as it would go. A throaty purr escaped her and she increased the tempo of her pumping hips.

"I'm close! So very close!"

So was Fargo, although he fought it, just as he had with her sister. Planting himself, he sought to bring Cyrena to the crest ahead of him. His hands were everywhere, his mouth feasted on every square inch of bare skin he could reach. He was beginning to think it would take forever when she cooed and stiffened and spurted. It was all he needed. The night spun and blurred, the stars whirling in a mad dance.

Caked with sweat, Fargo slowly sank to earth, bearing her with him.

Cyrena smiled contentedly, and chuckled.

"What?" he prompted.

"The frontier has more to offer than my sister and I thought."

7

Skye Fargo was surprised to see George Hagen up and about. The entire family was bustling about the corral, replacing broken rails. Even Rebecca was helping, hobbling on a crude crutch they had made out of a tree limb with a fork at one end. But his surprise was nothing compared to theirs at the sight of Thimbletree on the zebra and Walikali on Tembo. Their expressions were downright comical. Then Timmy squealed in fright and ran to his mother and wrapped his arms around her good leg, crying, "It's back, Ma! The monster is back!"

"Fetch my shotgun!" George bellowed.

Obediently, Margaret had taken several steps toward the house when Rebecca hollered, "Wait! Mr. Fargo is with them. They must be friendly."

Thimbletree lowered his pink parasol and beamed. "That we are, my good woman. Thaddeus T. Thimbletree, at your service. I am the proprietor of Thimbletree's Traveling Menagerie and Mystic Arcanum. Or a circus, if you will. And I regret to inform you that one of our attractions is responsible for the damage I see about me."

George Hagen advanced on him, hefting a saw.

"That brute is yours? It about killed me the other night."

Undaunted, Thimbletree slid off the zebra and handed his parasol to an astounded Priscilla. "So I have been informed, Mr. Hagen. My abject apologies, sir," he said contritely.

Fargo and the others were dismounting. Walikali had Tembo lower him down, then stood patting her leg and speaking softly. She was staring at the barn, perhaps remembering the oats.

"Saying you're sorry won't help my fractured ribs heal," George Hagen declared. "Or fix the holes in my barn and my house." He held the saw as if he were tempted to swing the serrated edge at Thimbletree's neck.

"George!" Rebecca said sternly. "Don't you dare."

"Thank you, madam," Thimbletree bowed to her. From under his jacket he produced a leather pouch which he opened and extended toward the incensed father. "Hold out your hand, if you please, sir, and I will make restitution."

"What are you talking about?" George angrily demanded, but he did as he had been asked.

"Perhaps in some small measure this will make up for the suffering and the inconvenience you and your lovely family have suffered." Thimbletree upended the pouch.

Fargo was as dazzled as the Hagens. Onto George's palm spilled over a dozen gold coins. Glittering brightly in the sunlight, they formed a small pyramid. Several slid off and fell to the ground and were snatched up by Margaret.

"God Almighty!" George exclaimed.

Thimbletree pulled the string on his pouch, closing it, and slid it under his jacket again. "If that won't suffice, I will happily return in a couple of days with more. I truly want to make amends."

Rebecca hobbled to her husband's side and selected a coin. "Solid gold, George! These are solid gold!" She bit it, looked at the dent her teeth made, and turned in astonishment to Thimbletree. "There's more here than we would earn in two or three years."

Probably more, Fargo reckoned. Hardscrabble farmers like the Hagens lived hand to mouth. Most of their income came from the sale of crops and cows, of which the Hagens at the moment had neither. Small wonder George Hagen was speechless. The gold was probably more wealth than he ever had at any one time in his entire life.

"You're satisfied, then, madam?" Thimbletree asked, and when Rebecca numbly nodded, he asked the same question of George.

"Mister, we're as right as rain. Why, if you want, you can have that critter of yours tear down the rest of the barn. I can always build a new one."

Like the rest, Fargo laughed. He happened to glance over his shoulder at the twins and saw Judson Richter staring at the coins. Richter had the same greedy gleam in his eyes that he had when he mentioned Thimbletree's chest.

"Where did you ever get so much money?" Rebecca asked their benefactor.

Fargo hoped Thimbletree would avoid answering, with Richter there. But Thimbletree's honest streak was too ingrained.

"My circus has performed before the crown heads of Europe and Asia, my dear. They think nothing of paying a king's ransom for an evening's entertainment."

"What's a circus?" Margaret piped up.

Thimbletree puffed out his cheeks like a flustered badger. "How can it be that you've never heard of one? Why, child, a circus is all your dreams come true, your fondest fantasies given substance, the child in all of us brought to enchanted life."

"Huh?" Margaret said.

Dacia walked past him and put a hand on the girl's shoulder. "Pay him no mind. He likes to talk flowery to impress others. A circus has animals like Tembo, there, and performers like you might see at a variety theater."

The mention of Tembo reminded the Hagens of the elephant, causing Rebecca to hobble closer to her offspring. "That thing won't act up again, will it? I don't mind admitting it scares the living daylights out of me. And I sure don't want my children harmed."

Walikali patted Tembo's leg. "If my daughter could talk, she would tell you how sorry she is for what happened."

"Your daughter?" Rebecca said, and glanced quizzically at Fargo.

"I'll let him explain." Fargo led the Ovaro, the zebra, and most of the other horses to the corral and tied their reins to the top rail.

Judson Richter was still on his mount, still staring at the gold coins George Hagen had clasped to his chest.

Since it was nearly noon, Rebecca invited them to share in the family's dinner fare. She also urged them to stay the night but Thimbletree politely declined, saying he had to return to the circus so they could get under way for Salt Lake City. He did allow Walikali to give the children rides on Tembo and regaled George with tales of his travels in foreign lands while the twins and Rebecca shared cups of tea.

Fargo made it his business to keep an eye on Richter. But once George had taken the gold coins into the house, Richter showed no more interest and stayed in the background, minding his own business.

It was shortly past two o'clock when Thimbletree said his good-byes and they departed. Fargo rode between the twins, who were unusually quiet. "Something on your minds, ladies?"

Cyrena gazed over her shoulder at the homestead. "Rebecca has a nice family. They're poor as dirt but her husband is devoted and dependable and her children are precious."

"It makes a woman think of what she might be missing," Dacia commented, and gave her head a little toss. "But we each must live with the decisions we make. Regrets are for those who can't leave the past where it belongs."

Richter was right behind them and broke his long silence to say, "I agree, Miss Fleetwood. I never feel guilty over anything I've done. All I care about is what tomorrow will bring."

"Who can predict what the future holds?" Dacia said offhandedly.

"We make our future by what we do today," Richter responded. "Seize the bull by the horns today and you'll have life by the tail tomorrow."

Dacia shifted in her saddle. "I'm not quite sure I understand."

Fargo thought he did, and it did not bode well for Thimbletree. "The thing to remember is that there are limits to what we can do. There's always someone who will make a man answer for it if he steps over the line." His veiled threat made Richter smirk.

"What line is that?" Cyrena asked.

Judson Richter answered. "The line that separates law abidin' folks, ma'am, from those who live as they damn well please." He smiled at Fargo. "And as far as that goes, the lawbreakers only answer for their deeds if they're caught."

The rest of the day was uneventful. They camped beside a pool at sunset and Fargo and Richter trimmed long limbs, sharpened them, and waded out to spear fish for supper.

Walikali happened to be watering Tembo, and when Fargo walked by her, she raised her trunk from the water and sprayed him. Caught off guard, he was soaked to the skin. Everyone else thought it was hilarious.

"Do not be mad, bwana," Walikali said. "It is a sign Tembo is fond of you, that is all."

Fargo supposed he should be thankful she didn't express her affection by sitting on him. Later, as he sat drying himself at the fire, the twins could not resist poking a little fun.

Nudging Cyrena, Dacia remarked, "You know, it's not every man who has an elephant fall in love with him."

"It's a good thing she isn't the jealous kind or we could be in trouble," Cyrena responded.

Fargo endured their peals of mirth by reminding himself there were few pastimes women enjoyed more than teasing men.

The next morning they got an early start. By the landmarks, they had less than a mile to go when Thimbletree brought the zebra alongside the Ovaro. "Might I have a moment of your time, Mr. Fargo?"

"What's on your mind?"

"It's my understanding that a day or two west of where my circus is encamped, there is a mountain range. The Uintas, I believe Mr. Richter called them.

Is it true they are largely unexplored? And the haunt of countless beasts and savages?"

Fargo never liked it when Indians were branded as less than human. "The Utes are no more savage than we are."

"I daresay they're not. It's how Mr. Richter described them." Thimbletree paused. "I'm more interested in the wildlife. He says the Uinta Mountains are crawling with grizzlies, to use his vernacular."

"Forget it," Fargo said.

"I can't. A caged grizzly would be a sensation, as big a draw as Tembo or Lord Sydney or Leo."

"How many of your people can you afford to lose catching it? No net will hold a griz. A pit might, but getting it from the pit into a cage will be next to impossible." Fargo couldn't believe how pigheaded Thimbletree was being. "You'd be better off trying to snare a wolverine. They're every bit as ferocious but they're a hell of a lot smaller and would be a lot easier to handle." He did not mean for the suggestion to be taken seriously.

"A wolverine, you say? I've heard of them. Pugnacious creatures with voracious appetites. Gluttons, I believe they are commonly called." Thimbletree thoughtfully twirled his pink parasol. "I think you are on to something, Mr. Fargo. A wolverine would eat a lot less than a grizzly bear yet have the same allure for the public."

"But finding a wolverine could take months. They're rarer than grizzlies and as crafty as an animal comes."

"So capturing one can't be done?"

"I didn't say that. Anything can be done if a man puts his mind to it. But it's not as if you can rig a trap and expect a wolverine to walk into it the very first day."

"What if I gave you a week? And agreed to pay you five hundred dollars whether you bring a wolverine back or not?"

Fargo had barely twelve dollars to his name. Five hundred would recoup his recent gambling losses and give him a sizable stake, besides. "A week isn't anywhere near enough."

"Then what will you lose besides time? Seven days is all I ask. If at the end of that interval you haven't caught one, there will be no hard feelings. Do we have a deal?" Thimbletree offered his hand.

The way Fargo saw it, the circus owner was wasting his money, but it was Thimbletree's money to waste. "I'll think it over and let you know."

"Don't take too long. Ideally, you should leave tomorrow so you reach the mountains well before we do. I'll send Richter and a few others along to assist with whatever you require."

"I work better alone."

"As you prefer. I will provide whatever supplies you need from our supply wagons." Thimbletree smiled. "Should you prove successful, I will name the wolverine after you in your honor. Imagine, if you will, thousands of people around the world gaping in awe at Fargo the wolverine!"

The man came up with the silliest damn notions, Fargo reflected. He glanced to the rear to be sure they could not be overheard and asked, "What about Richter and his pards? They won't sit out there forever biding their time." He thought of another problem. "And in case you've forgotten, the Uintas are swarming with Utes. They're not as hostile as some tribes but they're not friendly, either, and I'm fond of my hair."

"I never try to persuade anyone to do anything against his will," Thimbletree said. "Think it over and let me know before you turn in tonight."

The camp was as they left it. Most of the animals were dozing in the afternoon sun, and most of the performers and workers were sitting around doing nothing. That changed when Thimbletree arrived. Under his supervision the trapeze apparatus was erected. It consisted of two ladders and a giant metal frame from which the trapeze was suspended.

To Fargo it did not appear anywhere near sturdy enough to support the twins, but when the workers were done, Dacia and Cyrena appeared wearing their costumes and climbed to a small platform high on one of the ladders.

Almost everyone gathered to watch. Fargo had never seen trapeze artists perform, had never even heard of them until he met the twins, and mentioned as much to Thimbletree.

"It's a new discipline, started in France about two years ago but only now making its way to American shores. Exciting to watch but dastardly dangerous. Those young ladies take their lives into their hands every time they put on a show."

Dacia was at the edge of the platform holding the trapeze bar. Cyrena was adjusting her outfit.

"Wouldn't it be better if they used a net of some kind?" Fargo remarked. It was a thirty foot drop to the ground. If a fall didn't kill them outright, they stood the risk of being crippled or, at the very least, of sustaining broken bones.

"I have suggested as much," Thimbletree said, "but the girls think it would dilute the excitement of their act."

Dacia pushed on the bar and the trapeze swung

toward the other ladder and then back. On each return swing she pushed it again, each shove taking it farther than the last. Then, with a nod at her sister, she tensed, and when the bar came toward her, she leaped and caught it and whipped her entire body in an arc. At the apex of the swing she let go of the bar, spun completely around, and grabbed it again. When it reached the platform, she did a precise flip and landed lightly beside Cyrena.

The twins took turns practicing. Fargo marveled at their grace, skill, and confidence. Each death-defying act was greeted by a sharp intake of breath from those below.

"Here comes their finale," Thimbletree said. "You have to see it to believe it."

Dacia launched herself from the near platform and as the trapeze swung outward, she slid her legs over the bar and hung by her knees. Lowering both arms, she concentrated on her sister, who had moved to the end of the platform and stood poised to leap.

Fargo was as riveted as the rest. When Cyrena suddenly sprang into the air, he involuntarily took a step toward the ladder. For a few seconds she was suspended between the sky and the earth, her body a perfect bow, her hands outstretched toward her only hope of salvation. Their timing had to be flawless; a split second off either way would spell disaster. Dacia's hands snagged Cyrena by the forearms and on their return swing Cyrena flipped onto the platform. On the swing after that, Dacia performed an incredible double flip.

Spontaneous applause erupted. Thimbletree clapped loudest of all, saying, "No matter how many times I watch them, I'm always in awe."

Judson Richter was shaking his head and muttering

to himself. Louder, he said, "Those girls are plumb crazy. They'll be dead before they're thirty." Then he chuckled and added, "If they don't die a hell of a lot sooner."

Fargo did not think much about the comment at the time. That evening, seated around a campfire with the twins and Thimbletree, he was listening to Dacia relate why she and her sister had chosen to become trapeze artists.

"We were tomboys when we were little. We loved doing all the things our brothers and their friends did. Riding, swimming, running, we were always athletic. But nothing came of it until our parents took us to London to see our aunt perform." Both women smiled wistfully at the memory. "I don't know how to describe it other than to say that the moment we saw our aunt take her first swing, we knew we had found our life's calling."

Out of the shadows stepped Judson Richter, his rifle cradled in his arms. "If you ask me, that's no way for a lady to act. Dressin' all skimpy like you do and flauntin' yourselves in public."

Cyrena's mouth curled in contempt. "Would you rather we were chained to a kitchen stove? Woman have as much right as men to enjoy some adventure in their lives."

"Is that what you call it? Adventure? I call it indecent."

"No one asked you," Fargo said.

"Now, now," Thimbletree interjected. "Let's be civil, shall we? We have a long journey ahead of us and we should make every effott to get along."

Richter trained his rifle on them. "That's where you're wrong, fat man," he sneered. "This nonsense has gone on long enough."

More figures materialized out of the darkness, two or three near each campfire, all with rifles leveled. Among them Fargo recognized Proctor and Stewart. He inched his hand toward his Colt, only to have a rifle muzzle jab him in the spine.

"I wouldn't, if I were you," warned a stocky man who had come up on him unnoticed.

Thimbletree rose to his feet. "I say, Mr. Richter! What is the meaning of this? Who are these hooligans and what deviltry are they up to?"

"Don't play dumb," Judson Richter responded. "Make it easy on us and we'll make it easy on you. Play us for fools and your people will suffer."

"You're spouting nonsense," Thimbletree said.

"Is that a fact?" Richter glanced at Proctor. "Round them up and mosey them over to the tiger wagon. Our friend here wants to do it the hard way."

Fargo's Colt was snatched from its holster and he was given a sharp shove. He still had his Arkansas Toothpick in its ankle sheath but the Toothpick was useless against that many guns. He had to swallow his pride and let himself be herded with the rest.

Lord Sydney disliked the commotion. He was pacing and growling and twitching his long tail.

"Look at the teeth on that thing!" Stewart exclaimed. "Why, it could bite clean through a calf without half tryin'."

The Great Gandolpho, Lecter the Human Flagpole, the Mystic Swami, and several others looked fit to tear into their captors if Thimbletree would but give the word. But their employer had more sense than to let them be slaughtered, and stood with his arms folded in anger.

With Proctor and Stewart on either side of him,

Judson Richter spelled it out. "All we want is the chest of gold. As soon as we have it, we'll be on our way, and all you freaks can go on breathin'."

"Don't call us that!" snapped Juliette. "We're as normal as you or anyone else."

"Says the woman who is the worst freak of all," Richter replied. "No normal gal would cover her body with all those drawin's. I get queasy just lookin' at you."

"The feeling is mutual," Juliette said, and some of the others laughed.

Fargo wasn't one of them. The circus people didn't realize how serious the situation was, or how much worse it could become.

Proctor brought matters to a head by saying, "Why are we wastin' our breath on these idiots, Jud? Do what we have to so we can get the hell out of here."

Richter turned to Thimbletree. "I'll ask you one more time, old man. Where is the damn chest? And before you answer, keep in mind that what you say could cost someone their life."

Thimbletree said the worst thing he possibly could. "You're bluffing, sir. No one is as callous as you make yourself out to be."

"Mister, I don't even know what that word means." Richter scanned them and his gaze came to rest on Juliette. "You there. The freak who doesn't know when to keep her mouth shut. You'll do." He gestured and two gun sharks seized her by the arms and hauled her to Sydney's wagon.

Fargo took a step but stopped when several rifles were pointed at him. "Don't do this, Richter. There has to be another way."

"I could gun them down one by one, I suppose,"

Judson Richter said. "But why waste the ammo when there's a hungry Bengal tiger that can do the job just as well as we can?"

Shock and horror gripped the onlookers. "You can't!" Lecter the Human Flagpole cried. "She's never done anything to you!"

"Do *you* know where the gold chest is?" Richter asked him.

"No," Lecter admitted.

"Then shut the hell up," Richter said, and shot him in the hip. Lecter staggered and would have fallen but others cushioned him as he grit his teeth in agony and nearly blacked out.

"Anyone else want to flap their gums?" Richter barked. When no one answered, he nodded at the men holding Juliette. A third gunman dashed to the cage door and gripped the bar that secured it.

Thimbletree still refused to accept the evidence of his own eyes. "Enough of this, you scoundrel! We all know you're only attempting to scare us."

In two long strides Judson Richter gripped Thimbletree by the front of his shirt and shoved him at the wagon. Thimbletree fell to one knee, took hold of a wheel, and attempted to rise, but Richter pushed him down again. "No you don't! Stay right where you're at. I want you to have a good look." He swatted Thimbletree's hat and it fell to the ground, then seized the circus owner by the hair. "I want you to see every drop of blood that's spilled and know it's all your fault."

Uncertainty deepened the lines in Thimbletree's face. "You wouldn't."

"Do it!" Judson Richter commanded.

Juliette fought. She thrashed and kicked and struggled with all her might. The Great Gandolpho and two others rushed to aid her but stopped when Proctor sent a slug into the ground in front of them. Seconds later the deed was done. The door was flung open and Juliette was thrown inside.

Under the circumstances, Juliette did the only thing she could. She screamed.

8

There are moments in life a person never forgets, moments of extreme joy or unbridled terror, moments so filled with emotion, they are seared indelibly on the memory. Sometimes they are moments better forgotten but which never will be. Moments like the one Skye Fargo was experiencing.

With every fiber of his being Fargo yearned to save the tattooed woman from the grisly fate Judson Richter had in store. But with several rifles trained on him, he would be blasted into eternity before he reached the cage.

The Great Gandolpho tried anyway. Bellowing, "Hold on, Julie!" he barreled toward the wagon door but took only two steps when a rifle cracked and he spun around and fell.

Nearly everyone else was frozen in horror, Thaddeus T. Thimbletree foremost among them. He was as white as chalk, beads of perspiration dotting his forehead his mouth slack.

Juliette had scampered into a corner and crouched with her arms across her face, whimpering, "Please no! For the love of God, don't do this to me."

Lord Syndey had not moved. He stood with his tail swishing from side to side, his head bent as if he were puzzled by this new development and not quite sure what he should do about it.

"Come on, you dumb tiger," Judson Richter barked. "Kill the bitch so we can get on with this."

"Don't, Sydney!" Dacia cried. "Please don't!"

Of the entire circus menagerie, the tiger was the least tame. Its savage nature had not been dulled by captivity. Its predatory urges were as keen as ever, its natural instincts as strong as they were in the wild.

Fargo dreaded what it would do next, and felt his gut tighten when Lord Sydney suddenly crouched and slunk toward Juliette as if he were stalking a cornered fawn.

Judson Richter grabbed hold of Thimbletree. "One last chance to save her, old man. Where's your gold?"

Thimbletree was mute with shock.

"Still won't say, huh? Suit yourself. But remember. What happens next is on your shoulders and no one else's."

Then came the moment Fargo would never forget, the moment when Lord Sydney roared and sprang. Juliette screeched and curled into a ball but all she did was make it easier for the lord of the Indian jungle. His long fangs sheared through her arm into her skull and ripped outward, nearly severing her hand and taking a sizable part of her head with it, even as his front claws sliced into her shoulder and chest. Her screech faded to a bubbly groan as blood gushed from her ruptured throat and out of her mouth. She was dead before the tiger bore her to the floor, her eyes wide and glazing fast.

Lord Sydney bit her again and gave a powerful wrench, ripping her open from her shoulder to her sternum. Blood gushed like a geyser.

Many of the women and children screamed, and not

101

a few of the men. Fargo fought down bitter bile and clenched his fists in impotent rage.

As for Richter and his friends, they were chortling and laughing.

"Maybe we should throw a kid in next," Proctor suggested.

But their laughter died when Lord Sydney did the last thing anyone expected. Maybe the tiger had seen that the wagon door was ajar. Maybe it was a random reaction to the thrill of killing a hated human. But Juliette had barely stopped convulsing when Lord Sydney roared and threw himself at the door, which the outlaws had forgotten to bar. It exploded outward, knocking two of them off their feet, and before anyone could blink, Lord Sydney was gone, streaking into the forest like a bolt of orange and black lightning.

Judson Richter was transfixed with amazement, but not for long. "Damn you, Latham! Why the hell didn't you bar the door?"

Latham was on the ground, frantically running his hands over his body to see if the tiger had clawed him. "How the hell was I to know it would do that? I've never seen a critter like that before."

Thimbletree straightened and gazed forlornly at the crumpled figure in the wagon. "Sweet, gentle, Juliette. I beg your forgiveness. I never thought they would go through with it."

Richter spun him around. "Now you know it's no bluff, you fat bastard. So no more games. Tell us where your gold is or someone else will suffer."

"If I do the circus is ruined," Thimbletree said.

"What's more important? Your gold or the lives of these fools who work for you?" Richter gripped him by the collar and propelled him toward the lion cage. "You have about a minute to make up your mind."

Proctor fired into the dirt and hollered, "I want everyone to listen up. Give us any grief and we'll shoot you where you stand. Savvy?"

Once again Fargo had to endure being shoved and prodded. He counted ten outlaws, all told, and didn't dare resist.

Leo the lion sat calmly on his haunches, watching everyone gather in front of his cage. He had never been as excitable and nervous as the tiger. In fact, Fargo had never heard Leo roar or growl.

"So who will it be this time?" Richter said to Thimbletree. "Which one will die because you're a skinflint?"

"It's not that." Thimbletree's chin was bowed and tears streaked his cheeks. "I've had to work extraordinarily hard to make my circus a success. If you steal my money, all my work, all my sacrifice, will have been for nothing."

"Sure, sure," Richter said. "You don't give a hoot about the gold." In plain resentment he slapped Thimbletree across the face, rocking him on his heels. "What do you take me for, you bastard? Sugarcoat it all you want, but you're no better than anyone else. When it comes right down to it, your gold means more to you than these people do."

"No, no, no," Thimbletree said, scarlet drops trickling from his mouth.

Judson Ricther faced them. "Any volunteers?" he taunted. "Any of you feel like dyin' for this worthless gob of spit?"

To Fargo's consternation the twins stepped forward. He moved to stop them but a rifle barrel blossomed in front of his face.

"Take us," Cyrena declared.

"Or better yet," Dacia said, "give us guns so we can give you cowards a taste of your own medicine."

"Cowards, are we?" Judson Richter wrapped a hand around her wrist and sent her stumbling into the hands of the same two who had thrown Juliette into the tiger's cage. "Here you go, boys. Let's see how much guff she gives us when that lion is chompin' on her innards."

Fargo couldn't understand why Cyrena didn't try to stop them from tossing her sister into the cage. Dacia was pitched to her knees not an arm's length from the king of the beasts.

"This should be good," Richter said, rubbing his hands in sadistic glee.

Leo stared at Dacia, then sniffed her. He was so much bigger than she was, she seemed like a child by comparison. His mouth gaped wide, and he—yawned. Then Leo brought his great maned head down close to hers and licked her, coating her face with slobber.

"What the hell?" Richter blurted.

"The damn thing is as tame as a kitten," Proctor said. "They knew it the whole time and played us for jackasses."

Some of the circus people were grinning but they did not grin for long. Judson Richter turned red with fury, grabbed Cyrena by the hair, and pulled her none too gently toward the next wagon. "So you think you can make us look dumb, huh? You think you're so stinkin' clever?"

"Let her go!" Dacia yelled, and threw herself at the door to Leo's wagon. But Richter's friends had learned from their mistake with the tiger and replaced the bar. "Cyrena! Run for it!"

All her sister could do was futilely pound at Richter's

forearms as he brought her to a stop and spun her toward the bars. "How tame is this thing?" he rasped. "I bet it won't lick you and sit there like a pet puppy."

Fargo was not prone to fear but it knifed through him now. Cyrena didn't have a prayer. The creature in that wagon was a living testament to all that was cold and heartless in the world, a creature without feelings, without a shred of compassion or remorse, a creature more merciless than Lord Sydney, a creature whose sole purpose in life was to crush and eat anything it could catch.

"Not the python!" Cyrena exclaimed.

The giant reptile had been lying completely still, coiled in a corner, but the sudden activity caused its tongue to flick in and out and its head to slide a few inches higher on its mountain of coils.

"Yes, sir," Judson Richter crowed. "There's nothin' like a snake to put the fear of dyin' in folks." He gestured. "Open the door, boys. We'll be the ones laughing this time."

Fargo's legs moved of their own accord. He was almost to Richter when pain exploded at the base of his skull and the world faded to swirling hues of gray and black. He had a vague sense of being moved, and marveled that he was still alive. Since he had not heard a shot, he figured someone had struck him with a rifle butt. There were shouts, and what sounded like blows, and then he was pitched onto his stomach on a hard surface. His vision returned, and when he saw where he was lying, he jerked his head up, his pulse quickening.

At the other end of the wagon was the python, motionless except for the flick of its tongue.

Hands fell on Fargo's shoulders and pulled him to his knees. "Are you all right?" Cyrena asked.

Fargo nodded, unwilling to take his eyes off the python. Its own eyes, with their vertical slits and netherworldly iciness, had a mesmerizing quality. Placing an arm against Cyrena, he backed them to the door. "Let us out, Richter."

"You know better, Trailsman," the other scout replied. "Nothin' personal, you understand. But a man has to do what a man has to do."

Many of the circus troupe were pressed to the bars, Thimbletree among them. Tearing his gaze from the giant snake, Fargo turned and crouched. "Give them the gold, Thaddeus. It's not worth more lives." In a whisper he added, "I'll get it back for you. I swear."

Conflicting emotions had Thimbletree in their sway. He looked at the python, then at Richter, then at Cyrena, and finally at Fargo. "I'm sorry," he said plaintively. "I just can't."

Richter's disdain was no worse than Fargo's own. "So much for your grand notions and big words, mister. When you peel away your fancy airs, all that's left is a greedy worm."

"The circus must always come first," Thimbletree justified himself.

"Tell that to the tattooed gal. Or to these two when that snake gets done swallowin' them."

The bars were spaced only a couple of inches apart, but that did not stop Fargo from lunging and trying to squeeze his hand through to grab Richter by the throat. All Richter did was laugh.

"Nice try. But I'd save my energy. Sooner or later that serpent is going to get hungry, and you and your lady friend are the only treats on the menu."

Fargo glanced around. The door was too sturdy to break down, the bars were made of iron. That left the hardwood floor and the roof. Rising on the tips of his toes, he raised his arms and desperately searched for a weak spot, for a board that might be loose or a joint he could pry apart. There were none.

Richter did not let up on Thimbletree. He heaped insult after insult, calling Thimbletree everything from a yellow cur to a rotten liar, but the abuse rolled off the object of Richter's scorn like drops of water off a duck's back. In rising anger, Richter slammed Thimbletree against the bars and pointed at Cyrena. "You'd let a pretty woman like that die when you can save her? Hell, you're worse than I'll ever be. But that's always how it is with you uppity types. You think you're too good for the rest of us when you're not fit to lick our boots."

"I never claimed to be your superior," Thimbletree said indignantly.

"You didn't need to. How you feel is as plain as that bubble nose on your ugly face." Richter went to say more but glanced at the cage and grinned. "Looks as if the waitin' is over. It's feedin' time."

Fargo whirled.

The python's obscene triangular head had risen into the air and its devilish forked tongue was flicking faster than ever. Those hideous unblinking eyes, as big as saucers, were fixed on Cyrena and him. The patterns on its glistening skin rippled as the coils began to move.

Cyrena gasped and clutched Fargo's arm. "What do we do? It's stronger than both of us combined."

"We're too big for it to swallow," Fargo grasped at a straw. "Maybe it will leave us alone."

"Pythons can swallow things a lot bigger than they are by dislocating their jaws," Cyrena enlightened him. "I've seen this one swallow a full-grown deer." She glanced at Thimbletree. "Please, Thad. For me, if for no other reason."

"I wish I could, my dear." Thimbletree wouldn't look at her. "I only hope you can find it in your heart to forgive me."

Fargo had an overwhelming impulse to punch him. "Maybe she will but I sure as hell won't. You're not half the man I thought you were."

"Look!" Cyrena cried.

The python's head was on the floor, slithering slowly toward them.

"This is not how I want to die," Cyrena said.

That made two of them. The way Fargo saw it, they had one chance and one chance only. He was no match for the snake, brawn pitted against brawn. But he was quicker, and he had his Toothpick, and he would be damned if he would stand there like a lamb for the slaughter while he had a breath of life left in his body. He was a fighter. He had always been a fighter. And if it was his time to die, then he would die fighting. Bending, he slid his hand up under his pant leg and into his boot.

"Hey! He's got a knife!" Proctor shouted.

The python was only a couple of feet away when Fargo sprang. He leaped above its head and dropped, his knees bent to pin the neck, his left hand outstretched to grab hold of it just behind the jaws. That was where anyone who knew anything about snakes always grabbed them. He had done so many times with nonpoisonous snakes and some of the poisonous ones, besides.

But the difference between a gopher snake or a garter snake and a python was more than one of degree. Just as a grown man was many times stronger than an infant, so, too, was a python many times stronger than its smaller kin. Exactly how much stronger Fargo found out when he slammed onto its back and seized it by the neck. He had hold of a whirlwind and the whirlwind was enraged.

Fargo stabbed at the reptile's head but missed as the python came up off the floor in a blinding explosion of power and speed. It felt as if a battering ram slammed against his chest. The impact upended him and he flew head over heels against the bars. He heard Cyrena scream, but as if from a distance. Dazed, aching, unsure whether he still held the Toothpick, he rose onto his hands and knees, resisting a tide of dizziness.

The python was crawling toward him.

Fargo's mind shrieked at him to move, to get up, to defend himself, but his body wouldn't budge. Part of him was so mesmerized by the approaching snake, he couldn't control his limbs. Its mouth was opening to clamp onto his arm when another scream from Cyrena pierced the strange fog benumbing his brain. With an effort of sheer will, he broke the invisible chains binding his body, heaved erect, and sprang back.

The python's sinuous body curved first right, then left, as it sought to corner him, just as it would a rodent or other mammal it was fed.

Fargo backed up until there was nowhere to go. Bracing a foot against the wall, he saw the python suddenly streak toward him, and skipped aside. The snake hissed and twisted. He vaulted off the floor, his knees tucked to his chest, and the reptile slithered under him.

His respite was brief, a few heartbeats in duration. Then gravity took over, and he came down hard on the python's spine. His left hand closed around the base of its jaw but it was like trying to hold on to a bucking bronc. Something struck his legs and he wound up on his back with the snake beside him, rearing to attack.

"Don't let it get its coils around you!" Cyrena yelled.

Fargo did not need to be reminded. Thimbletree had told him pythons were constrictors, and he had seen enough king snakes to know how constrictors killed prey. As the blunt snout swept toward him, he rolled and struck, burying the Toothpick's double-edged blade.

The python recoiled, its body whipping violently about.

Scrambling up, Fargo crouched with the Toothpick held low in front of him. Blood dripped from the tip and some was on his hand. He watched for sign of another attack but the python continued to thrash about. A hush had fallen outside the wagon, and over near the door Cyrena had a hand to her throat in undisguised fear.

Judson Richter laughed. "You're a bundle of surprises, Fargo. I never knew you carried that pigsticker. I should shoot you and let the snake fill its belly but I want to see how long you hold out."

"I've got ten dollars that says he won't last two more minutes," Proctor called out.

"And I've got ten that says he'll last five!" Stewart took him up on it.

More bets were exchanged but Fargo didn't listen. The python was sidling to the left to outflank him and he pivoted to keep it in front of him. Suddenly it lashed out but he met it with a swipe of his knife and opened up the flesh above one eye. Whipping back, it hissed again.

Sweat caked Fargo from head to toe. Some got into

his eyes, stinging terribly, and he blinked to clear his vision. His eyes were only shut for a fraction of a second but it was enough. He felt his legs bowled out from under him and then a vise closed around them, paralyzing him from the waist down.

The python had him in its coils.

Fargo saw its body but not the head. Something brushed his lower back and slid higher. With a start he realized the thing was under him and about to coil around his neck and shoulders. Twisting, he grabbed as high up on its neck as he could and tried to pull its head from under him but it resisted. For long moments they pitted sinew against sinew, and it became apparent to Fargo that the snake would win unless he did something drastic. Three, four, five times he stabbed it, aiming at the spine, and on his fifth blow the python unraveled with incredible rapidity. A sweep of its coils flung him across the floor and he struck the wagon door.

Warm hands helped him sit up. "Are you all right?" Cyrena asked.

Fargo was sore and bruised but so far he had been spared serious injury. He spun toward the python, figuring it would be on top of them, but it was coiling in on itself in the corner.

Faces were pressed to the bars on both sides. Those of the circus crowd were hopeful; those of the outlaws were disappointed.

"Hell," Proctor said sourly. "My grandma could beat that thing with one hand tied behind her back."

"Maybe we should just stake them out and skin them alive," Stewart proposed. "Startin' with money-bags."

Judson Richter had other ideas. "Fetch some rope. I want these pilgrims hobbled so they can't run off on us. Then we'll help ourselves to their food while I do some ponderin'."

For the moment Fargo and Cyrena were safe. He tried to catch a glimpse of Dacia in the lion's cage, but he couldn't see it from where they were.

"I hope Leo leaves Dacia alone," Cyrena voiced his thoughts aloud. "He's as gentle as can be most of the time, but he's a lion, after all."

Fargo sagged against the bars. The struggle had taken more out of him than he thought. His right palm was slick with blood and sweat so he switched the Toothpick to his other hand, wiped his palm dry on his buckskins, then gripped the knife in his right again.

The python wasn't moving. It lay much as it had been when they entered the wagon, only now the coils hid its head except for one baleful eye.

"I'm sorry I wasn't any help," Cyrena said. "I'm scared to death of snakes. Always have been. When I was a girl, my younger brother stuck one in my bed one night and I about died of fright."

"We're still alive," Fargo said.

"No thanks to me. Or to Thaddeus. I thought I knew him but I guess I don't. Poor Juliette is dead because of his selfishness, and more of us might join her before these terrible men are through."

Judson Richter and Proctor were huddled nearby, talking in low tones. Fargo tried to overhear what they were saying but all he caught were snatches.

Rope was brought, and the circus troupe was gathered together and forced to submit to having their wrists and ankles bound. All except Thimbletree, who was made to stand off by himself, under guard, until Richter beckoned.

"My patience is wearin' thin, old man. Where's the damn chest?"

112

"Look for it," Thimbletree responded.

"Don't you think I already have? Three times since we left Denver I've searched your wagon when you weren't looking. Three times I came up empty-handed."

"Do your worst but I still won't say."

"Reckon so, do you?" Richter grinned. "I've had a brainstorm. You keep sayin' you won't turn over the chest because your circus needs it. But what if there is no circus?"

"How's that?"

"You heard me. What good is your precious gold if all of this is gone?" Richter motioned at the wagons.

"Only a heartless fiend would shoot all my animals."

"You're not payin' attention, old man." Richter poked Thimbletree in the chest. "Why should I bother with just your critters when I can go you one better?" Richter smiled. "I'm talkin' about all your wagons, all your equipment, all your provisions, everything. I aim to burn it to the ground."

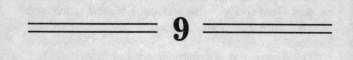

It didn't take Judson Richter's men long to gather armloads of dead branches and pile them under the wagons and vans.

Skye Fargo stood at the bars watching as a lanky gunman kept returning with firewood and shoving it under the python's wagon. On his last trip the man's face split in a wicked grin.

"That should do it, hombre. In a little bit, you and the pretty lady, there, will be roasted to a crisp. You might want to spend your last minutes cuddlin'." Laughing, he left them.

Thaddeus T. Thimbletree observed the preparations without saying a word. Even when Richter stepped to the nearest campfire and selected a burning brand, Thimbletree did nothing.

"What will it be? The gold or your circus?" Richter waved the crackling brand in front of Thimbletree's face.

Thimbletree stared at the burning brand without the slightest flicker of recognition. He appeared to be in a daze induced by the violence and deaths.

"Thad!" Cyrena cried. "Snap out of it!"

Blinking, Thimbletree looked at her, then at Richter. "My circus means everything to me."

"Then you'd better rustle up that chest of yours, old man."

"I can't. It's my life's earnings. I would rather die before I gave it up."

Balling his other fist, Richter smashed Thimbletree across the jaw. It folded him like an accordion and left him hurt but conscious. "How can one peckerwood be so stinkin' stubborn?" Richter fumed. "What does it take to get it through that thick skull of yours? *I'll do whatever it takes to get my hands on that gold.*" Richter kicked Thimbletree in the side. "I should stave in your ribs. Maybe some pain will change your mind." He kicked him again.

Thimbletree groaned but made no attempt to defend himself.

"Leave him alone!" Cyrena shouted. "You won't get the gold if he's dead."

Judson Richter controlled himself and stepped back. "So help me God, old man, I've never wanted to kill anyone as much as I want to kill you." Bending, he jabbed Thimbletree in the neck. "For the last time. Where's the chest?"

Thimbletree raised his head. He was crying again. Twice he tried to speak and couldn't but at the third attempt he said softly, "I'm sorry. I can't and I won't and that's all I will ever have to say."

Richter leaned down and made as if to shove the brand into Thimbletree's face, but at the last moment he straightened and swore. "Proctor! Get over here!"

The gunman with the pearl-handled Colt hustled past a wagon. "What has you so riled?"

"Get the redhead out of the lion cage and the other one out of the snake wagon. We're takin' them with us."

"Where to?" Proctor asked.

"Just do it!" Richter was practically beside himself. "I aim to make this geezer wish he'd never been born." Proctor and several others scrambled to obey, and Richter yanked Thimbletree to his feet. "I want you to watch, you son of a bitch. I want you to see what it's like when someone is burned alive. Maybe then you'll change your mind."

Fargo doubted it. Thimbletree's gold meant more to him than life itself. He heard the wagon door open, and spun, but a rifle muzzle dissuaded him from interfering as Cyrena was hauled out. The door slammed shut and he heard the bar slap home.

In another minute Dacia was brought over. Fargo was relieved to see she was unhurt. Both sisters looked at him in dismay, Cyrena wringing her hands.

Richter slapped Thimbletree to get his attention. "Listen good. If you haven't told us where the gold is by the time your wagons burn down, we're takin' the redheads off a ways and spendin' the night by ourselves to give you and your hired help a chance to talk things over. In the mornin' we'll be back, and you either have the gold waitin' or not one of you will ever reach Salt Lake City." Richter slapped him again, then turned to the rest. "Did you hear that? Make him understand or your hours are numbered."

Rustling behind him galvanized Fargo into whirling but the python hadn't moved.

"Let's do it, boys," Judson Richter bawled, and advanced with the burning brand extended. "You and the snake go up first, Fargo. Any last words?"

"Go to hell."

"Is that the best you can come up with?" Richter snickered. "Let me know if it gets a little warm in there." With that, he pitched the brand onto the pile of wood under the wagon and leaped back as the wood ignited and flames shot from underneath.

Almost immediately the temperature in the wagon jumped five to ten degrees. Fargo stepped back from the bars as flames licked around their base, nearly singeing his boots. It wouldn't be long before the floor caught on fire, and once that happened, the rest of the wagon would soon follow.

The door was the only way out. Although Fargo knew it was pointless, he kicked it again and again and again in a vain bid to dislodge the bar. The cutthroats mocked him. Some of the circus crew were yelling for Richter to let him out but Richter ignored them.

The temperature climbed higher. Tongues of flames crept up the bars and the wagon filled with smoke. Covering his mouth with a forearm, Fargo continued kicking the door. His eyes smarted and his nostrils were filled with the acrid odor, but still he kicked, kicked, kicked. He drew back his leg to do so once more and felt something brush against his other foot.

It was the python. The fire had agitated it and with an instinct borne of self-preservation it was seeking a way out.

Fargo turned to ice, one leg in the air. The snake showed no more interest in him than it would in a lump of coal and crawled back the way it came. As soon as its tail looped past him, Fargo assaulted the door anew.

Sweating profusely, his eyes streaming smoke-induced tears, Fargo crouched and attacked the door with the Toothpick. He might be able to chip his way out but that took time and the smoke and heat would overcome him first.

Loud voices were raised excitedly, and Judson Richter bellowed. Then Fargo heard a sound he had not heard since that night at the Hagens: the booming trumpet of an African elephant. With all that had happened, he had forgotten about Tembo. He also realized he hadn't seen Walikali since early in the evening, and was sure Walikali had not been among the captives.

A gun cracked. Someone cursed. More guns blasted, and were punctuated by a loud, confused babble.

The smoke was so thick by now, Fargo couldn't see what was happening. He imbedded the Toothpick in the door and twisted, tearing off a piece about the size of his thumb. But it was nowhere near enough. At the rate he was going, it would take hours to break out and he had at the most minutes.

Pressure on his leg caused Fargo to glance down. The python had returned and was just lying there, the tip of its tongue brushing his boot every time the tongue darted out. Any other time he would have stabbed it or leaped back. But it did not try to bite him or wrap around his legs so he went on chopping.

Then, much to Fargo's astonishment, the python suddenly battered at the door with its blunt snout. The only explanation he could think of was that the snake had seen food tossed in to it so many times that in the dim recesses of its reptilian brain it, too, realized there was only one way out.

Over and over Fargo drove the blade into the wood but he had made little headway when flames spouted from the center of the floor, gusting nearly to the ceiling. The heat was blistering. Fargo moved toward the bars, as much to evade the flames as to avoid the thrashing python. It had been burned, and in the throes of agony, it was whipping madly about.

Fargo's lungs felt as if they were on fire, too. His

eyes were watering so badly, he couldn't see. And to make his predicament worse, the heat was rapidly sapping his vitality. He barely had strength to lift his arm.

The ruckus outside had risen to a riotous din. Guns banged, but from farther away. Tembo trumpeted again.

Suddenly, the entire wagon shook from a tremendous impact. The jolt knocked Fargo off his feet and he sprawled across the convulsing python. Almost instantly its jaws closed on his left leg. The pain was excruciating, but it was eclipsed by the pain of being thrown against the bars when, without warning, the entire wagon canted at an angle. Two of its wheels had risen up off the ground. Wood creaked and splintered. He felt it start to go over and clutched at the bars for support.

The crash was deafening. Half the roof crumpled, and the flames shot higher. The python let go of his leg. Fargo seized the instant and dived for the opening. As he shot through, something coiled around his waist. Thinking it was the python, he started to stab it, only to discover it wasn't the python, it was Tembo's trunk.

The elephant lifted him clear and carried him a dozen yards. He sucked in the clear air as a man dying of thirst would gulp down water, only vaguely aware of Walikali talking to Tembo and of the bedlam of many people yelling all at once. He also heard the crash of undergrowth and the drum of hooves. Above it all a man suddenly bawled, "Stop them! We can't let them get away!"

"Bwana Fargo," Walikali called to him. "Are you hurt? Can you stand if Tembo sets you down?"

"Do it!" Fargo commanded, and the second his

boots touched the ground he was off and running, around the burning wagon to where he had last seen the twins. They were not there. Neither were Judson Richter nor Proctor nor any of the other outlaws except for one who lay in a pool of spreading blood, his head split like a melon. A few of the circus crew were also sprawled here and there. Others were dashing about in confusion.

Out of the darkness came the Great Gandolpho, a bloody metal bar in his right hand. It explained the dead outlaw. His left shoulder was stained red.

"I thought you were dead," Fargo said.

"So did they, my friend. But I crawled under their noses to a supply wagon and got this crowbar." Gandolpho brandished his weapon. "Walikali spotted me, and we hit the hyenas from two sides at once." His broad face creased in triumph. "Lord, you should have seen their faces when Tembo lit into them! They didn't want any part of her."

Fargo rolled the dead gunman over and helped himself to the man's revolver a Remington. "Where are Richter and his gang now?"

"They made it to their horses." The Great Gandolpho glowered westward. "They took the Fleetwood girls along. Richter shouted that they'll be back at ten tomorrow, elephant or no elephant."

"And Thimbletree?"

Gandolpho shook his head. "I have no idea where he went. I was only interested in bashing heads."

"Call everyone together," Fargo said. "We need to take stock." He ran toward Thimbletree's private wagon and nearly tripped over another body. This one was Stewart, and tucked in the gunny's waistband was his Colt. Now he had two revolvers.

The door to Thimbletree's wagon was shut. He

knocked, and when there was no answer, tried the latch. The door wasn't locked. He only had to stick his head in to confirm no one was there.

Scouring the camp, Fargo shouted the circus owner's name several times. If Thimbletree heard, he didn't respond.

Fargo headed for the horse string, worried what he would find. But fate granted him another stroke of luck. In their haste to escape Tembo's wrath, Richter and company had neglected to run off the horses and mules. He took the Ovaro to where he had left his saddle and bedroll, and saddled up.

By then everyone else had gathered near the burning wagon, and Fargo led the Ovaro toward them.

"I am glad you are safe, bwana." Walikali had climbed down from Tembo and was hurrying over.

"It took you long enough to do something. Juliette is dead and I was almost burned alive."

The African spread his hands. "I am sorry, bwana. I was afraid for my daughter. Afraid those bad men would shoot her." His regret was genuine. "But Gandolpho said we must do something. And Tembo, when she saw you in the fire, I could not stop her."

"Are you saying she saved me on her own?" Fargo gazed across the clearing to where Tembo stood, and damned if she didn't raise her trunk as if she was waving to him.

"I told you, bwana, remember? My daughter is very fond of you. If she did not have me, I think she would choose to live with you."

"I'm flattered," Fargo said dryly.

"An elephant's affection should not be laughed at. You are special, bwana. Among my tribe you would be held in high honor."

Fargo had heard enough about elephant love for

one night. "Get back on her and patrol the camp. Make sure none of Richter's men are skulking anywhere around." Walikali nodded and turned to go, and Fargo glanced at Tembo. "And be careful. We don't want anything to happen to her."

For some reason Walikali grinned. "Will do, bwana. Do not fear. I love my daughter, too."

"Too?" Fargo said, but by then the man was halfway across the clearing. Shaking his head, Fargo led the Ovaro to where the Great Gandolpho was having his gunshot wound examined by one of the clowns, an Englishman named Brent. "Any sign of Thimbletree yet?"

"I was hoping you had found him," Gandolpho said. "He has a lot to answer for."

"What about us, mate?" Brent asked. "Those blokes are bound to come back, and next time they won't let Tembo chase them off."

The others hemmed closer to hear, among them Lecter, the Human Flagpole, who was being helped by two others. "I'm more worried about the twins. Who knows what those skunks will do."

Fargo had a fair idea, which was why he said, "I'm going after them before they can get very far."

"How can you find them in the dark?" Gandolpho asked. "You're not an owl."

"I'll do what I can. If I'm not back by midnight, circle the wagons and post guards. I doubt Richter will try anything before dawn but it's better to be safe."

"What if they do try something?" Gandolpho held up the crowbar. "This won't stop bullets."

Fargo handed him the Remington. "Take the other revolver, rifles, and gun belts from the two you killed and hand them out." He turned to the Ovaro and hooked his boot in the stirrup. "And don't forget to bury Juliette."

"Be careful out there," Gandolpho said.

Once beyond the firelight, a black veil enveloped him. The night was cloudy and few stars were visible. Fargo trotted west but slowed after a quarter of a mile in order not to tire the Ovaro too soon. He was relying on luck again since he had no idea whether Richter had stuck to the trail or gone in some other direction.

Soon he came to a low hill. From the top he had an unobstructed view of the surrounding countryside. He could see the fires of the circus, burning bright. But no others. Dismounting, he paced in a circle for over an hour. He was counting on Richter's killers to start a fire of their own, but either they were clever enough to do it where it couldn't be seen or they had made a cold camp.

"It was worth a try," Fargo said to the stallion as he climbed on. And there, a few miles to the northwest, blazed a small red and orange triangle.

Fargo rode as fast as the darkness permitted. He had no plan short of saving the twins and killing Judson Richter. Proctor, too, while he was at it. Without their leaders the rest might give up.

He found himself thinking about the burning wagon, and the python, and how close he came to pushing up mesquite. He could kick himself for not confronting Richter sooner. If he had, Juliette might still be alive.

Once he smelled smoke, Fargo slowed to a walk. He secreted the pinto in a ravine about three hundred yards from the fire and stalked on foot to a brush-covered knoll, the Henry in hand. Reaching the top without making noise taxed his skill but at last he was below the rim, and removing his hat, he craned his neck.

Instead of Judson Richter's bunch, below him were eleven swarthy warriors in buckskins. A Ute hunting party, since neither they nor their horses were painted for war. They were talking and joking, relaxed and at ease.

Fargo figured they were on their way north to their village. They were no danger to the circus, so he saw no reason to stick around. He placed his hands flat to slide back down the knoll, then stiffened.

From out of the night to the southeast rumbled a ferocious roar. A roar never heard in the Rockies before, because the carnivore that made it came from a jungle halfway around the world. Lord Sydney was abroad, and he had caught the scent of the Utes and their horses.

The warriors jumped up, brandishing their weapons, and faced in the direction of the roar.

Lord Sydney roared again, closer now, by Fargo's reckoning only sixty yards from the knoll. It dawned on him that the tiger might catch *his* scent and come after him instead of the Utes. He started to slide down but again stopped.

The Utes had spread out and were coming to investigate. Little did they realize their bows and lances were no match for the fierce meat-eater they were up against. Fargo was torn between his urge to get out of there and a twinge of conscience. The Utes should be warned. But the only way to do that was to show himself, and the Utes were liable to fill him with arrows.

Lord Syndey roared a third time. He was less than thirty yards from the knoll now, and if he hadn't caught Fargo's scent, he would soon.

The twins had told Fargo that tigers were the most widely feared predators on the Asian continent. Their senses were extremely sharp, their smell and hearing in particular. Like most cats, they could move as silently as a shadow. In some provinces in India they were known as "striped ghosts."

The Utes weren't eager to face the source of the roars. They had halted and several were holding torches aloft.

Fargo turned to make himself scarce and spotted the inky silhouette of Lord Sydney highlighted against the backdrop of underbrush due east of him, blocking his retreat. He thought the tiger would keep circling but it had stopped and was staring at the top of the knoll. The tiger knew he was there. Fargo was sure of it. He was trapped between Lord Sydney on one side and the Utes on the other and soon the Utes would spot him, too. The light from their torches was growing brighter as they neared the other side of the knoll.

Lord Sydney suddenly crouched and slunk toward him.

Fargo wedged the Henry to his shoulder but held his fire when the tiger was swallowed by shadows. He needed a clear shot. Killing Sydney would be as hard as killing a grizzly, and their capacity for absorbing lead was legendary.

The tiger's head appeared, seemingly detached from its body. Steadying the Henry, he tried to fix a bead on one of its eyes. But in the dark they were next to invisible. All he might do was wound it.

Lord Sydney growled and vanished again. A sudden splash of light over the knoll explained why. Some of the Utes were almost to the top. Others were flanking it. As yet they had not seen the feline invader of their domain, but it was only a matter of moments.

It was also a matter of moments before they spotted Fargo. He was in high weeds and about to drop onto his belly when he spied the tiger again.

Lord Sydney was only twenty yards away, poised to charge.

Just then a torch appeared over the top of the knoll, and in a streak of incredible speed, the huge cat bounded off.

One threat was gone but the other remained. Fargo flattened a heartbeat before his side of the knoll was bathed by torchlight. Four Utes were above him, others on either side. At a shout from a warrior wearing an eagle feather, the rest halted and gazed into the woods beyond.

Fargo scarcely breathed as he waited for them to turn back so he could rush to the Ovaro. Lord Sydney hadn't gone in the direction of the ravine but that did not mean he wouldn't change direction. Seconds passed, and Fargo chafed with concern for the stallion.

Some of the Utes made for their camp but the rest were in no great hurry. They were gesturing at the woods as if debating whether to search further.

Fargo was elated when the Ute with the eagle feather motioned and the rest turned back. But his elation was short-lived, for the very next instant the night was shattered by the loudest roar yet, and out of nowhere sprang Lord Sydney.

10

Shock rooted the Utes in place. They had never seen a tiger before. They had no idea such a creature existed. To them it was the unreal made real. Many must have doubted their senses as it hurtled from out of the night and leaped onto a hapless warrior before any of them could lift a bow or lance.

Lord Sydney's weight bore the warrior to earth, and in the blink of an eye his fangs penetrated the man's skull. The body went into convulsions as the tiger bit into the Ute's shoulder and started to drag him off.

Several warriors recovered their wits and the tall one with the eagle feather sent an arrow flying but in his haste he missed. Another cocked an arm to throw a lance.

Lord Sydney let go of his prey and roared. It froze the Utes to a man. One paw on the dead warrior's chest, his teeth gleaming like sabers in the torch light, he was a living, breathing nightmare, the embodiment of ferocity cloaked in stripes, claws, and fangs. Then, seizing hold of the dead man, Lord Sydney whirled. The darkness closed around him, and although a few of the braver Utes ran after him, they were much too slow to have any hope of catching him.

There was nothing Fargo could do. He had not had

a clear shot. Several of the Utes had been in the way. He lay there as the tall warrior gave a yell and those who had gone after the tiger gave up the futile chase and hurried back. A few passed within a dozen feet but didn't see him. Those already at the fire were adding wood so it would blaze brighter, maybe with the idea of discouraging the tiger if it came back for a second helping.

At last Fargo was able to slip away unnoticed. His relief at finding the Ovaro unharmed was unbounded. Forking leather, he retraced his route to the hill where he had first glimpsed the Ute fire and spent the next hour searching for the glow of another. There was none. He had to resign himself to the fact that for the time being Dacia and Cyrena were at the mercy of Judson Richter.

Tired, sore, and depressed, Fargo bent the Ovaro's hooves eastward. The circus troupe had done as he told them and formed the wagons and vans into a circle. Brent, the clown, was one of the sentries and nervously challenged him with, "Who goes there? Speak quick or I'll shoot!"

Fargo identified himself and rode into the firelight. Others came running but when they saw he was alone, they stopped and frowned or hung their heads.

The Great Gandolpho had a revolver strapped around his waist. "No luck, I gather?"

"I saw the tiger," Fargo said, wearily sliding down.

"The python is missing, too. In all the confusion no one saw it crawl off." Gandolpho's wide shoulders slumped. "This has to be the worst night of my life."

"Any sign of Thimbletree?" Fargo asked.

"As a matter of fact, yes. He came back about an hour after you left and locked himself in his wagon.

We've tried to get him to open the door, or at least to talk to us but all he'll say is to go away."

"Let me try." Fargo took a few steps and Gandolpho started to follow. "Alone, if you don't mind."

The wagon was on the south side of the circle. Fargo knocked several times without receiving a response. "Thaddeus, it's Fargo. Open up or I'll bust in the door."

"Leave me alone," came the forlorn reply.

Fargo kicked it, rattling the door on its hinges. He kicked it a second time and was drawing back his foot for a third when Thimbletree pounded on the other side.

"Didn't you hear me? I don't want to see anyone."

"I don't give a damn." Fargo planted his boot next to the latch. Another couple of times should do it.

"Curse you, sir!" The door was jerked open and Thimbletree filled the doorway. His eyes were misty and his nose and cheeks were red and in his left hand was a half-empty bottle of whiskey. "Why can't you let me be?"

Fargo hit him. He slugged Thimbletree full on the jaw, not with all his strength, just hard enough that the portly circus owner tottered and fell, spilling whiskey over himself and the floor. Entering, Fargo slammed the door and threw the bolt.

"Wh-wh-what are you doing?" Thimbletree stammered.

"That was for Juliette." Gripping the front of Thimbletree's shirt, Fargo hoisted him up. "This is for me." Fargo hit him again, in the gut this time. Again, he pulled his punch, but Thimbletree still doubled in half and staggered against the wall, gurgling and gasping.

"No more," he pleaded. "Please."

"You wish," Fargo said, and slapped him across the mouth. This time he didn't hold back and the blow sent Thimbletree crashing to the floor where he covered his bloody lips with his hand and whined.

Fargo folded his arms and waited for him to get up. The wagon was spacious and comfortably furnished. Twice as wide as most of the others, there was room for a full-sized bed and a table and several chairs. Ingeniously, the furniture had been bolted to the floor so it wouldn't be tossed about when the wagon was on the move. "Where is it?"

Red drops were rolling down Thimbletree's pudgy chin. "Where's what," he hedged.

"Do you want me to hit you again?"

"Mr. Richter struck me several times, too, if you'll recall, and I never told him," Thimbletree boasted.

"It means that much to you." Fargo was stating a fact, not asking a question.

"It means that much to me. Nothing you can say or do will ever persuade me to tell you. So do your worst."

Fargo shrugged. "I aim to." He slowly drew his Colt and slowly thumbed back the hammer and slowly took aim at Thimbletree's right leg. "I'll count to five." He paused. "One."

Thimbletree grinned through the blood and the pain. "You're not Richter. You could never shoot someone in cold blood."

"Normally, no. But two lives are at stake. The lives of two people I care about." Fargo's face hardened. "Two."

"What is that expression I heard in Denver? Oh, yes. You can fill me full of lead, but my lips will still be sealed."

"Three."

"Honestly, Mr. Fargo. Desist in this folly while you retain some semblance of dignity."

"Four."

"I can overlook your striking me. It's understandable, your being upset at the abduction of the twins. But there are limits beyond which civilized individuals do not trespass, and you, in contrast to Mr. Richter, are civilized, whether you will admit it or not."

"Think so?" Fargo said, and shot him. He aimed at the fleshy part of the calf and the slug tore clean through and out the other side, boring a hole in the floorboards.

Howling like a stricken wolf, Thimbletree wrapped his hands around his leg and hopped back and forth. "Oh God! Oh God! Oh God! You did it! You really did it!"

Fargo cocked the Colt. "I'll count to five again. Then I'll shoot the other leg. You might want to hold still so I don't hit the bone."

Thimbletree stopped hopping, and blanched. Blood was seeping through his fingers and down his pants but not so much that he was in danger of bleeding to death anytime soon. "My other leg?"

"And then your arms. After that, if you still won't say, it will be your feet and then your hands."

Thimbletree's eyes narrowed. "I believe you would!" He licked his bloody lips. "You're not at all the kind of man I thought you were."

"One," Fargo said.

Fists pounded on the wagon door and the Great Gandolpho shouted, "What's going on in there? We heard a shot."

"Save me!" Thimbletree cried. "I'm trapped in here with a lunatic! If you don't do something, he'll shoot me to pieces."

"Fargo? Open the door!" Gandolpho yelled, and pounded some more. "This isn't the way to go about it."

"Two," Fargo said.

Thimbletree leaned on the table. "Break it down, Anthony! Hurry! I'm a dead man if you don't!"

"Three."

The door shook to the impact of Gandolpho's shoulder. "Damn it, Fargo! Open up! I have others here with me and we'll batter it down if we have to."

"Did you hear that?" Thimbletree gloated.

Fargo shifted and put a shot through the door high up so no one would be hit. From the sound of things, they quickly scrambled for cover. "Keep away until I'm done," he warned, and pointed the Colt at Thimbletree. "Where were we?" He paused. "Oh. I remember. Four."

"You are a contemptible cad, sir. Worse than Richter and all those other ruffians combined."

"*I* didn't feed Juliette to Lord Sydney." Fargo centered the front sight on Thimbletree's leg. "Five."

"All right! All right!" Thimbletree bleated, and deflated like a punctured bubble. "I know when I'm beaten. I will show you where it is if you will be kind enough to give me your word you will not give any of it to Richter."

"Quit stalling." Fargo had liked the man once, but he would not let that stop him from doing what needed to be done.

Thimbletree limped to the next chair and from there to a cabinet beside a long counter. "I have never misjudged anyone so badly in my life. I thought you were a man of honor, a noble knight errant of the wilds. But I see now you possess the same streak of viciousness Mr. Richter does."

Fargo didn't say anything.

"Primitives, the whole lot of you." Thimbletree fished in a vest pocket. "I should never have brought my show to America. I saw it as the land of untapped economic opportunity."

"Less gum flapping," Fargo said.

"Or what? You'll shoot me again?" Sullenly, Thimbletree slid a small key out. Instead of inserting it into the cabinet, though, he inserted it into a barely noticeable hole in the wall next to the cabinet. It was a secret compartment and hidden inside was a safe with a combination lock. "This might take a while, the condition I'm in."

"If it takes more than ten seconds you'll be in a lot worse condition."

Mumbling to himself, Thimbletree spun the dial first right and then left and then right again. There was a loud click and the safe door popped open without being touched.

Fargo sat at the table and placed the Colt beside him. "Let's see it."

From the safe Thimbletree removed an exquisite ivory chest. Ornately hand-carved and gilt with gold, it was worth a small fortune. He set it on the table and pried at the gold clasp with a thumbnail. "I hope you're satisfied."

Gold coins from various countries were heaped to the rim. Mixed with them were a few silver coins and a smattering of rare gems; rubies, diamonds, and emeralds.

"The chest was given to me by a rajah in Bombay in appreciation for the fine show we put on at his palace," Thimbletree said. "It had been in his family for generations."

"And these?" Fargo asked, tapping the coins and

gems. It was more wealth than most men saw in a lifetime. Hell, he thought, make that *ten* lifetimes.

"The reward for all my hard work over the years. Given to me by kings and princes and other royalty for command performances and the like. One day I shall be too old for this life, and when I am, I intend to live out the remainder of my years in the luxury to which my thriftiness has entitled me. Perhaps now you can understand why I refused to turn my chest over to a despicable cad like Judson Richter."

"Understand, yes," Fargo said. "Approve, no."

"Oh, come now. You would have done the same were our circumstances reversed. It's easy to part with riches when the riches aren't yours."

Fargo selected a ruby and held it to the lamplight, admiring how it sparkled with an inner fire. "No amount of money is worth a human life."

"Spoken like someone who has never had a lot of money of his own," Thimbletree countered. "I was like you, once. When I was younger I was as poor as the next man, and I hated it more than I can describe. I hated it so much that when I eventually crawled out of the gutter, I vowed never to go back. Call me miserly if you must, but there you have it."

"You were generous to the Hagens."

"Out of my largesse I bestowed a pittance. And don't forget, I had an ulterior motive. I didn't want them to complain to the authorities. Tembo brings in too much income for me to risk having her put down."

"What about Juliette? Wasn't she valuable enough to be saved?"

"The insult, sir, is duly noted. Blame me if you must for putting my financial welfare before all else, but I'll have you know that if I had it to do over again, I would do exactly the same." Thimbletree sank into a chair across from him. "I am not a saint, Mr. Fargo. Far from it. I am a human being with the same weaknesses and foibles as everyone else."

"So I'm learning." Fargo had made the mistake of judging the man by his looks, by his friendly features and white hair, rather than looking past them to the real man who lurked underneath.

"What now? Will you appropriate my riches for yourself? That is what most everyone else would do. Gandolpho and Lecter and the rest included."

"You should give them more credit," Fargo said. Dropping the ruby into the chest, he pushed the chest toward Thimbletree. "Take out all the gems and divide the gold in half."

"Why? So you can keep some for yourself?" Thimbletree's mouth was a slash of scorn. "I knew it. For all your posturing, you're as much a scoundrel as Judson Richter. More so, since Mr. Richter doesn't pretend to be something he is not."

"Just do it." Fargo's patience with the man had worn thin. It would not take much to trigger his anger. He watched as Thimbletree made stacks of the gold coins and piles of the various jewels. Thimbletree then counted out half the coins and pushed the stacks toward him.

"There. Eighty-three altogether."

"Find me a pillowcase," Fargo said.

"Eh?" Thimbletree nodded. "Oh. I see. You need something to carry the gold in." Propping his hands on the table, he stiffly rose and hobbled to a closet. "I'm surprised you're only taking half. I wouldn't, were I in your shoes."

Fargo accepted the pillowcase without comment and began dropping the coins inside.

"What do you plan to do with your ill-gotten

gains?" Thimbletree sarcastically asked. "Fritter it away gambling? Or on women, perchance?"

"I'm going to swap it with Richter for Dacia and Cyrena," Fargo revealed. He wrapped the excess length of pillowcase around the bulge the gold made, twisted it, and tied a large knot.

Thimbletree had cocked his head to one side. "I don't understand. Richter demanded all my gold, not just half." He fondled one of the stacks on the table as if it were a woman. "He won't accept what you give him."

"Richter has no idea how much you have." Fargo hefted the heavy pillowcase. "For all he knows, this is all of it." Rising, he walked to the door.

"Hold on a second," Thimbletree said. He was confused. "Why aren't you taking it all? After what I've done, I'd expect no less."

"Like you said, if you go broke, the circus folds." Fargo opened the door. "The people who work for you deserve better."

The Great Gandolpho and fifteen or sixteen others were waiting outside. Fargo shouldered through them, saying, "Your boss needs doctoring." He went straight to the Ovaro and stuffed the pillowcase into a saddlebag, fastened it, and led the stallion to a fire near Prince Maylay's wagon. The orangutan was clinging to the bars, quietly contemplating all that went on around him.

Fargo poured himself a cup of coffee and raised the cup to the orang in a mock toast. "To jackasses everywhere. May they rot in hell."

Prince Maylay bared his teeth as if he understood and was grinning.

The coffee was not as hot as Fargo liked and someone had added too much sugar but he drank it anyway. In another five hours the sun would rise and Judson Richter would pay the circus a visit. He had preparations to make before the outlaws arrived.

Gandolpho stomped across the clearing like a bull spoiling for a fight, his brawny fists clenched. Others trailed in his wake, equally mad. "You had no call to do that, to beat him and shoot him like you did. It was wrong."

"Do you want to save the twins or not?" Fargo demanded.

"Need you ask? But I'd never stoop to Richter's level to do it."

"It was the only way he would give me the gold."

Gandolpho glanced at Fargo's Colt, and after a moment he let his thick fingers relax, and he squatted. "You have my help if you want it."

"Same here," said one of the women who had followed him.

"The twins are our friends," Lecter the Human Flagpole declared. "We'll do whatever it takes to save them."

Fargo took another swallow. "There's more to it than that. Richter can't afford to let any of you live."

"You're saying that to scare us," said the woman.

"I'm saying it because Richter can't leave witnesses. He and his men won't let you reach Salt Lake City to report them to the law." Fargo looked at each one, then said, "It's them or you. Get that through your heads or you're as good as dead."

"But we're performers, not killers," the Great Gandolpho said. "We like to make people smile and laugh, not snuff out their lives." He pressed a hand to his metal helmet and sighed. "How do bad things like this happen to good people like us?"

It had been Fargo's experience that misfortune

never played favorites. Nor did fortune, for that matter. Life was what you made of it, a roll of the dice with the dice rigged in death's favor. "Call everyone else together. Tell them what I've told you and ask them what they want to do. Take a vote. If you decide to fight, I'll help. If you would rather be slaughtered, once Dacia and Cyrena are safe, you're on your own."

They left him to his thoughts. And to more coffee. While he awaited their decision, Fargo studied the lay of the land, particularly the positions of the wagons in relation to the river and the woods. He figured Richter would come from the west, and if so, there were several spots where an ambush could be sprung.

About twenty minutes had gone by when the last person Fargo expected came limping toward him. "What do *you* want?"

Thaddeus T. Thimbletree was using a cane. His pants had been cut at the knee and a bandage applied to his calf. His lips were split, his jaw puffy, and he had to try twice to talk. "I want to apologize."

"It's a little late for that."

"You misunderstand. I don't want to apologize for Juliette or the Fleetwoods or any of the rest. I made my decisions and I'll stand by them." Thimbletree stood close to the fire. "I want to say I'm sorry to you, personally, for misjudging you. You're more honest than I thought."

"Go to hell."

Thimbletree's eyebrows met over his nose. "That's not exactly the reaction I anticipated. I realize you think less of me than you once did, but my sincerity should be taken in the vein it's intended."

"Sincerity my ass. You want to stick close to me so you can be close to your precious gold. If I let you,

you'd try to stop Richter from taking it, even if it cost the twins their lives."

"If you let me?" Thimbletree said, and firmed his hold on the cane.

The Colt was in Fargo's hand before the circus owner could twitch a muscle. "I've seen that kind of cane before. It's a sword cane, popular with gamblers and the like."

Thimbletree smiled thinly. "Nothing escapes your notice, does it? But you're wrong if you think I would do you harm. I've never hurt anyone in my life."

"There's always a first time," Fargo said. "Do us both a favor and stay in your wagon until this is over. If not, I can't guarantee I won't shoot you again just for the hell of it."

"Coming from anyone else I would take that as a melodramatic threat," Thimbletree remarked, "but if I've learned nothing else from our association, it's that you are first and foremost a man of your word." Leaning on the cane, he turned. "I will do as you want, but under protest."

"Just so you do it." Fargo watched over the rim of the tin cup until Thimbletree had gone inside. The wagon door had barely closed when the circus crew came toward him in a body, the Great Gandolpho at the forefront.

"We've made up our minds. You've been right about everything else, so we have no cause to doubt you about Richter. If you say he wants us dead, we believe you. And we'll do whatever it takes to stop him."

"Even if that includes killing?"

It was Lecter the Human Flagpole who answered. "We'll be honest with you. Some of us don't know if we can take another life or not. We've never done anything like this. But we don't want to die, either."

"Pulling a trigger is never easy the first time," Fargo conceded. "And if all goes well, most of you won't have to. All I need are four of you who think they can."

"Count me in," Gandolpho said. "Shooting them is no different than splitting their skulls, and they must pay for what they did to Juliette."

"You can count me in, too," Lecter offered. "She was the sweetest girl alive and meant the world to me."

The juggler stepped forward. He had curly brown hair and well-muscled shoulders. "When I was younger I did a fair amount of hunting with my father and grandfather. I've never shot a person but I'm willing to try."

"That makes three," Fargo said.

A young woman in pants and a shirt strode from the crowd. "My name is Cynthia Tilson. The Fleetwoods are good friends of mine and I'd like to do my part to save them."

Fargo had his doubts. As he recollected, her job was tending to some of the animals. "I don't know."

"Why? Because I'm a woman? Because I'm younger than most?" Cynthia gestured. "Do you see anyone else stepping forward? It seems to me you can't afford to be choosy."

The hell of it was, Fargo mused, she was right. Draining the rest of the coffee, he set down the cup and rose. "We have a lot of work to do before we can turn in so let's get started."

The wagons and vans were in a circle. Under his supervision, the four nearest the trail to the west were taken from the circle and repositioned alongside the trail, two on either side. In effect, it served as a funnel into which he hoped to lure the outlaws.

Next Fargo had the wagons that still lined the circle placed as close together as possible. There were still gaps. But he solved that problem by having the men bring torches and search out logs which were dragged or rolled to plug any and all openings riders might exploit to enter the clearing.

He armed the rest of the circus people with whatever was handy: knives, a couple of axes, metal bars, and wooden clubs.

They did not have a lot of ammunition to spare but Fargo still set up several bottles as targets and had Gandolpho, Lecter, Vaughn the juggler, and Cynthia take turns firing a couple of shots so they knew how to load and fire their guns.

It was close to three in the morning when Fargo advised everyone to get what sleep they could, and turned in himself after posting sentries. He lay with his head on his saddle, staring at the stars and reviewing all he had done and all that he must still do to give the circus troupe a chance of making it through the morning alive. Because, if Judson Richter had his way, before another day went by they would all be dead and their bodies left for the vultures and coyotes.

Maybe, just maybe, he could prevent that from happening.

11

Dawn broke cool and clear with a stiff breeze stirring the trees. Skye Fargo was up well before the sun peeked above the horizon. He had more preparations to make and he couldn't make them alone. After waking the Great Gandolpho and having him see to it that everyone else was roused from their wagons, he ordered the fires to be rekindled and coffee put on to boil and breakfast made.

The circus people were unusually quiet and nervous. Little was said, and many an apprehensive glance was cast westward.

Fargo kept them busy to try to take their minds off the impending clash. He had them go into the woods and gather large piles of brush close to the wagons as additional obstacles. At a few points he had ropes stretched from tree to tree. The end result was that none of Richter's horsemen could get anywhere near the wagons from the outside, only through the opening he had made.

Inside the circle, Fargo had furniture and more brush brought to give the defenders something to take cover behind.

And finally, Fargo asked that a table be placed in the middle of the clearing where Judson Richter could see it. Unwrapping the pillowcase, he upended it over the tabletop, and out cascaded the glittering gold coins.

One rolled to the ground and the Great Gandolpho picked it up. "All this violence and bloodshed over metal men dig from the earth." He added the coin to the pile. "Sad, is it not, that some men will do anything to be rich? Even kill if they must."

Fargo had never had a hankering to be neck deep in money. From time to time he toyed with the notion of prospecting for gold or silver but something always came up and he had to put it off. Maybe one day he would get serious about it. Until then he would go on living as he liked, wandering where the wind took him and indulging his fondness for poker, whiskey, and women, not necessarily in that order.

"What about those of us with guns?" Lecter intruded on his thoughts. "Where do you want us to be when those awful men get here?"

To catch Richter's men in a crossfire, Fargo instructed Gandolpho and Lecter to hide under wagons to the south and Vaughn the juggler and Cynthia Tilson to climb up on top of a wagon to the north. "Wait until I give the word. And whatever you do, don't shoot unless you're sure what you're shooting at."

As ten o'clock approached Fargo sent the rest of the women and the children off into the trees, and instructed the rest of the men on what they should do when the shooting started. His ambush as complete as he could make it, he stood with his hands on his hips trying to think of anything he had overlooked.

There was one thing.

Over Thimbletree's objections, he locked the circus owner in his wagon and pocketed the key.

"Are you sure that's necessary?" the Great Gandolpho asked.

"We can't trust him," Fargo bluntly stated. "And I want the twins alive, not dead."

All that was left was to wait. Fargo poured himself a cup of coffee and sat in a chair he had placed next to the table. He expected Richter to show up early and watched the trail to the west closely. An hour later he was still watching.

Ten o'clock came and went and Fargo began to pace. Something was wrong. He could feel it. Richter had said he would be there by ten for the gold.

Fargo began to worry that Richter had sent someone on ahead to check things out and the spy had seen the trap being laid. Even now, Richter and his men might be surrounding the camp. To satisfy himself that wasn't the case, he told the others to stay where they were while he made a circuit of the adjoining woods. He saw no one.

Shortly before eleven Fargo asked one of the acrobats to climb a tall tree as high as the limbs could bear his weight. The man shouted down that the trail to the west was empty for as far as he could see.

By noon Fargo had come to a decision. He had Gandolpho and the other three come out of hiding, replaced the gold coins in the pillowcase, and gave the pillowcase to Gandolpho.

"Hold onto these. I'm going to look for Richter. Post lookouts and don't let anyone stray off. And keep your eyes peeled for those Utes I told you about."

"What do we do if Richter shows up while you're gone?" Cynthia Tilson asked.

Fargo had already considered that. "Don't let him see the gold. Tell him I have it and that as soon as I get back, we'll trade it for Dacia and Cyrena." He went to saddle the Ovaro and they tagged along.

"I don't much like being left on our own," Lecter

mentioned. "You're the only one of us who knows what he's doing."

"I don't like leaving," Fargo admitted. But he was worried Richter had run into the Utes, in which case Dacia and Cyrena might be in more trouble than ever.

"What about Mr. Thimbletree?" Cynthia wondered.

"What about him? He's to stay in his wagon. Even if he begs and promises to behave, no one is to let him out."

"That's awful cruel."

"So is being eaten by a tiger." Presently he was ready and a tap of his spurs sent the Ovaro down the trail at a trot. The tracks left by Richter's outfit were easy to read in the daylight, and he soon learned why he had not spotted their camp the night before. Only a mile from the clearing they had turned north, crossed the river, and headed for the Uinta Mountains. A long way to go, given that Richter intended to be back by ten. But there were no tracks coming from the mountains toward the river, which meant Richter hadn't returned, which confirmed Fargo's hunch that something was amiss.

It took an hour and a half to reach the mountains. Dense forest blanketed the high, steep slopes, broken here and there by clusters of boulders and occasional cliffs. Many of the peaks were over ten thousand feet high, some over thirteen thousand, and the highest mantled with snow.

The Uintas were imposing and formidable, and one of the least explored regions on the continent. The Mormons had bypassed them and settled around the Great Salt Lake. Only a few trappers and mountain men had ever penetrated the range, and of those who did, even fewer made it out alive to say what they had seen.

The tracks climbed to a switchback and from there to an upland bench. Fargo came to the top and instantly reined up. He dropped his right hand to his Colt, then sat staring in bewilderment.

Judson Richter had camped at a spring. Since it had been so late, Richter and his men spread out their blankets and turned in without making a fire. That much Fargo could tell at first glance. It did not take any great skill at reading signs: *the blankets, saddles, and saddlebags were still there.* But the men who owned them, and the horses the saddles were meant for, were missing.

Fargo warily kneed the Ovaro forward. It made no sense for the outlaws to have abandoned their belongings. Since he could conceive of no earthly reason for them to ride off bareback, it had to be an extraordinary circumstance.

At the spring Fargo found his answer. Large pug marks were imprinted in the mud at the water's edge. Lord Sydney had been busy last night. After filling his belly with the Ute warrior, the tiger had traveled north into the mountains and sometime before dawn had caught wind of Richter and his men. The jumble of tracks were hard to read, but as best Fargo could unravel them, Lord Sydney had crept close to Richter's camp, probably intending to indulge his fondness for man-killing, but the horses spooked and ran off to the northwest. The picket rope still lay in the grass, snapped in half. The commotion had awakened Richter and his boys, who went after their animals on foot, taking Dacia and Cyrena with them.

Then Lord Sydney brazenly came to the spring to drink, and loped off to the east.

Fargo scratched his head. The horses ran off hours ago, yet Richter and his men never came back. He gigged the Ovaro up the next slope and over the crest into a long winding valley. The panicked horses had been galloping like mad, the men doing their best to catch up. In the predawn gloom and shadow, it was unlikely Richter saw what Fargo now beheld in the bright sunlight.

A Ute village lay below. The valley was dotted with tepees arranged in customary fashion. Painted symbols adorned many. In the center of one of the circles were scores of Utes, warriors, women, and children.

Even from that far off Fargo could hear their excited whoops and cries. He quickly entered a belt of pines so as not to be seen and descended until he was fifty yards from the valley floor. Climbing down, he looped the reins around a sapling, shucked the Henry, and stalked the rest of the way on foot.

The Utes had taken captives. Four posts had been imbedded in the ground and lashed to them were four of Judson Richter's men. One had been stripped to the waist and carved on with a knife—his nose and ears had been sliced off. Two more were sprawled in the dust, bristling with arrows.

Nearby were several dead Ute warriors, laid out in a row.

Fargo did not see Richter himself. Nor the twins. They might be in any one of the lodges.

He had a fair notion of what happened. Thanks to Lord Sydney, Richter's horses had stampeded into the valley with Richter and his cutthroats hard after them. Much too late, the outlaws had spotted the village. Indians were early risers, so most of the Utes must have been up and about when the alarm was sounded. They came pouring from their dwellings, probably in the belief they were being raided by another tribe. Instead they spied the whites, and a skirmish took place. It didn't last long. Richter had been badly out-numbered. His men shot three Utes but were overrun. Those not slain outright had been taken captive, and would soon be a lot worse off.

Fargo didn't feel the least bit sorry for them. They had brought it on themselves, and he wouldn't lift a finger to help. But the twins were another story. He had to find them and spirit them out of there before they took their turn at the stake or were chosen as wives. But with the Utes buzzing about like a swarm of riled bees, he had to bide his time.

A scream echoed across the valley. A stocky Ute had taken a bone-handled knife and stabbed one of the gunmen, down low. The outlaw bubbled hysteri-cally and frenziedly tried to wrest free of the rawhide straps binding his wrists and ankles. But the Utes had bound them good and tight.

Fargo had a disturbing thought: What if the Utes sent scouts out to see if more whites were in the area? They might stumble on the circus. He had to get back but he refused to leave without Dacia and Cyrena.

Another scream pierced the village. A second cap-tive had been cut by a different warrior. But the Utes were not out to kill them, not yet, anyway. First the Utes would whittle on them some.

Fargo leaned against the bole of a pine and scanned each lodge, seeking a clue to the one the Fleetwoods were in.

After a while the Utes quieted down. A council of older warriors got under way, and the women and children moved to one side and made themselves comfortable.

Not long after, a shout went up, heralding the ar-rival of warriors on horseback who filed out of the woods a hundred yards to the west of Fargo. In the lead rode the tall Ute with the eagle feather in his hair.

The hunting party had returned.

The tall Ute addressed the council, telling them about Lord Sydney, Fargo surmised. Quite a stir resulted. Indians were big believers in omens, and the tiger was bound to be regarded as bad medicine. Indians were also patient by nature. Their leaders took turns giving long speeches.

Fargo regretted not eating anything since breakfast. He was famished, and his stomach wouldn't stop growling. Prying off a piece of bark, he used the Toothpick to remove a strip of inner pulp, chopped it into pieces, and popped one in his mouth. As food went it was bland but it beat an empty belly. The remaining pieces he stuffed into his pocket.

Whatever decision the council came to was not reached until midafternoon. The women were talking and gossiping in small groups, the younger children were scampering playfully about, when the tall warrior with the eagle feather rose and said something that brought everyone to their feet. They moved toward the stakes.

Not once had Fargo caught a glimpse of the twins. He wondered if Richter might already be dead. Good riddance to bad rubbish, as a gentleman friend of his from New Orleans might say.

He stretched to relieve a cramp in his back, and in doing so, gazed eastward toward where many of the littlest children continued to play. Only Fargo saw the striped form slinking toward them through the high grass.

Lord Sydney was making up for the many months

he had spent in a cage. He had attacked the hunting party; he had scared off Richter's horses; now he was about to pounce on one of the Ute children.

Fargo couldn't sit there and let a child be killed. He had to warn them. The Utes might take him captive, too, but that was the chance he had to take. He stood and cupped a hand to his mouth to shout, but even as he did, there was a tremendous roar.

In a blur, Lord Sydney was in among the little children. Three fell to powerful sweeps of his flashing claws. A fourth, he seized in his mighty jaws, and whirling, he was off into the forest before a hand could be lifted against him.

Screams and shrieks greeted the slaughter. Warriors and women rushed to their panic-stricken children. Other Utes sprang for their mounts. In the extremeness of the moment, their captives were forgotten.

Fargo hunkered before anyone noticed him. He watched a mother kneel beside a torn and bloody husk and wail and tear at her dress; saw other mothers clasp unharmed children to their bosoms and cry in relief; saw fathers shake fists at the sky and vow vengeance.

Soon most of the warriors in the village were in pursuit of the Bengal tiger. Those not in pursuit, and everyone else, were gathered around the children.

The captives were all by themselves. There would never be a better opportunity.

Fargo ran to the Ovaro and swung up into the saddle. Shoving the Henry into its scabbard, he reined toward the village. At a gallop he burst from the trees and flew toward the circle. It was a few seconds before one of the Ute women spotted him and cried out. Warriors immediately rushed to intercept him but they were on foot and had farther to go to reach the captives.

One of the captives raised his head. He had been badly beaten, and his face was split and bruised to where it was nearly unrecognizable. As Fargo reined up in a swirl of dust, he licked his swollen lips and croaked, "Help us, mister!"

"Where are the sisters?" Fargo demanded. "Dacia and Cyrena Fleetwood?"

"I don't know," the man said. "Honest to God I don't. They were with Richter. He and some of the others caught their horses right before the Utes hit us, and got away."

"Which way did they go?"

"I didn't notice," the battered gunman said. "I was too busy tryin' to stay alive."

Onrushing warriors, yipping and whooping, were almost to the circle. In seconds they would be within bow range.

"I'm obliged for the information," Fargo told the gunman, and reined the pinto around.

"Wait! You can't leave us like this. Don't you know what they'll do?" The man struggled against the straps. "Take me, if no one else. Please! I'm beggin' you."

"Did you help the tattooed woman when she begged to be spared?"

"I couldn't. Richter would have splattered my brains all over creation." The man made a last appeal. "For the love of God. One white man to another. You can't let these heathens torture us."

"I should," Fargo said. But he didn't. The Colt filled his hand and he fired four times. At each blast an outlaw sagged.

An arrow whizzed out of the blue and bit into the soil only a few feet from the Ovaro. More rained down as Fargo reined around. One missed his ear by a whisker's width, another glanced off his saddle, a third nearly clipped one of the pinto's ears.

Fargo galloped toward the forest a few yards ahead of a few last shafts. He looked back and saw two young warriors on horseback giving chase. They were young but they were eager, and they held long lances they could throw with great skill. He fled up the slope, confident he could elude them. He didn't count on a rut, didn't count on the Ovaro pitching forward and nearly going down. He didn't count on being thrown, either.

It had been ages since Fargo was last unhorsed. He had forgotten how much it hurt to hit the ground with the force of a cannonball. He rolled and tumbled a dozen or more feet but was spared serious injury. The delay cost precious seconds, though, enabling the young Utes to come almost within lance-hurling range.

Dashing to the stallion, Fargo gripped the saddle horn and pulled himself up. The summit seemed impossibly far away. He rode hell-bent for leather, making no attempt to pull his rifle. The young Utes were yipping and screeching, unaware that he could kill them whenever he wanted. But he chose not to. They were protecting their village, nothing more, and unless they left him no other choice, he would let them live.

The final forty yards were the steepest. Fargo reached the spot where he had crossed over into the valley, and drew rein. The young warriors were a credit to their people but they had pursued him far enough. Yanking the Henry out, he wedged the stock to his shoulder and sighted on the ground in front of their horses.

Five shots in rapid cadence rang out, and as the last echoed across the valley, the pair did what any seasoned warrior would do. They decided discretion was the wiser part of valor.

Fargo trotted down to the bench, and the spring. The first thing he noticed was that some of the saddles and blankets were missing. Judson Richter and those with him had been there and left. The saddlebags belonging to their friends had been dumped out and picked through. Honor among killers was as rare as honesty in politicians. Their tracks pointed southeast, in the direction of the circus. Four horses, but the depths of the tracks showed that two were bearing extra weight. The twins?

The Ovaro had covered a lot of ground that day; now it had to cover a lot more. Fargo lashed his reins, trying not to think about the fact that Judson Richter was a couple of hours ahead, or what Richter would do once he got there. He hoped the Great Gandolpho had done as he advised.

The ride to the river seemed twice as long as the ride from it. Fargo was fording a short distance from the circled wagons when he heard loud weeping. It was his first inkling something had gone wrong. His second were the bodies near the table he had set up, only now the table was on its side. Steeling himself, he drew rein.

Lecter the Human Flagpole was on one knee beside the still figure of the Great Gandolpho. A few feet away lay Cynthia Tilson. Off toward Prince Maylay's wagon was Vaughn the juggler, a bullet hole in his forehead. The performers and workers were gathered about the bodies, downcast.

"Where *were* you?" Tears brimmed Lecter's eyes. "Richter has been here and left."

"Richter wasn't to blame for this, though" Brent the clown told him. "It was Thaddeus. He shot them when they tried to stop him from taking his coins."

"What?" Fargo glanced at the circus owner's wagon, and sure enough, the door was wide open. "I left orders Thimbletree wasn't to be let out," he said, dismounting.

Lecter placed a hand on the human cannonball's shoulder. "It was Gandolpho's doing. Thad begged and begged and finally Gandolpho said he would unlock the door if Thad promised to behave."

"Damn," Fargo said.

"For a while Thaddeus acted like his old self," Lecter said. "Smiling and friendly to everyone. Then he pulled a gun no one suspected he had and commanded Gandolpho to hand over the coins you took from him."

Fargo clenched his fists so hard, his fingernails dug into his palms.

"Gandolpho was going to but Cindy wouldn't let him. She reminded him they needed the coins to trade for Dacia and Cyrena."

Fargo stared at the dead woman, at the blood trickling from a hole high in her left side.

"She pointed her pistol at Thaddeus and told him to drop his gun. He started to, and when she reached for it, he shot her. Gandolpho and Vaughn came to help her and Thad shot them, too."

"Where were you while all this was going on?"

"Right there." Lecter nodded at the upended table. "My hip was bothering me something awful where Richter shot me, and I was sitting down, resting. When I tried to stand, I tripped. The table tipped over and I dropped my revolver." He crossed himself. "Why Thad didn't shoot me, too, I will never know."

"Where did he get to?"

"Thad took his zebra and rode east. His last words to us were that we were on our own from here on out." Lecter bowed his head. "I'm sorry. We let you down."

"You let yourselves down." Fargo raked the clearing. He was sure someone else was missing but he couldn't think of who. "How long ago was Judson Richter here?"

"An hour, maybe more. He has the twins with him. He sure was mad when he found out what Thaddeus had done."

Fargo could imagine.

"I remembered what you said about him not leaving any witnesses, so I gave Richter our word none of us would turn him in. And do you know what he did? He laughed and said we were the least of his worries. He said the Utes will be on the warpath soon and will solve his problem for him by wiping us out." Lecter slowly rose, grimacing from the pain. "Is that true?"

"The Utes might pay you a visit," Fargo admitted.

"Then you must guide us to safety You're the only one who can."

Every last one of them was looking at him. His insides churning, Fargo said, "I'll do what I can." But it would mean a delay in going after Dacia and Cyrena, and since they were no longer of use to Richter in bargaining for the gold, they were in more peril than ever.

"There's more bad news, I'm afraid," Lecter said.

"How can it get worse?"

"It's Walikali. I've never seen him so upset. He and Gandolpho were good friends, you know. About ten minutes after Thaddeus left, he climbed on Tembo and went after him."

"Walikali can take care of himself." Fargo was relieved that's all it was. "He has Tembo to protect him."

"Oh, that's not the bad part," Lecter corrected him. "Before he left, Walikali said to tell you that he thinks Thaddeus will head for the Hagen homestead. And in his current state of mind, there's no predicting what Thaddeus will do once he gets there."

Fargo swore. As the old saying had it, when it rained, it damn well poured.

12

The late afternoon sun beat down on the plodding caravan, sapping the vitality of men and animals alike. Skye Fargo rode at the rear of the column to keep watch for Utes. Although some of the circus people had objected, he was taking them east, back to Denver. To try to push on to Salt Lake City with the Utes stirred up was asking for more trouble than they could handle.

The slow pace chafed at Fargo's nerves. He was anxious to head out after Judson Richter and the twins, but if the Utes attacked while he was away, the circus would be wiped out to the last man. He felt obligated to stick with them until they were out of danger, but he didn't like it, he didn't like it one bit.

By common consent, Lecter the Human Flagpole was now in charge. He was in the first wagon, unable to ride a horse due to his hip.

Fargo was tempted to ride on up the line and tell Lecter to speed things up, but the horses and mules pulling the wagons and vans were toiling the best they could.

A rider came trotting from the front, a performer who billed himself as the Mystic Swami. All Fargo knew about him was that he hailed from India, and that his name was Dansay. He was a small, wiry man, with a swarthy complexion and a beaked nose. He always wore a turban and a tunic, both a bright blue, and girded his waist with a red sash. He handled his horse skillfully, and reined it around to fall into step beside the Ovaro.

"I bring you greetings, sahib, from Harold Lecter. He would like to know, at your convenience, how long we will travel today?"

"Until the animals drop dead from exhaustion," Fargo grumbled.

"Sahib?" Dansay said, his keenly intelligent eyes narrowing. "If I may be so bold, you seem to be upset."

"There's no 'seems' about it," Fargo responded. "It's one of those days when I want to shoot someone for the sheer hell of it."

"I trust, sahib, you will not choose poor Dansay as your target. I am but the bearer of Lecter's tidings."

Fargo rode a bit, then commented, "Your English is better than most whites I know. You almost sound British."

"My humble thanks for your kind compliment," Dansay said, and smiled. "And yes, sahib, I was taught by an Englishman in a school in Delhi. My accent has betrayed me again."

"What does that word mean you keep using?" Fargo asked. "Sahib?" He had never heard it before.

"It means 'master.' "

Fargo looked at him. "Call me something else, then. I'm not your master or anyone else's."

"A thousand pardons, *tuan*. If you do not want me to call you sahib, then I will refrain."

"What's that other word you just used? *Tuan*?"

Dansay's sly grin was disarming. "It is a Malay term, sir. It, too, means 'master.'"

"How about if you call me by my name and I call you by yours?" Fargo proposed. "That's how it's done in our neck of the woods."

"You Americans and your expressions," Dansay said, and surveyed the expanse of forest and river ahead. "This is fine country, sir. Not at all like the jungles and swamps of my native India. Yet it has its appeal."

"Do you miss your home much?" Fargo asked to make small talk.

"At times very much, yes. Especially my wife and my fifteen children. I worry about them constantly."

"Fifteen?" Fargo laughed for the first time that day. "Are you sure you have enough?"

"In my country, sahib, large families are a necessity. The more sons and daughters, the less work for the fathers and mothers. To you it sounds like a lot, but I love each and every one of them with all my heart." Dansay's affection was undeniable. "I would give anything to be back with them right this minute."

"Why did you leave?"

"Why does a man do anything in this world? Money, sahib. There was a flood, and much of our farm was underwater for weeks. Our crops were ruined. My family was close to starving and there was nothing I could do to fill their empty bellies." Dansay wore his heartbreak on his sleeve. "Then I heard about Sahib Thimbletree. How he was looking for animals and acts for his circus. So I went to him and offered myself to him for one year if he would pay the year's wages in advance, which he graciously consented to do. Now here I am."

"How much longer before you can go back to India?"

"Three months. I will sing with joy when that day arrives." Dansay glanced at him. "To a man like you, with no attachments, you probably think me silly to be so devoted to my family."

"Never put thoughts in another man's head," Fargo replied. "Truth is, I respect men like you, even if I'll never be like you. Your wife and kids must be proud."

Dansay turned away and coughed. His voice, when next he spoke, was thick with emotion. "I thank you, sahib, for your kindness. You are a lot like this land, I think. Rough on the outside, but once you look under the surface there is much beauty."

Fargo chuckled. "No one has ever called me beautiful, as I recollect."

The Indian chuckled too. "From this day, sahib, you have a new friend. I am your humble servant. Ask anything of me and I will do it."

"Know much about tigers?"

Dansay sobered. "Indeed I do. My own mother was killed by one. Dragged off when she went to the well for water. I was with the men who tracked the smears of blood to where her body was found. To this day the memory wakes me up at night in a cold sweat."

Fargo told him about seeing Lord Sydney attack the Ute warrior and the Ute children.

"There is no more vicious animal in the world than a man-eater, sahib. Whether it be a tiger or a leopard, they never stop killing until they are killed."

"Are there a lot of these man-eaters in India?"

"Very few, actually. It is rare for a tiger to turn from eating deer and wild pig to eating people. But when they do, it is most terrible. A few years ago a tiger in Chowgarh killed one hundred and twenty-seven people over a three year span. Another tiger killed eighty-six."

Fargo whistled. That was more than all the grizzlies and mountain lions ever born had killed. "Why so many?"

"India is not like your country, sahib. Here, guns are everywhere. There, guns are few, and to kill a tiger with a bow or spear or knife is not easy." Dansay paused. "Then too, our jungles are vast and thick, and a tiger may hide in them forever without being found."

"What can you tell me about Lord Sydney?"

Dansay frowned. "I told Sahib Thimbletree not to buy him. I warned him man-eaters cannot be tamed as other tigers can. But he would not listen. He said Lord Sydney would bring him much money. That was all he cared about."

"How many did Lord Sydney kill in your country?"

"Before I answer, permit me to explain about man-eaters. They are known by the towns or villages where their first victim is claimed. So in India, Lord Sydney was known as the Kot Kindri tiger, because the first person he ate was a small girl from there. She was picking mangos in full sight of her family when he pounced and carried her off. They did not go after him because they had no weapons, and they were afraid. A government hunter was sent but by then the Kot Kindri tiger had killed thirty-eight more. For half a year the government hunter tried to end the tiger's reign of terror but the tiger always outwitted him. Then an Englishman, Lord Sydney, a famed hunter in his own right, decided to try his luck."

"I know what happened to him," Fargo said.

"But his death was not in vain. It brought about the tiger's capture. For when the government hunter

161

found Lord Sydney's body, he rigged a great net to drop on the tiger if it returned to feed, and that is how the tiger was taken alive."

"Then along came Thimbletree," Fargo guessed.

"The tiger's capture was in all the newspapers. The government planned to kill him after displaying him at all the villages in the district to prove to the villagers they had nothing more to fear. Sahib Thimbletree read about it and hurried there to buy him before he was slain."

"And now he's killing folks here." Fargo had to marvel at the strange twists of fate that resulted in a Bengal tiger running loose in North America.

"Lord Sydney will kill many more times unless he is stopped," Dansay said. "His craving for human flesh will drive him far and wide."

"The cold weather will stop him," Fargo predicted. "Our winters are a lot worse than those in your country. A cat used to the jungle won't last long in ten feet of snow and forty below."

"Cold weather is not unknown in India, sahib, and the tigers still survive. In the north of my country are high mountains much like your Rockies where many tigers live, year round, amid snow and ice."

Fargo mulled that over a while. It could be that Lord Sydney would go on killing for years, running up a tally as high as some of those Indian tigers. "How do you stop a man-eater?"

"It is never easy. They become clever at avoiding traps, and stay away from men with guns. The best way is to track them until you are close enough to shoot, but few men are that brave. Their senses are better than ours, and once they know a hunter is after them, they often turn on him and kill him." Dansay looked at him. "Remember this above all else, sahib.

If you get a shot, you must go for the head or the heart. Nothing else will do. And remember, too, that when tigers know they are dying, nothing can stop them from slaying their killer."

It was clear by now that Fargo had to do something about Lord Sydney. But first he had the twins to think of, and the Hagens. That evening around the campfire he came to another decision, which did not go over well with Lecter.

"You're riding off and leaving us? With Utes on the warpath?"

"We don't know the Utes are on the prod. If they haven't shown by noon tomorrow, odds are they won't. I'll wait until then to head out."

"You're gambling with our lives," Lecter was right to point out. "Why not stay with us another couple of days to be sure?"

"You know why as well as I do."

"I just pray you're right," Lecter said.

Fargo walked off to be by himself. Ever since his encounter with Tembo, he had been like a stick bobbing in a stream, swept along by currents over which he had no control. And he was damned tired of it. Sitting on a log, he propped his boots on a stump and regarded the night sky. The way he saw it, he had four problems: Judson Richter, the Utes, Lord Sydney, and Thaddeus T. Thimbletree. All four were a danger to others but at the moment Richter and the tiger posed the greatest threats and should be dealt with first.

Footsteps crunched on fallen leaves and out of the darkness came Dansay. "Here you are, sahib. I have been looking all over for you."

"Come to offer your help in hunting the man-eater?"

Dansay shook his head. "I am not that brave, sad to say. But in India I have talked with others who are, and I will share what they told me, if you are willing."

"I'm all ears." The secret to tracking an animal, Fargo had learned, was to know the animal as well as he knew himself. Animals, like men, were creatures of habit, and once a hunter knew what those habits were, the rest was easy.

"Tigers have a sharp sense of smell, sahib. They can smell a person from half a kilometer off when the wind is right. Perhaps because they think all creatures have a nose as keen as theirs, they always stalk their human prey from downwind, never upwind, and always from behind."

"Mountain lions do the same," Fargo mentioned. Cats were cats, whether big or small, New World or Old World.

"When tigers know a hunter is after them, often they circle back and lie in wait for the hunter to come by," Dansay revealed.

"I've known grizzlies to do the same."

"Then you know to watch your back." Dansay paused. "Tigers are more active during the day than at night but man-eaters will strike at any time. They can move without making noise, and can lie still for hours. Their only weakness is that they do not look up, which is why most hunters shoot them from blinds in trees."

"Anything else?" Fargo said when the Indian stopped.

"Only that you should always watch a tiger's tail. Right before he charges it will twitch. When it stops, that is when you must ready yourself."

They sat a while talking about India, its other wildlife and its customs, and then Dansay excused himself to go to sleep.

Fargo lingered, too restless to turn in yet. A lot had happened the past few days, and he had a feeling the worst was yet to come. He tried to shake it off but it was midnight before he crawled under his blankets and one before he drifted off. It seemed like no more than five minutes had gone by when a hand on his shoulder woke him.

"Mr. Fargo?" Brent said. "It's your turn." As always, Brent was in full clown makeup, his face painted white, his bulbous nose red.

Fargo had almost forgotten he volunteered to stand watch from four until six. Throwing off his blanket, he sat up and yawned. The camp lay dark under the stars. He had ordered the campfires extinguished to avoid advertising where they were.

"Nothing much has happened," Brent informed him. "We heard some coyotes and what might have been a bear grunting from across the river."

"How long ago?" Fargo wondered if it might have been Lord Sydney.

"Oh, an hour or so. We only heard it a few times and after that it was quiet." Brent ran a hand through his frizzy hair. "That's all there was, except for the strange light we see now and then."

"What are you talking about?"

"No one told you? Rufio spotted a light east of us. We'll see it for a while and then it will disappear and then it's back again. None of us know what to make of the thing."

"Show me," Fargo said gruffly. They should have reported it sooner.

"This way." Brent hurried between two wagons and

skirted a thicket. "You can see it best from right about here."

Fargo looked but saw nothing except an unending veil of darkness.

"You need to watch a while sometimes," Brent said. "But if you blink you'll miss it."

"It's not there now," Fargo noted, and started to turn. Out of the corner of his eye he caught a glimmer of light. He stepped to the right and saw it more clearly, the unmistakable glow of a campfire. After a few seconds it blinked out, a trick of the wind and the intervening vegetation.

"Did you see it?" Brent asked. "Just like I told you."

"Wake up Lecter. I'll meet him here in five minutes." Fargo had plenty of time until sunrise but he wanted to reach the distant camp while it was still dark. Throwing on his saddle blanket, he saddled the pinto, tied on his saddlebags and bedroll, and walked the Ovaro to where Lecter and Brent were waiting.

Lecter did not look happy. "You're leaving us?"

"Someone is camped a few miles east of us. It might be Richter."

"It might be Utes."

"Indians don't let their fires burn all night. It has to be white men." Fargo climbed onto the stallion.

"Shouldn't he be a lot farther ahead of us by now?"

"There's only one way to find out. Keep pushing east and I'll rejoin you as soon as I can." Fargo rode off, glad to be on his own for a while.

At night the woods were an obstacle course of boulders, thickets, and logs. Occasionally Fargo saw the campfire but the light never appeared for long. He blamed the wind which was bending the tops of the trees and whipping the lower branches.

Based on the position of the Big Dipper, it was close to five in the morning when Fargo reined up, shucked the Henry, and snuck to within a stone's throw of the fire.

A man sat beside it, a rifle across his lap, his chin on his chest. He was sound asleep. So was another man rolled up in a blanket. Two others were on the other side of the fire, near their hobbled horses, mired in shadow.

Snaking to a chest-high bush, Fargo studied them. Neither the man by the fire nor the one bundled in blankets was familiar. They might be Richter's men; they might not. Richter was supposed to have three gunnies with him, plus the twins, but Fargo only saw four blankets. Equally puzzling, there weren't any horses.

Fargo decided to wait. The sun would rise soon and he would have his answers.

It wasn't long before the squawk of an early rising jay caused the man by the fire to stir and look around. Slowly rising, he arched his back, then fed a few pieces of wood to the flames. With the toe of his right boot he nudged the one bundled in blankets, who mumbled something about jumping off a cliff.

"Wake up, Shorty, damn it," the first man said. "It's almost dawn and Jud wanted us to get an early start, remember?"

Shorty poked his head from the blankets. "Jud ain't here, is he? So how will he know? I say we're entitled to an extra hour of sleep. Wake me then, Crane, and not before." His head ducked back under.

Crane bent over a coffeepot and removed the lid to examine the contents. "Sleep as long as you want. But the rest of us are lighting a shuck and catching up with Jud as fast as we can."

"Afraid the Utes will get you?"

"Damn right I am, and I'm not ashamed to admit it," Crane said. "You would be scared, too, if your brain was any bigger than a pea."

Shorty poked his head out again. "I don't like bein' insulted."

"And I don't like the notion of being gutted and strangled with my own innards. I saw what the Sioux did to some buffalo hunters up in the Black Hills once. About made me sick to my stomach."

"Jud wouldn't have left us if the Utes were close."

"Your problem, runt, is that you're too damn trusting." Crane replaced the lid and set the pot on the fire. "Jud doesn't give a lick about us. All he cares about anymore is that chest."

Grumbling, Shorty sat up and rubbed the stubble on his chin. "I reckon I might as well stay up if all you're going to do is jabber."

Fargo's interest switched to the other two sleepers. The sky had brightened but not enough to tell who they were.

That was when Crane said, "I'll wake up the ladies. You saddle up."

"Why should I do all the work?" Shorty objected, rising. "You saddle one and I'll saddle the others." He buckled on his six-shooter, turned and took a step, and stopped as if he had walked into a wall. "Wait a minute. Where the hell are our horses?"

Crane turned. "The Utes must have taken them!"

"Think a second. If it was the Utes, why didn't they slit our throats while they were at it?" Shorty glanced at the undisturbed blankets. "I've got me a bad feelin' about this."

"They couldn't have!" Crane exclaimed. Dashing to the blankets, he cast them aside, revealing piles of grass and weeds arranged to mimic the shape of a human body. "They're gone! Both of them! They snuck off right under our noses. But how?"

Shorty was livid. "I'll tell you how, you peckerwood. You fell asleep, didn't you? That's the only way, since I sure as hell never dozed off when I was keepin' watch." He swore and slapped his leg. "Jud will have our hides for this, you idiot. He was mighty partial to those females."

"So am I," Fargo said, stepping into the open.

The pair whirled.

"You!" Crane blurted.

Shorty peered past Fargo into the trees. "So it was your doing? You snuck the females off? Where are they?"

"I'll ask the questions." Fargo flicked his eyes from one to the other. "And all I want to know is if Richter or anyone else has laid a hand on them."

"Those she-cats?" Crane said. "Hell, they'd claw out the eyes of anyone who tried. Besides, when did any of us have time?"

Shorty glared at his companion. "Jabberin' must be in your blood."

"What did I do?"

Now that Fargo had satisfied himself the twins had not been molested, he could attend to one other matter. "What will it be?"

"What will what be?" Crane asked.

At that Shorty snorted. "You must be the dumbest hombre this side of the Divide. He's givin' us a choice, lunkhead. We can go for our hardware or we can unbuckle it and there won't be gunplay."

Fargo waited.

"But what if we do shed our hog legs? What then?" Crane inquired. "Do we get to go our own way?"

"Who cares?" Shorty answered before Fargo could. "What chance do we have in Ute country without guns?"

Crane licked his lips and glanced behind him as if he was thinking of running. "This day sure stinks and the sun ain't hardly up yet." He looked at Fargo. "What will you do with us?"

"Turn you over to the first marshal I come across."

"That's what I was afraid you would say." Crane sighed. "You see, we're wanted down Texas way. And Kansas. And Missiouri, too, now that I think about it."

"There you go again," Shorty snapped. "Tellin' him our life's story when you should be fillin' him with lead."

Fargo shifted slightly. "I don't suppose there is any way I can talk you out of this?"

"You make it sound like we don't stand a prayer. But I've got news for you, big man," Shorty said. "I've bucked out more than a few in my time. In Kansas City I shot three men in a saloon before any of them could clear leather." He glanced at Crane and nodded.

Just like that, both killers exploded into motion.

13

Skye Fargo sometimes wondered why every gun shark west of the Mississippi thought he was the fastest man alive. He had lost count of the badmen who believed they were chained lightning and then found out the hard way there was always someone deadlier.

Shorty was a living example. He grinned as he clawed for his revolver. He thought he could draw and shoot before Fargo leveled the Henry and fired, and he was as wrong as wrong could be. The Henry boomed before Shorty's weapon rose an inch in its holster and the jolt of the slug smashing into his sternum spun him completely around. A stupefied look came over him as his legs gave out, and the last lesson he learned in life was that in a gunfight, as in everything else, nothing was ever certain.

Crane was a shade faster. He jerked his rifle up and snapped off a shot at the same instant Fargo did but his slug whizzed past Fargo's shoulders while Fargo's slug caught him in the ribs and lifted him off his feet. Crane thudded onto his back but he still had plenty of life in him. Enough to push onto an elbow, lever a new round into his rifle's chamber, and take aim.

Fargo shot him again.

Crane was knocked flat. Blood gushed from his

mouth as he twisted his head and stared at the gun-smoke curling from the Henry's muzzle. "Told you this day stunk," he croaked, then groaned and was still.

Fargo gathered up their revolvers, gun belts, and rifles, wrapped them in one of Shorty's blankets, and tied the bundle to the Ovaro, tucked behind his bedroll. The circus crew could use the guns.

Taking the reins in hand, Fargo walked past the bodies to where the horses had been tied. Tracks revealed that Dacia and Cyrena had walked the two horses over a hundred yards to prevent wakening Crane and Shorty, then climbed on. He was glad they had escaped but why had they gone east, instead of west, to the circus?

Mounting, Fargo trotted along the trail. Dawn had broken and the woods were alive with the chirping and warbling of birds. He rode hard but the twins had been going like bats out of Hades. After a bit the reason came to him, and filled him with dread. He remembered how much they liked the Hagens, how highly they thought of Rebecca. He recalled the children, particularly Margaret, and he applied his spurs to eke out a little more speed from the pinto.

The entire family were as decent and kind as anyone could be, and if anything happened to them, he would not take it well. He would not take it well at all.

Soon the Ovaro was flecked with sweat. Fargo slowed and tried not to think of the many miles he had to go. The sun was almost directly overhead when he came around a bend and had to rein up to avoid colliding with a horse lying in the middle of the trail. It was one of the animals the twins had taken, and its left front leg was shattered.

As near as Fargo could reconstruct the series of

events from the hoofprints, Dacia and Cyrena had raced around the same bend and one or the other had failed to spot a rain-worn hole. The horse had stepped into it, breaking its leg, and throwing its rider, who then climbed on behind her sister and continued on. They had no way to put the horse out of its misery so they left it lying there.

Fargo hated shooting horses. Even when it was necessary, he hated it. He would rather shoot anything than a horse. Of all the animals known to man, they were the ones man most relied on. Dogs were loyal in their way, but a good horse, in his estimation, had a dog beat six ways from Sunday. He had been around them all his life, and killing one, even when it was necessary, struck a nerve.

The bay raised its head to look at him as he cocked the Colt. "I'm sorry," Fargo said. He sincerely wished there were some other way but a horse with a broken leg never lasted long in the wild. Either it died of starvation and thirst or was devoured by scavengers.

Fargo stroked the trigger, splattering the bay's brains all over the grass. Climbing back on the Ovaro, he pressed on. As the hours went by he thought of all those who had lost their lives because of Judson Richter's greed. Thought of all the suffering Richter had caused. Richter had a lot to answer for, and Fargo aimed to see that he did.

It was not long after this that Fargo glimpsed a horse ahead. A foam-flecked sorrel barely a breath this side of exhaustion, carrying two riders. When he was close enough he shouted, "Dacia! Cyrena! Hold up!"

The twins heard him, and reined in. They slid off and were eagerly waiting for him when he caught up and alighted. Both ran at him and flung their arms around him and for a short space the three of them just stood there.

"Are you all right?" Fargo asked when they stepped back.

"We are now," one said.

Their ribbons were missing but Fargo saw that her lips were slightly fuller than her sister's. "Dacia?"

She nodded. "What are you doing here? Where's the circus?"

"They're a ways behind."

Cyrena pecked him on the cheek. "We heard about Thaddeus. Richter is dead set on getting his hands on that chest, no matter what it takes. But I guess you know that, don't you?"

"I think Richter was afraid of touching us for fear of what you would do," Dacia commented. "He talks big but deep down he's afraid of you. We could see it in his eyes."

Nodding, Cyrena said, "When Proctor wanted to rape us, Richter wouldn't let him. He said that would only make you madder than you're already bound to be."

"Richter was right."

"We're worried sick about the Hagens," Cyrena said. "Richter was there when Thad gave them all that gold, and he kept saying as how he thought it should be his."

"Surely he won't harm those darling children?" Dacia remarked. "Not even Richter would stoop that low."

Fargo didn't answer. There may have been a time when he believed most people were basically good at heart. But that just wasn't true. For every good person, for every person who would give a stranger in need the shirt off his back, there was another who would as soon knife the stranger and take what little he had.

"One of our horses broke a leg," Dacia said. "We've been riding double ever since."

Fargo told them about finding and shooting the animal. "One of you can ride with me. Your horse is about done in so we can't push as hard as we would like. But we still might reach the Hagen homestead by midnight."

The twins flipped a coin and Dacia lost so Cyrena got to ride with him.

Once an hour Fargo rested the horses for five to ten minutes. It delayed them even more but without the rest the sorrel would give out completely. By six that evening they had covered enough ground that Fargo announced they would rest for half an hour, then make a last long ride to the farm.

The twins sank to the grass, Dacia rubbing her eyes. "We hardly got a wink of sleep last night. Don't be surprised if we pass out on you."

Cyrena nodded. "I've never been so tired in my life. If it weren't for how worried I am, I'd curl up and sleep for a week."

"I can leave you some rifles and ammunition and ride on alone, and you can catch up on your sleep," Fargo proposed. "It should be safe enough."

"No," Dacia said. "We've come this far, we'll go the rest of the way."

Cyrena nodded. "We like the Hagens. We like Rebecca. She was nice to us, and we owe it to her to help her if we can."

Fargo did not point out that they were too far behind Richter to prevent the unthinkable. Or that Thimbletree was even further ahead. He let them nap forty-five minutes instead of thirty, then roused them.

Once the sun set and the cool of night claimed the countryside, it wasn't quite as bad. The rest had done wonders for the sorrel and the Ovaro was as dependable as ever. At eight Fargo stopped again but only for a quarter of an hour.

The twins were fighting exhaustion and hunger but they didn't complain. As sluggish as snails, they rose and mounted. It was Dacia's turn to ride double on the Ovaro, and she wrapped her arms tight around his waist, her breasts molded to his back, her chin on his shoulder.

"For a while there my sister and I thought we would never see you again."

"For a while there I thought the same thing."

"If we make it through this alive, we've decided to go to Europe and sign a contract with another circus. Thaddeus isn't the man we thought he was."

"You'll make it through alive," Fargo said, but they both knew it was not an ironclad promise.

"Funny how life works out." Dacia had to raise her voice to be heard above the clomp of hooves. "A few days ago we would have followed Thad to the ends of the earth and back. We thought he was the sweetest man ever born. Then he went and let Juliette be torn apart, and stood by and did nothing when Richter dragged us off."

"You're not the only one he fooled," Fargo said.

"But we knew him a lot longer than you have. What's our excuse for not recognizing his true nature sooner?"

"Some people don't show their true natures until they're put to the test," Fargo observed. "Until then they hide it behind a smile and a clap on the back."

"Has anyone ever complimented you on your intellect?"

Fargo laughed. "Not in the past twenty years or so, no."

"I wish we weren't in such a hurry," Dacia said. "I'd very much like to have you to myself for a few hours."

"I'd like that myself," Fargo declared. "But first things first."

"I know. You're as concerned about the Hagens as we are. I shudder to think what Richter will do if they refuse to give him their gold."

"Or what he might do anyway even if they do," Fargo said.

"You should have heard him. After he took us from the camp, practically all he talked about was the gold in Thad's chest. He's obsessed with it."

Fargo had known many a prospector and miner with gold fever. Most ended their days as poor as paupers with nothing to show for their years of searching and digging but filthy fingernails and skin as weathered as rawhide.

"I hope I never become that fanatical about anything," Dacia said, and giggled. "Except men."

The trail climbed to a low rise and as Fargo reached the top he spied a campfire ahead. He promptly reined up and Cyrena followed his example.

"Is it Richter and Proctor, do you think?"

"It could be." Although Fargo wouldn't have thought they would stop for the night when they were so close to the Hagen place. "Climb down. We'll go have a look-see." On foot, leading the horses, they crept close enough to see the lone figure beside the small fire, a skinny black man in a loose-fitting beige shift.

"Walikali!" Dacia exclaimed happily, dashing toward him.

The African heard her and jumped up. "Both Miss

Fleetwoods! And Bwana Fargo!" he beamed. "Truly, my heart sings for joy!"

Fargo had just reached the ring of firelight when an enormous shadow heaved out of the woods, making no more noise than would a breath of breeze, and towered over them. "Tembo," he greeted her. "We're friends, remember?"

The elephant remembered, all right. Her trunk snaked around his waist, and before Fargo could call out to Walikali to stop her, Tembo lifted him and carried him to the fire where she set him down as gently as if he weighed no more than a feather.

"I wish she would stop doing that."

"An elephant in love is the same as a woman in love," Walikali informed him. "She shows her love by doing things for the person she is fond of."

Fargo glanced up into Tembo's inscrutable eyes. He found it hard to accept that her interest in him was anything more than some strange form of animal infatuation. "Does this happen a lot in your country?"

"Elephants are wonderfully affectionate, bwana. But I have only ever seen this sort of thing once, when I was no older than a lion cub. A friend of my grandfather had an elephant named Ophar who was marvelously devoted to him and gave her life to save him from a charging rhino."

"Did I hear correctly?" Dacia asked with a grin. "Tembo's little heart is going pitter-patter over tall, dark, and dressed-in-buckskins?"

"Just when you think you've heard everything," Cyrena teased.

Fargo could think of better things to talk about. "Did you see any sign of Judson Richter and Proctor?" he asked Walikali.

"I have seen no one since I started after Bwana Thimbletree." The elephant man scowled. "He has a heart of darkness, that one. There is only one thing he loves, his riches. Now some of us will be stranded unless I can find him."

"Stranded how?" Fargo asked.

"It will cost much money to transport Tembo home," Walikali said. "Money I do not have. Bwana Thimbletree said he would take care of it when the time came. Without his help, Tembo and I will never see the veldt again."

"So that's why you're after him?" Fargo went to the Ovaro for his coffeepot and coffee. Since they had stopped anyway, a brief rest would do them all some good.

"That, and the murder of the Great Gandolpho and my other friends," Walikali replied. "I am a man of peace but there are things no man of peace should stand for."

Dacia was staring eastward. "I don't understand where Richter and Proctor got to. They were behind you."

Fargo suspected they had seen the African's fire and given it a wide berth. By now their horses must be as tired as the Ovaro and the sorrel, and they probably weren't far ahead. He handed the coffee to Dacia. "I'll be right back." Wheeling, he made for the river to fill the pot.

"Want some company?" Cyrena's arm slipped through his. "I need to stretch my legs."

"Just so that's all you want." Fargo was well versed in how devious the female gender could be, and he had noticed how her leg was brushing against his with every step she took.

"Why, whatever do you mean?" Cyrena batted her eyes. "You make it sound as if I have an ulterior motive."

"Show me a woman who doesn't."

Cyrena grinned and squeezed his arm. "You're a credit to men everywhere. But honestly, is this the right time and place for what you're implying?"

"No. So get the notion out of your pretty head."

"You slander me, sir." Cyrena laughed and gave him another squeeze. Her hand slid down his arm to his hand. "Not that I would mind if you decided to take advantage of me."

"I won't." They were threading through the trees, their footing uncertain in the dark, and Fargo hooked his other arm around her waist in case she slipped.

"My, my. Your mouth says one thing but your body says another."

Fargo glanced at her in irritation. Her eyes were twinkling playfully but she didn't fool him. "For two cents I'd throw you over my knee and spank you."

"You shouldn't get my hopes up like that." Cyrena pinched his backside, once on each buttock.

They reached the river and Fargo disentangled himself and dipped the coffeepot in the water. He ignored her when she rubbed his shoulders and when her finger traced the outline of his ear. "You listen about as well as a mule."

"You sure can flatter a girl."

"Keep it up and I'll throw you in the river." Fargo felt her hand slide across his neck to the front of his shirt, and under it.

"Go ahead. I dare you," Cyrena challenged him.

The coffeepot was full. Fargo set it beside him, stood up, and turned. She was so close, their bodies caressed one another, and the warm press of her bosom and her hips was enough to ignite stirrings in his groin. "Damn you."

Cyrena kissed his neck. "Why, another compliment like that and you'll sweep me right off my feet."

"I thought you were tired."

"I'm never *that* tired."

Fargo grabbed hold of her hips, thinking to give her a scare by pretending to heave her into the water. But the feel of his fingers on her soft, yielding flesh and the pressure of her bosom gave him pause.

"What are you waiting for, handsome? Or can it be your bark is a lot worse than your bite?"

"I don't know if you can swim," Fargo said, but he wasn't fooling anyone.

"Like a fish." Smiling seductively, Cyrena rose onto her toes and planted a moist kiss full on his mouth.

Fargo tasted the silky sweetness of her tongue and could not help growing warm all over.

"You big fibber," Cyrena said huskily. "You want it as much as I do."

"We don't have the *time*," Fargo stressed.

"Not if we take forever, no. But who says we have to? Who says we can't treat ourselves to five minutes of pleasure and go back with no one the wiser?" She nibbled on his chin. "Five minutes. Is that too much to ask?"

"You're a hussy."

Her grin was infectious. "And damn proud of it." She lowered her right hand to the hardening bulge in his pants. "Look at this. Part of you agrees with me. A *big* part of you at that."

"It's the night air. It always does that."

"Have any other fairy tales you want to share?" Cyrena ran her hand up and down his shaft and it grew harder still.

In the recesses of Fargo's mind an unconvincing

181

voice said not to do it but was immediately smothered by the volcanic surge of raw passion that coursed like liquid fire through his veins. There was no denying he wanted her as much as she wanted him.

"Five minutes," Cyrena repeated. "My sister and Walikali will never suspect."

Fargo hesitated.

"What will it be, lover?" Cyrena tugged at his belt. "Are you going to stand here like a bump on a log or show me what you're made of?"

"You asked for it," Fargo said. He peeled off her form-fitting costume and ran his fingers from her knees to the silky junction of her smooth thighs.

"Mmmm. Nice," Cyrena cooed, and shivered. "I've thought about you all day. About you and me, and this."

Fargo felt her hand close around his pole and nearly exploded then and there. By sheer force of will he held off, and gripping her slender waist, raised her high enough off the ground for what he had in mind next. "Just remember this was your idea."

"Do you hear me complaining?" Cyrena bantered. "Regrets are for those who feel guilty about everything they do. Me, I haven't felt guilty about anything since I was twelve." She ran the tip of her tongue across his lips. "I make my bed, I lie in it, come what may."

"Too bad we don't have a bed here," Fargo said, and rammed up into her. He did not bother being gentle. She asked for this, she would get it.

"Ahhhh!" Cyrena threw back her head and dug her fingernails into his shoulders. Her mouth parted wide, and for a few moments it appeared she would yell out. But all she did was moan and press against his chest.

"Yessssss. Oh, yesssssss."

Fargo wrapped her long legs around his waist and locked her ankles at the small of his back. Then, sliding his hands under her bottom, he began to stroke her. His manhood was throbbing.

"Do me hard, lover," Cyrena whispered. "Hard and fast."

"Exactly what I had in mind." Fargo rocked up onto the balls of his feet, thrusting to the hilt. Her velvet sheath contracted, heightening his sensation. His next stroke caused her to sink her teeth into his shoulder. His third triggered a geyser.

Cyrena tossed her head wildly about in a paroxysm of rapture. Her thighs kept opening and closing, her hips bucked like a bronco's. Cresting, she slumped in fatigue and her legs started to slide down his to the ground.

Fargo speared into her anew. Each time he rose up onto the balls of his feet for greater penetration. Each time her inner walls clung that much tighter.

Cyrena suddenly covered his mouth with hers and inhaled his tongue. She was panting hot and heavy, and whimpering.

Fargo glanced toward the fire. Dacia and Walikali were seated beside it, talking. The horses were nipping grass. He clasped Cyrena's waist and slammed up into her as never before. The friction built, and with it the pleasure. Fargo rocked up into her. Four, five, six more times, and then the night shimmered and faded, and for a few heartbeats there was just the two of them locked together as one.

"I'm there! Oh, I'm there!"

Cyrena clung to his buckskin shirt, her red tresses half over her face, nearly breathless.

They fixed their clothes, he picked up the coffeepot, and arm in arm they walked back.

14

When Fargo rode out less than half an hour later, he rode out alone. He left the twins with Walikali and told them to come on at their own pace. With Tembo to protect them and scare off everything under the sun, he figured they would be safe. Dacia and especially Cyrena were not pleased about being left behind but accepted it when he reminded them of the danger the Hagens were in, and how important it was to reach their homestead quickly.

The Ovaro was tired. The brief respite had restored a little of the pinto's flagging stamina but what it really needed was a day of nothing but rest. Fargo rode no faster than a trot and then only for short spells.

The whole time, Fargo's gut was in a knot. He was not a big believer in intuition or premonitions but he had a feeling he would not like what he found when he got there. Again and again he thought about the children, and how Margaret had taken such a shine to him.

It was with a sense of deep dread that Fargo rose in the stirrups when at long last he spied the gleam of lamplight from the cabin windows. That alone was troubling. It was past midnight and the family should have turned in long ago. Frontier folk were not like city dwellers. They didn't stay up to all hours. Not when they had to be up at dawn and spend the entire day at backbreaking chores.

There were three rectangles of light, which was odd since to the best of Fargo's recollection the cabin had only two windows. As he came nearer he saw that one of the rectangles was wider and higher than the others, and his dread climbed. It could only be light spilling through the open front door, and the Hagens would never leave the door open at night.

Drawing his Colt, Fargo slowed. He left the trail and crossed a cleared space that George Hagen had told him he intended to plow and plant with corn. He thought he saw a shadow flit across the doorway. Richter and Proctor might still be there. If he was right, if the Hagens had been harmed, the minutes the two killers had left to live could be numbered on the fingers of one hand.

Near a stump in the yard, Fargo drew rein and slid from the saddle. It creaked under him but not loud enough to be heard in the cabin. Bent low, he stalked to the open door, careful not to step into the light. No sounds came from within.

Fargo was so intent on the doorway that he nearly tripped over a body. It was George Hagen, lying in the shadows on his side, one hand outstretched as if in appeal, surprise etched into the lines of his face. He had been shot twice, once in the chest, again in the face.

Throwing caution to the breeze, Fargo barreled inside and instantly crouched, his eyes sweeping the room for movement. All he saw was another body. This time it was Rebecca. She lay in front of the bedroom door, her features set in defiance, the bosom of her dress caked with dry blood. She had been shot once through the heart.

A chill came over Fargo. A sensation of icy rage that knifed through him clear to the bone. He had to force his legs to move. He reached for the latch and heard movement in the bedroom. Darting to one side, his back to the wall, he pushed the door open. But it only swung inward about a foot. It could not go any further because another body lay on the floor.

Fargo stared down into little Timmy's glazed eyes and wanted to scream his fury to the rafters. Bending, he gently rolled the boy aside and opened the door the rest of the way. A groan was torn from deep within him.

Priscilla was sprawled at the foot of the bed, a jagged chunk missing from the back of her head. Fargo did not roll her over. He moved past her to check the other side of the bed but did not find Margaret.

Racing back out, Fargo searched the entire cabin. Margaret was missing. He ran outside and around the corner to the corral. The Hagens had finished repairing it and three horses were huddled at the far end.

The barn door was open. Fargo ran to it but did not see anyone inside. Turning, he hollered Margaret's name several times, no longer caring if Richter and Proctor were lurking nearby. He wanted them to hear. He wanted them to try to kill him so he could repay them for what they had done to the Hagens. "Margaret?" he called out again but received no answer.

His emotions a churning whirlpool, Fargo took a step toward the cabin. He would take a lamp and search more thoroughly. She had to be around there somewhere.

From within the barn came a whimper.

Whirling, Fargo ran back in. A lantern hung on a hook and he quickly lit it and raised it over his head. "Margaret?" A sound from under the hayloft drew him to a crumpled form. For a few seconds his legs felt weak but the spell passed and he dropped onto his knees, saying through clenched teeth, "God, no."

Margaret's eyes blinked open and focused on him and her mouth creased in a weak smile. "Mr. Fargo? Is that you?"

"It's me." Fargo's voice did not sound like his own, and his face was burning as if it was on fire.

"I thought I heard you." Margaret tried to raise her head but sank back. "I feel so strange. Like part of me is missing."

"Lie still." Fargo put a hand on her shoulder.

"Are the rest of my family?—" Margaret could not bring herself to say the word.

Fargo nodded.

"I was afraid of that. I tried to run and hide like Ma said." Margaret coughed, and her mouth and chin grew dark. Her child's eyes bored into his. "I'm dying, aren't I?"

Again all Fargo could do was nod.

"I don't want to. There's so much I haven't done. Places I wanted to see." Her small hand limply rose and found his. "You won't leave me, will you?"

"No," Fargo said. He had to force the word out past a constriction in his throat. "I will get the men who did this to your family if it is the last thing I ever do."

"It was just one man," Margaret said.

"Judson Richter or Proctor?"

"I don't know who they are. The man who did this

was the one who came with you and those nice ladies with red hair. Mr. Thimbletree. The one who gave my pa all that money."

The world spun and reeled. "What?" Fargo said.

"He came riding up on that zebra of his. Pa went out to say howdy and Mr. Thimbletree shot him." Margaret was speaking so softly he could barely hear her. "Then he came in the cabin and shot everyone else. He shot me, too, but I made it past him and out the door." She stopped. "Funny thing. The whole time, he was crying and saying he was sorry."

Fargo could not remember the last time he shed a tear but one trickled down his cheek.

"I came in here to hide but Mr. Thimbletree followed me in and stood right where you are and said, 'I am not the man I thought I was, child.' Then he shot me again." Margaret's grip on his hand grew slack. "What did he mean by that?"

How could Fargo explain?

"Then Mr. Thimbletree went out and after a while I heard horses ride up and there was a lot of shouting and shots. I think Mr. Thimbletree rode off and whoever else was here went after him." Margaret closed her eyes. "All this talking is tiring me something awful."

"Lie quiet. I won't leave you."

"You're nice, Mr. Fargo. I like you a lot."

"I like you, too." Fargo felt like he was fit to choke. He thought of Thimbletree and fury filled him. Total, near-blinding fury, along with the determination to do to Thimbletree as he had done to the Hagens.

"Mr. Fargo?"

"Call me Skye."

"If I had been older would you come courting? I

always wanted a beau some day. Ma liked to say how special her courting days were."

"I'd have been honored to court you." Fargo had never hated anyone as intensely as he hated Thaddeus T. Thimbletree at that moment.

Margaret smiled. "I bet I'd be a good wife. Pa always bragged on how Ma was the best wife anyone could—" She suddenly stopped and seemed puzzled. "It's getting all dark. Not out here, inside of me. It's a strange feeling?"

"I'm so sorry," Fargo said.

"For what? It's not your fault." Her fingers plucked at his. "Will you do me a favor?"

"Anything."

"Would you hold me a second. Please. I'm terribly scared."

Awkwardly, Fargo enfolded her small crumpled body in his big arms. He could not bring himself to look at her for fear he would lose control. Stroking her hair, he whispered, "I'm proud to be your friend."

Margaret reached up and touched him, then went limp.

Fargo was in the barn a long time. When he came out he was carrying Margaret, and a shovel. He set her next to her father, then went into the cabin and one by one brought out the rest of the Hagens. Rolling up his sleeves, he began digging. He made the graves deep so scavengers couldn't get at the bodies. The soil was iron, the work hard. He was at it for hours. Blisters soon covered his palms and burst open and every muscle in his body ached but he stayed at it, digging, always digging, until finally the graves were ready and he lowered each of the bodies into the dank earth after wrapping them in blankets. He paused when he began to lower Margaret in, and touched her head. He was tamping down the last of the mounds when the night disgorged Walikali and the twins.

The African stared sadly down from on top of Tembo. "Truly, this is a life of many sorrows."

Cyrena and Dacia dismounted and walked over to the graves.

"Richter murdered them all?" Cyrena raged. "The bastard!"

"It was Thimbletree."

Dacia started to cry. "No, no, no."

Fargo leaned the shovel against the cabin and went in and sat in the rocking chair. He felt numb, inside and out, and gazed at his bloody hands without feeling the pain he knew he should. He heard the others come in but he did not look up.

"At first light I'm going after Thimbletree, Richter, and Proctor." Fargo couldn't wait. As a general rule he never killed unless he had to, but this was one occasion when he would kill and kill gladly.

"So Richter and Proctor did show up?" Cyrena squatted beside the rocking chair. "What happened? Did they go after Thad?" She saw his hands and blurted, "Good God! Look at those blisters. You sit here while we boil some water and see if there's any salve or medicine to be had."

Fargo did not care what they did. He did not care about his hands. He did not care about anything except the one who was to blame and the two who had driven him to do it. They were all he would care about until he had done what needed doing. Then, and only then, could he get on with his life, but he would never be quite the same again.

"We came as fast as we could," Walikali was saying, "but their horse was very tired."

The mention jarred Fargo into standing. Without a word he went out and unsaddled the Ovaro and led it to the barn. He avoided glancing at the spot where he had found Margaret as he ladled out oats.

"You should have asked me to do that." Dacia had followed him. "It's what friends are for."

Fargo tried to walk past her but she snagged his arm.

"You can't keep it all inside. Talk to me. I'm a good listener, and there's only the two of us."

"I suggest you and your sister stay here with Walikali until I get back." Fargo walked on and she fell into step beside him.

"That's it? No remorse to get off your chest? No anger simmering around in there like a pot on to boil?"

Fargo stopped so unexpectedly she took several steps past him before she stopped, too. He stared at her. That was all. Just stared.

Dacia slowly nodded. "So that's how it is? But killing Thaddeus won't bring the Hagens back."

"Are you defending what he did?"

"Never." Dacia bowed her head. "What he's done is hideous. It's why he did it that baffles me. Thad was always the sweetest person you would ever want to meet. You saw yourself how kind he can be." She gazed off into the night. "Something has happened to him. Something has snapped deep inside. He's not the same man."

"Maybe he is. Maybe this is how he was all along and he had everyone fooled." Fargo strode on.

She caught up and said, "You're being unfair. He deserves the benefit of the doubt."

Fargo gestured at the row of freshly dug graves. "All he deserves is one of those. Or better yet, to be staked out and skinned alive."

Dacia was aghast. "You wouldn't! That would be barbaric."

"And what do you call what he's done?" Fargo snapped. Entering the cabin, he went straight to the rocking chair.

Walikali and Cyrena had been talking in hushed tones but now they fell silent and looked at Dacia, who slumped down on the settee.

"We have been thinking, bwana," the African said. "Maybe it is not wise for you to go alone. Maybe Tembo and I should go, too."

"No."

Cyrena squatted in front of the rocking chair, her hands on Fargo's knees. "You should look at yourself in the mirror. You're worn out. You need rest. You need food. In the shape you're in, you could get yourself killed. Why not lie up for a day and then go after them?"

"No."

"Damn it, I only want to see you get through this alive. Too much hate can make a person careless."

Fargo leaned back. "Ever hear of Hugh Glass?"

"I can't say as I have."

"Glass was a trapper. One day he was hunting and a grizzly mauled him so badly, his friends didn't expect him to live. But when he took a long time dying, they helped themselves to his weapons and his possibles bag and went off and left him. He begged them not to but they did it anyway. Glass hated them for that, hated them with all his heart and soul, as he liked to say. That hate kept him alive. That hate helped him mend. That hate carried him across hundreds of miles of hostile country, eating nothing but carrion. That hate brought him all the way to Fort Kiowa, and safety." Fargo paused. "So don't tell me about hate."

Cyrena rose and went over to sit beside her sister.

"The bed is yours if you want it," Fargo said. "There's plenty of food in the root cellar. More than enough to last until Lecter and the circus show up. If I'm not back by then, go on with them." He closed his eyes and was asleep almost instantly.

Years of life in the wild had instilled in Fargo the habit of waking at sunrise. Standing, he stretched, and saw Walikali curled up on the settee. The closed bedroom door explained the absence of the twins. He did not bother eating.

The sight of the graves rekindled his seething emotions of the night before. He saddled up, left the bundle of guns he had taken from Crane and Shorty just inside the front door, and stepped into the stirrups.

The door opened. Walikali was rubbing sleep from his eyes and looked toward the barn, where Tembo was tied. "You were not going to say good-bye, bwana?"

"Tell them for me."

"I wish you much luck. The state you are in, I fear you will need it." Walikali nodded toward the elephant. "My daughter is worried about you, too."

Tembo was staring at Fargo in that peculiarly human way she had. She came toward him as far as the rope permitted.

"You're a good man, Walikali. If we don't see each other again, I wish you and Tembo the best." Clucking to the Ovaro, Fargo rode to the trail. He assumed Thimbletree had fled east but there were no new tracks. Riding in a wide circle, he discovered the zebra's prints northwest of the cabin, bearing toward the far distant mountains. Paralleling them were the tracks of two shod horses: Richter's and Proctor's.

It beat all, Fargo reflected, why Thimbletree was

heading for the Uintas. The only thing there were Utes, plus more grizzlies and mountain lions than anyone could shake a stick at. And a man-eating tiger.

It made little difference, though, where Thimbletree fled. Fargo would chase him to the ends of the earth, if that was what it took. And if, along the way, he ran into Judson Richter and Proctor, so much the better.

Fargo was in no hurry. There wasn't a cloud in the sky, so he need not worry about rain washing out the sign. He would take his time and pace himself, and like the plodding tortoise that won its race with the much faster hare, he would catch up to them eventually, and there would be an accounting.

As he rode, Fargo recollected other places, similar times. Like that day in New Mexico when he came upon a small wagon train, the wagons burned, the seven families massacred. He had tracked the renegades responsible to their lair and brought their days of slaughtering innocents to an end. Then there were the emigrants in the Cascades, butchered and left to rot, and the bandits he had tracked for a week before they, too, were left to rot under the sun.

Atrocities were a fact of life on the frontier. Savagery was all too common, in men as well as beasts, although when it came to wreaking slaughter, few animals were a match for man. A mountain lion might kill thirty or forty sheep in an excess of bloodletting, or a fox might wipe out all the hens in a chicken coop, but such frenzies were rare.

Man killed in war, for revenge, out of spite, out of a craving to kill for killing's sake. Man had a thousand and one reasons for why he killed but they all boiled down to one: it was in man's nature.

To Fargo's way of thinking, inside of everyone lurked the potential to spill blood. All it took was the right set of circumstances and the inner walls that usually held the craving in check came tumbling down. With Thimbletree, it was the fact he could not bear to part with his precious hoard. To keep it, he would spill as much blood as was necessary, and even blood that wasn't.

The tracks revealed that Thimbletree had not given the zebra a breather until it came to the base of the mountain range. By then it must have dawned on Thimbletree that in his panic he had gone the wrong way. Either he didn't give a damn or he knew Richter was after him, because he pushed on into the Uintas.

It was noon before Fargo came to where Thimbletree had stopped for a while, maybe to get his bearings. If so, Thimbletree's woodlore was as meager as an Apache's knowledge of opera, because Thimbletree headed due west, into the very heart of the range, and into the very heart of Ute country.

Judging by the gait of Richter's and Proctor's horses, they were moving half as fast as Thimbletree. Which could just be a sign they were being cautious.

Midafternoon saw Fargo draw rein on the bank of a swiftly flowing stream. Judson Richter and Proctor had halted at the same spot so their mounts could drink. He saw where the pair had crossed to the other side and gone off up a pine covered bluff.

Swinging down, Fargo sank onto one knee and dipped a hand in the crystal clear water. It was cold and delicious. He drank a few more handfuls, then walked to an oak and sat with his back to the trunk to rest a while. His lack of a decent night's sleep was wearing away at him. Removing his hat, he squinted up at the bluff, noting that from up there a man could see for miles.

Hardly had the thought crossed Fargo's mind than

a rifle lever rasped and he was warned, "If you so much as sneeze, you die."

Out of the brush stepped Proctor wearing a sadistic grin.

Fargo held himself still. His hat was in his right hand so he could not stab for the Colt if he wanted, and the Henry was in its scabbard on the Ovaro. "Let me guess. Richter and you spotted me from up top?"

"Smart hombre." Proctor chuckled. "But if you were really smart, you'd have figured that out sooner and not waltzed into my gunsights."

"Where's your partner?"

"He'll join us shortly. I came on foot to spring this little surprise. Now that I have," Proctor fired into the air and jacked the lever again before Fargo could think to draw, "that's the signal to let him know it worked."

"I'm not the only one who isn't too smart," Fargo commented. "Up here sound carries a long way. Thimbletree or the Utes might have heard that shot."

"The Ute village is miles off," Proctor said. "And all the old man will do is ride that striped horse of his into the ground that much sooner." He came and stood between Fargo and the Ovaro. "I want you to take that hog leg of yours and toss it as far as you can. Use two fingers, and only two fingers, and do it mighty slow."

Fargo did exactly as he had been directed.

"Now do the same with that knife of yours, the one you used on the big snake. No fancy tricks, you hear? I've seen men throw a knife and stick it in a bull's-eye ten times out of ten, but a knife isn't faster than a bullet."

Again Fargo complied.

Proctor smiled. "Now we'll just wait until Jud gets here. He wants the honor of rubbin' you out."

"Why did he send you down instead of waiting for me himself?" Fargo asked. "You must not be much of a friend."

"Tryin' to turn me against him won't work. We've been pards since we were knee-high to grasshoppers."

High up on the bluff a rider appeared. Judson Richter was leading Proctor's horse by the reins. The trail down was narrow and winding, and it would take him a while.

Fargo gauged the distance between himself and Proctor and decided against trying anything unless he could lure Proctor closer. "It's a shame, you going to all this trouble for nothing."

"What the hell're you talkin' about?"

"The gold. You think Thimbletree has it but he doesn't. The chest is with the circus."

Proctor laughed. "Nice try but we know better. They told us how he went loco and killed some of his own people and then lit out with it."

"They lied. Thimbletree went crazy but he left the chest in his wagon. I saw it with my own eyes." Fargo was playing a bluff, and it worked. The outlaw took a couple of steps toward him.

"You're the one who's lyin'."

"Am I?" Fargo placed his hat on his head. "Did you really think they would hand over a fortune to you? The only gold Thimbletree has with him are the coins he took from the Hagens."

Gnawing on his lower lip, Proctor glanced up at Judson Richter, then took another step. "I still say you're lyin', mister, and I know how to prove it." He fixed a bead on Fargo's right knee. "You have until I count to five to tell the truth or I start shootin' you to pieces."

15

Not that long ago Skye Fargo had forced Thaddeus T. Thimbletree to reveal where his treasure chest was hidden by doing the very thing Proctor was about to do to him. Proctor was right; he was lying. But it was in his best interests not to admit it no matter what the gunman did. "Count to five or fifty, it won't make a difference. Go ahead and shoot. What do you care if I know where the chest really is?"

"You do?" Proctor raised his cheek from the rifle.

"Don't let that stop you," Fargo baited him. "You can always make the circus people tell you."

"What are you up to?" Proctor lowered the rifle a few inches. "If they lied to us once, they'd lie again. And if I accidentally kill you, we might never find out." He glanced up the bluff. "I think we'll wait until Jud gets here. He'll know what to do."

"I don't know if I'd count on Richter all that much," Fargo said. "What has he done so far except get the rest of your friends killed?"

"I warned you before. Don't try to turn me against him. It won't work. Jud and me have been through a lot. He'd do to ride the river with any day of the week."

Fargo shifted so his feet were flat on the ground

and draped his forearms across his knees. Proctor wasn't quite close enough yet. He had to draw him nearer. "Never trust anyone when it comes to gold. You're loco if you believe he'll share with you."

"We've agreed to split it fifty-fifty. And Jud has never broken his word to me in all the years I've known him."

"There's always a first time." Fargo plucked a blade of grass and stuck the stem between his front teeth. "But I'm wasting my breath. You don't have the brains God gave a turnip or you wouldn't let Richter make a jackass of you."

Bristling, Proctor took another step. "Not one more insult, you hear? Or I'll stomp you to a pulp."

"I'd like to see you try." For a moment Fargo thought it worked. Proctor snapped the rifle overhead to bash him in the face and started to take the step that would bring him close enough to spring, but at the last instant Proctor snapped the rifle down and stepped back instead.

"No you don't! I'm not as dumb as you make me out. Keep your mouth shut until Jud gets down here."

Fargo had no illusions about what Richter would do. He looked for a downed tree limb or a rock or anything else he could use as a weapon but nothing was within reach.

Then the unexpected reared its head.

Judson Richter was three-fourths of the way to the bottom when Fargo saw him gaze to the south, stiffen in the saddle, and suddenly lash his reins. He descended the last part of the trail at a trot, which was much too fast given how narrow it was, and twice his mount almost pitched over the side when its hooves came down too close to the edge.

"What the hell?" Proctor stepped back a few paces,

never taking his rifle off Fargo. "Is Jud tryin' to kill himself?"

The answer was provided by Richter when he reined up and barked, "Utes! Twenty to thirty of them! They're not more than half a mile away and comin' in our direction. They must have heard the shot you fired."

Snatching up Fargo's Colt and Toothpick, Proctor dashed to his horse, then nodded at Fargo. "What about our friend, there? Do we shoot him and be done with it?"

"And have the Utes pinpoint where we are?" Richter shook his head. Drawing his revolver, he pointed it at Fargo. "On your feet and on your pinto. And remember the Utes will lift your hair as quick as they'll lift ours."

Fargo rose, and with his hands in the air, he stepped to the stallion. He would just as soon the Utes did spot them. In the confusion he might give Richter and Proctor the slip.

"Hurry it up, you damned turtle," Richter growled. "I'm not hankerin' to be turned into a pincushion."

Fargo was about to swing up when he realized the Henry was still in its saddle scabbard. Proctor had neglected to take it and Richter hadn't noticed it yet. Quickly reining around so the Henry was on their off side, he said, "Back up the bluff?"

"No. They'd see us. Head north and don't try anything. You wouldn't be the first man I've shot in the back."

Fargo was constantly alert for a chance to yank out the Henry and use it but the opportunity never came. Richter was always too close behind him, and always too watchful. It surprised him that neither had noticed the Henry's stock jutting from the scabbard, but then they were preoccupied. Several times they stopped to scour the country they had covered.

"I think we gave them the slip," Proctor commented as they were climbing toward a sawtooth ridge.

"Think again," Richter said.

A line of riders were smack on their trail and coming on fast.

"Son of a bitch," Richter spat. "We've got to lose them soon or we'll lose Thimbletree and the gold."

Proctor told Richter what Fargo had said about the chest.

"And you believed him?" the renegade scout scoffed. "He was tryin' to trick you. Probably wants the gold for himself."

Red with anger, Proctor kneed his horse up next to the Ovaro and flourished his revolver. "Ever been pistol-whipped, mister? I should split your skull, you think you're so damn smart."

"We're both smarter than Richter," Fargo responded. "Or hasn't he wondered why Thimbletree bothered taking the gold coins he gave the Hagens if he has a chest full of it?"

The question gave Proctor pause. "Damn you. You confuse the hell out of me sometimes."

"Ignore him," Judson Richter said. "We'll hash this out later." He, too, brought his horse up beside the pinto, but on the other side. "Right now we've got to—" He stopped, his gaze fixed on the Henry. "Damn you, Proctor! Are you *tryin'* to get us killed?" Richter pulled the Henry out and shook it at his friend. "What if he had gotten his hands on this when we weren't lookin'?"

They were both mad enough to hit him so Fargo gave them something else to think about. "Aren't you two forgetting the Utes?" he asked, riding on. It worked. For the moment their fear for their scalps eclipsed their anger, and they followed.

The terrain was typical of the Rockies—steep forested slopes sprinkled with boulders and broken by ravines. There was talus and deadwood to be avoided. Terrain that quickly tired a horse, and after another hour, all three of their animals were in need of a rest. But the Utes were still back there, sticking to their scent like bloodhounds, and so long as they were, Judson Richter refused to stop.

"It'll be a cold day in hell before a stinkin' savage counts coup on me."

"I heard you lived among the Flatheads for a while," Fargo mentioned.

"That I did," Richter confirmed. "For pretty near a year, back when I was green as grass. The Bloods had taken my horses and supplies and I was lost and near-starved when the Flatheads found me and invited me to their village."

"I also heard you repaid them by stealing one of their horses and killing a warrior who tried to stop you."

Judson Richter laughed. "It was three I killed. One was the pa of a squaw who took a shine to me. I'd trifled with her and she was in a family way, and her pa thought I should shackle myself to her for life. Later I heard she was so brokenhearted, she walked out into a lake and drowned herself. Can you imagine? A heathen gal gettin' that upset over a little thing like a baby."

Fargo would have liked to kick his teeth in.

Throughout the long, hot afternoon, they wound deeper into the mountains. One time, and one time only, Fargo had the opportunity to slip away. It came as they were negotiating a slope covered with loose stones. He reached the crest first and galloped toward a stand of heavy timber, convinced he could reach it before Richter and Proctor came to the top. But he had twenty yards to go when a rifle cracked and a slug whistled past his ear. He reined up.

"Try that again and I'll splatter your brains all over creation," Richter snarled as he came to a stop. "I should do it now but you have a few questions to answer about Thimbletree first."

By evening they were a lot farther into the Uintas than Fargo had ever gone. He liked what he saw. The towering mountainous ramparts laced by streams and rivers, the thick forests and many meadows and fields of grass, the abundance of game of every kind, created a paradise. He would not mind returning some day to explore the entire range.

"Are we stoppin' soon?" Proctor called out. "Those savages aren't likely to follow us once the sun goes down."

"Which is exactly why we're *not* stoppin'," Judson Richter declared. "As soon as the sun sets, we'll show these heathens they can't outfox white folks."

Richter's plan called for waiting until they saw the glow of the Ute campfire, then swinging wide to the west and then south after Thimbletree. But the sun had been down a good long while when Richter said, "Something is wrong. They should have stopped by now. Either they made a cold camp or they're still after us."

"Why not wait here and see?" Fargo suggested. It was dark enough now that he could try to slip away at any time.

"Oh, sure," Richter said. "You'd like for us stop so the Utes can jump us. You figure you can get away in the confusion."

"But that's not about to happen," Proctor said. "We're not stopping until we see their fire. So keep going."

They entered deep forest. Limbs and bushes hemmed them in. It was like riding through a tunnel. Fargo could barely see his hand when he held it front of his face. Smiling, he sat straighter.

Just ahead a low branch appeared. Normally Fargo would duck but this time he grabbed hold and pushed, bending the branch as far as it would go. He was glancing back as he did. Judson Richter was looking behind them. Proctor was fiddling with his rifle.

Suddenly reining to the left, Fargo let go. There was a shout and the blast of Richter's rifle but the slug missed and when Fargo next glanced back, Richter was on the ground, swearing luridly, and Proctor was starting to give chase. Inexplicably, Richter called him back.

Fargo did not slow down until he had put over a mile behind him. Reining up, he listened, and when the only sounds to reach his ears were the hoot of an owl and the bleat of a deer, he headed southwest.

He was unarmed, but as long as he fought shy of hostiles and grizzlies, he should make out all right. Eventually he would strike Thimbletree's trail. At night he might miss it, though, so after another mile, when he came upon a small clearing, he stopped. Stripping off his saddle and saddle blanket, he spread out his bedroll and was soon asleep.

How long he was out to the world, Fargo was uncertain, but it could not have been long when he found himself lying there with his eyes open, staring at the stars, and wondering why he was awake. He rolled onto his side and was about to close his tired eyes again when he noticed the Ovaro, its head high and its ears pricked, staring off into the woods.

Fargo sat up. Night was when predators were abroad and there might be a bear or a mountain lion or wolves roving about. He looked but did not see anything and he was lying back down when the pinto stamped a hoof and whinnied.

Rising, Fargo turned. Too late he heard the rush of stealthy feet. Much too late he tried to leap aside. Arms encircled his own, others encircled his legs. He was slammed to the earth. He did not need to see his attackers to know they were Indians. Only Indians smeared fat in their hair, and the smell of bear fat was strong. He lashed out with an elbow, felt it connect, and heard a grunt. The arms around his chest slackened, as did those about his legs when he smashed a fist downward.

Springing upright, Fargo tried to reach the Ovaro. But his first two attackers had brought friends, six altogether, who rushed him from all sides. The fact they did not use their knives or lances told Fargo they wanted to take him alive, and the only reason hostiles took white men prisoner was to torture them later.

It was all the motivation Fargo needed to fight with a fury born of pure and primal desperation. His fists flailed right and left. Indians were grapplers and wrestlers, not boxers, and his flurry broke their charge, leaving several in the grass. But their numbers prevailed and they overwhelmed him. Hands clamped onto his wrists. Strong fingers wrapped around his ankles.

Fargo refused to give up. He slugged a burly Ute on the jaw, hit another in the cheek. He gouged a third in the eye, eliciting a howl, and kicked a fourth where it always hurt males the most. Momentarily in the clear, again he sought to reach the stallion, but as quick as he was, they were equally quick, and three of them plowed into him and bore him to the earth. They were fast learners, these Utes, and they rained punches of their own. Most were absorbed by his shoulders and neck but enough landed to hurt and sting and bruise.

Twisting, Fargo drove a knee into a crotch. He punched an exposed ear. He connected with a combination that stretched out a stocky warrior like a poled buffalo. But it was not enough. Nowhere near enough. Again they swarmed him, all hands and fists and a tangle of limbs, and this time when they slammed him onto his back, he stayed here. Utes were on his legs, Utes pinned his arms, yet another Ute was astride his chest.

Words flew in the Ute tongue. Fargo was rolled onto his stomach and his wrists were bound. He was hauled erect, pushed to the Ovaro, and thrown belly-down over its back. He hated leaving his saddle and other possessions but then saw that some of the Utes had collected everything and carried it to where the warriors had concealed their horses off among the pines.

"Do any of you speak the white man's tongue?" he asked.

"I do," one said.

"I am not your enemy. I have not come to harm your people. Untie me and we will talk with straight tongues."

The warrior was the one Fargo had kneed in the groin. "Do not talk, white-eye, unless I say," he said harshly. "Or maybe you not talk again, eh?"

Being forced to ride on one's stomach was never

comfortable. At night, bareback, over the roughest of terrain, and sometimes at a trot, it was sheer hell. Fargo's gut became so sore that before long he winced whenever the Ovaro was made to move at any gait faster than a walk.

The Utes rode all night. Sunrise brought a surprise. Twisting his head, Fargo recognized the warrior in the lead. It was the tall Ute with the eagle feather. When the warrior looked at him, he smiled, but the warrior merely looked away. The glances the others bestowed left no doubt how they felt.

Their destination was no surprise. Never stopping once to rest or eat or water their mounts, by early afternoon they reached the Ute village.

Fargo spied sentries posted around the perimeter, a precaution usually taken only when enemies were known to be nearby.

A pall of sorrow and gloom hung over the village. The faces of the women were downcast, the children in the grip of fear.

The tall warrior led the Ovaro to the largest lodge and the tall warrior reined around and unceremoniously dumped Fargo to the dirt. Fargo's shoulder took the brunt. He grit his teeth against a sharp stab of pain and slowly sat up.

Utes converged from all over. Soon every man, woman, and child ringed him, their collective ill will enough to give a man the chills. At a shout they parted and the tall warrior came up to Fargo and stood over him, arms folded, contemplating him as he might an elk he was fixing to slaughter. "I am Nevava."

"The Sioux know me as He Who Tracks."

"Your skin white."

"I am not one of those who hates Indians because

they *are* Indians," Fargo said. "I have lived with the Sioux and other tribes."

"That not make you friend." Nevava squatted and took hold of Fargo's jaw. "I see you before."

"When I rode into your village after the tiger attacked," Fargo said. "I did not hurt any of your people, only the whites you were torturing."

"The Ti-ger?" Nevava slowly repeated.

"That's what whites call the big cat with stripes," Fargo said. "It comes from a land far away where there are many animals not found here."

Nevava said something to a group of elders and after they replied, he glanced down again. "How this ti-ger come to Ute land? White men brought, yes?"

"In a wagon with metal bars," Fargo said. "The whites were taking it to the Mormons by the Great Salt Lake but it escaped."

"This ti-ger come back two times," Nevava revealed. "Kill more of my people."

"I'm sorry."

"We want ti-ger dead."

"I would, too, if I were in your moccasins," Fargo said. But finding it would take more luck than skill. The Utes knew next to nothing about its habits.

"We want you kill ti-ger."

"Me? I've never hunted one before. I'm not sure I can kill it."

"You not kill, you not live." Nevava slid a hunting knife from a beaded sheath and lightly pressed the razor-sharp blade to Fargo's throat. "You not kill, I cut neck."

"You have many warriors. Many hunters. Why not have them try?"

"Seven go out after ti-ger, none come back. Five go out after ti-ger, only one come back and he not live long. Now no more go." Nevava pressed the knife a little harder. "Now you go."

"Why me? I'm not one of the whites who brought it here."

"One moon past, warriors see whites, see wagons, see animals not see ever. See big gray one with horns at mouth. See big snake. See hair man. And see ti-ger."

Fargo should have suspected the Utes had known about the circus all along. "That still doesn't tell me why it has to be me."

"Whites bring ti-ger. You white. You kill ti-ger."

Their logic was hard to dispute but Fargo had a few demands of his own. "I can't do it without my guns. Those two whites you were chasing have them."

"Other warriors still chase whites. Maybe catch. Maybe not." Nevava held the knife in front of Fargo's eyes. "We not wait. You take bow. You take lance. You take knife. You go when sun come up. You go on foot."

Fargo was dumfounded. They expected him to hunt down and slay one of the most fierce man-killers in the world with weapons he had rarely used since his days spent with the Sioux, back when he wasn't old enough to shave. They were demanding the impossible.

"We keep horse so you come back," Nevava informed him. "You kill ti-ger, you bring head. We give you horse, you free to go." He paused. "What you say?"

A few choice words were on the tip of Fargo's tongue but he bit them off. It wasn't as if he had much choice. "What makes you think the tiger is still around? It could be far away by now."

"Night past we hear ti-ger roar, hear ti-ger growl."

Nevava pointed at a tableland to the west. "There."
Rising, Nevava stepped behind him and slashed the
rope binding his wrists with a deft stroke. "Stand."

Fargo's wrists were sore and chafed. He rubbed
them as he rose, conscious of the bitter looks he received. By virtue of his skin color, the Utes blamed
him in part for the deaths of their loved ones. It wasn't
fair, it wasn't right, but it was understandable and no
worse than the hatred heaped on them by whites for
the same reason.

Nevava tugged on his arm. "Come."

An empty tepee was to be his jail for the night. A
pile of firewood had been gathered, and his bedroll,
saddle, and saddle blanket had been placed to one
side. A waterskin lay near them.

"All the comforts of home." Fargo opened the
waterskin and chugged until water sloshed over his
chin and chest.

Nevava was the only Ute who had entered. "You
want deer meat? We bring deer meat. You want elk
meat? We bring elk meat."

The mention of food reminded Fargo how long it
had been since he last ate. "Some venison would be
nice."

"That all?"

"The prettiest woman in your village would be nice,
too," Fargo said with a grin. He felt like a condemned
criminal being offered his last request.

"We bring deer meat," Nevava said, and went out.

Fargo sat cross-legged. He was tired enough to sleep
for a week but he would wait for the food.

It wasn't long in coming. There was a sound at the
flap and it parted to admit a young Ute woman bearing a battered tin plate heaped high with roast venison. She set it in front of him and stepped back.

Rubbing his hands in anticipation, Fargo dug in. As famished as he was, he forgot about the young woman, taking it for granted she had left until he smelled woodsmoke and looked up to find her kindling a fire.

"Thank you," Fargo said, and smiled to show his gratitude. He resumed eating and didn't stop until his gut was fit to burst. Wiping his greasy fingers on his buckskins, he leaned back, as content as he could be under the circumstances.

The young woman was still there, on her knees by the fire, her hands folded in her lap. When he looked at her, she bowed her head and made a few comments in the Ute tongue.

"I'm sorry. I don't speak your language." Fargo motioned at the flap. "You can go now."

The woman rose. But instead of leaving she came over and knelt in front of him. Again she made a comment.

"What is it you want?" Fargo asked.

She motioned to show she did not understand.

About to try again, Fargo could have slapped himself for being so stupid. Even if he didn't speak their tongue, he was fluent in the universal language of most mountain and plains tribes. He moved his hands and fingers to form, "Question? You want?"

She seemed nervous. Swallowing, she answered him, her slender hands flowing fluidly. "Nevava sent me."

"Thank him for the food," Fargo signed. "You can go now."

"Is there not more you want?"

"Sleep," Fargo answered.

"Before you sleep?"

Fargo couldn't think of anything and signed as much.

"What about me? I am yours to do with as you please."

16

Among some tribes it was customary to offer a visitor a woman for the night but the Utes were not one of them. Fargo wasn't quite sure why Nevava had done it. Not that long ago the warrior had threatened to cut his throat.

He sat staring at the lovely maiden on her knees in front of him, debating how to reply. He had never been one to refuse the attentions of an attractive member of the opposite sex but this was a special situation. On the one hand, he might insult the Utes by refusing. On the other, some of the Utes were bound to resent a white man sleeping with one of their own.

"Did you see what my fingers said?" the woman signed when he did not respond.

"Yes," Fargo signed, and thought of a way to back out without placing the blame on his shoulders. "Was this your idea or did Nevava send you? I will not do it if you are being made to do it against your will."

"I do this because I want to do it," she assured him.

"Why?" Fargo needed to know. A lot of Indian women wanted nothing to do with white men, just as a lot of white men looked down their noses at Indian women as being lowly "squaws."

"I had a man once. Broken Horn. He was a great warrior. He counted many coup on our enemies. A winter ago he led a raid against the Cheyenne. Nineteen of our warriors went. They stole many horses but the Cheyenne came after them. The youngest of our warriors was wounded. Broken Horn went to help him and the Cheyenne killed them both."

For a few years now, as Fargo was aware, there had been intense ill will between the Utes and the Cheyenne. Each tribe held a grievance against the other and neither was willing to smoke the pipe of peace.

"My heart has been heavy. I have been alone since," the woman signed. "I have not wanted to share my blankets with a man." She looked him in the eyes. Hers were wonderfully dark and more than a little frightened, like those of a doe about to give herself to a buck in rut. "Now I do."

Fargo was puzzled. She had danced around his question rather than answer it directly. He pegged her age in the early twenties. She had a high forehead and high cheekbones that blended into ripe, full lips and a pointed chin. "Why me?" he signed.

"We will never see one another again."

A woman after his own heart, Fargo mused. A woman who did not want a deeper attachment than the joining of their bodies. Or was there more to it? "What will your people think?" Some tribes treated women who slept with white men harshly, going so far as to scar them or banish them.

"I do not care."

"Will they hurt you?" Fargo tried to pin her down.

Her eyes narrowed and she answered his questions with one of her own. "What am I to you that you care what they do?"

Reaching out, Fargo stroked her cheek, then signed,

"You are beautiful. A flower in bloom. I would not see that flower harmed."

"This I did not expect. You are not as I was told whites would be."

"Do you have a name?"

"Utina," she said aloud, and pointed at his chest.

He had to say his name several times with her repeating it before she could pronounce it to her satisfaction. She then asked if there was anything else she could get him, but he patted his stomach and said no. On second thought, he signed that he would like a cup of coffee. He had used the last of his the night before when he and the twins caught up with Walikali. He was skeptical the Utes had any since they seldom traded with whites.

Utina was not gone long, and when she returned, she brought enough coffee in a clay bowl to make a potful. He asked where the Utes obtained it and she replied that they traded with a tribe that traded with whites but she did not say what the name of the tribe was. She was fascinated by his coffeepot, and turned it over and over in her hands. He filled it with water from the waterskin and showed her where to add the coffee grounds, then placed it on the fire to brew.

While they waited, Fargo asked whether she had heard any word about the two whites he had been with. She answered that the rest of Nevava's party was still in pursuit, the last she heard. He asked if the Utes had seen anything of a white-haired man on a striped horse and she signed that they had not.

The mention of the zebra prompted Utina to broach another subject. "How will you kill the striped long-tail cat if you find it?"

"Long-tail cat" was sign talk for mountain lion. "I do not know," Fargo admitted. A bow and arrows and a lance seemed puny compared to the raw might and unbridled ferocity of a tiger.

"The striped cat has killed many," Utina signed, and grew sad. "One of the children was my niece. A sweet, happy girl, whose laughter I will never hear again."

"I will do my best to make sure no more young ones lose their lives," Fargo pledged.

Utina appraised him a moment. "You are a good man, I think."

Fargo could end up a dead man before another day was out but he didn't bring that up. Instead, he checked the coffeepot. The fragrant aroma had filled the tepee. Soon it would be done. He fished in his saddlebags for his tin cup, then signed, "I hope you do not mind sharing."

"I have only tasted coffee once," Utina signed. "It made my thoughts rush through my head."

"Firewater makes your thoughts rush even more." The thought of whiskey made Fargo's throat go dry.

"Firewater is bad. Utes who drink it are no longer Utes. They want only to drink more and more."

"The same with some whites," Fargo told her.

Just then the coffeepot chirped, and Utina jumped. Fargo added a spoonful of sugar from his meager store, stirred it, and handed the tin cup to her. "Be careful. The cup is hot."

Utina did not hide her surprise at being allowed to drink first. Among more than a few tribes, the women always fed the men before sitting down to their own meals. She gingerly sipped, then grinned and smacked her lips.

Fargo admired the swell of her bosom against her doeskin dress and the enticing flair of her thighs. Her raven black hair was done up in pretty braids that framed her lovely face like the frames of a portrait. "My eyes could feast on you all night," he signed.

Coyly averting her gaze, Utina smiled. After taking a few more sips she handed the tin cup to him and sat so her legs were curled under her. "Your coffee is sweet like honey."

Fargo set down the cup to sign, "Women taste sweet too. I would like to learn how you taste."

Utina gasped. "Are all white men so bold?"

"Are all Ute women as ripe as wild plums?"

"You remind me of my husband when we would stand under a blanket, before he took me for his own."

It was the custom among some tribes for courting couples to stand under a blanket outside the tepee of the girl's parents. "Did you like that?"

Utina brightened. "I was never happier. Broken Horn loved me as no other. My heart hurts, I miss him so."

Placing a hand on her shoulder, Fargo gently squeezed. She kissed his hand, then looked away again, embarrassed by her show of affection. Unwilling to rush things, he signed, "Are you hungry?" and offered her a piece of venison.

She accepted it and took a tiny bite. Setting it in her lap, she signed, "Answer with a straight tongue. Are you this kind to everyone?"

"No," Fargo admitted. "Only with those I like." He let a few seconds go by. "I like you a lot."

Utina did not comment until she was done eating, and then, after daintily licking her fingers, she signed, "I like you, too. When I first saw you I thought you were handsome for a white man. But I did not know what you would be like inside."

"I can show you later." Fargo grinned and winked.

"Why not now?"

The next instant Utina was tight against his chest, her arms encircling his neck, her lips on his. Her hunger was undeniable. Fargo slid his tongue into her mouth and entwined it with hers in moist, velvety foreplay. Her body gave off more heat than the fire.

Utina was a Ute, and Ute ways were not white ways, but under her soft beaded dress she was a woman, all woman, and she responded to his caresses and kisses as any woman would. As her passion climbed, her lips covered his face and neck with small kisses while her hands molded to the muscles of his arms and legs. When he pulled back they were both breathing hard. He touched a braid, then signed, "Do you mind?"

Shaking her head, Utina helped him undo them, releasing her rich black hair to cascade over her shoulders and midway down her back. Fargo ran his fingers through it, savoring its soft silken luster. She took off his hat and repaid the favor.

Their lips locked anew. Fargo could feel the tension drain from her like water from a sieve. With each passing moment more of her inhibitions were melting away. When his left hand roamed down her back to her pert bottom, she sighed and ground her hips against him.

Fargo had long been of the opinion that there was nothing quite like the feel of finely cured buckskin. Silk was smoother but lacked the full-bodied texture. Wool was rough by comparison. Caressing doeskin was like caressing skin. He ran his hand down her legs to her calves and rubbed them in small circles.

Utina's breath fanned his neck. She lightly nipped at him, then inhaled an earlobe and lathered it with her tongue.

Ripples of pleasure tingled Fargo's spine. He slid her moccasins off without hindrance, then slowly glided his right hand up under her dress and along her leg to her knee. His brazenness caused her to stiffen. Rather than make her uncomfortable, he slid his hand back down. They had all night. Plenty of time to do it right.

Suddenly Utina lowered her cheek to his shoulder and nestled against him, her hands clutching his shirt. Fargo sensed she was trying to decide whether she would go through with it. It was one thing to agree to offer her body to a stranger, and a white man at that, and another to actually be in his arms. He was content to stroke her hair and massage her neck and not go any lower.

"I am sorry," Utina signed.

"No reason to be."

Utina sat back. "I did not think I would feel as I do. It scares me."

"I would never hurt you," Fargo signed.

"It is not that. I am scared because I like your touch much more than I expected. I am scared because you stir me in ways I have not been stirred in many moons."

"We can stop."

Utina developed an interest in the fire. "You will be gentle?" she signed after a while.

"If you want me to be."

"I do not know what I want. My head is in a whirl. You have kissed many women, I think. A man is not as good as you if all he has ever kissed are his horse and his dog."

Laughing, Fargo signed, "My lips have touched the lips of two or three women, yes."

"You speak with a forked tongue, white man." Utina grinned. "Twenty or thirty is more the truth."

If she only knew, Fargo thought.

Uttering a low moan, Utina threw herself at him and rained hot kisses all over his face. He cupped her breast, and for a few seconds she was completely still. Then, unleashing her innermost desires, she glued herself to him and delved her tongue deep into his mouth.

Fargo felt her hands hitching at his shirt. Rolling her onto her side, he stretched out and cupped her other breast. It brought a louder moan.

Now that she had made up her mind, Utina was insatiable. She could not get enough of him. Her hands were constantly in motion, seeking, tantalizing. She removed his empty holster and helped him shed his boots and spurs. She practically tore his shirt off, and when she beheld the layered muscles of his chest and stomach, she ran her hands over them in sheer delight, like a child playing with a new toy. In her glee she lavished kisses and tiny nibbles on his shoulders, his ribs, his stomach.

Fargo lay back and enjoyed it. He plied his fingers in her hair. He kneaded her shoulders and back. Eventually, hungry for more, he pulled her up to him and glued his lips to hers while molding his palms to her globes. A low cry rose in her throat and her nether mound brushed the growing bulge in his pants.

Time lost its meaning as they kissed and petted, adrift on an idyllic cloud of sensual sensations.

Fargo grew warm all over. His manhood acquired the temper of steel. He eased Utina onto her back and began to remove her dress. It was halfway up when her hand gripped his wrist and she looked searchingly into his eyes. Whatever she saw there pleased her because she smiled and let go and raised her arms over her head to make it easier for him to slip the dress all the way off.

Her body was superb. Nary an ounce of excess weight anywhere. She had been toned by hard work and the outdoors, sculpted by nature into the epitome of what a female body could be. Her arms were lean and supple, her legs twin willows, her waist narrow but her breasts full, and it was to them Fargo devoted his attention. Sucking a nipple, he rolled and stretched it with his tongue and teeth, and it hardened more than it already was.

Utina was sensitive there, and each time he flicked one nipple or the other, she mewed and squirmed. He rubbed her flat stomach and massaged the contours of her hips, then slid his hand to her inner thighs and stroked them from her knees to within a few inches of her core. But he did not touch her there. Not yet.

Not one to lie like a log and let the man do all the arousing, Utina caressed his neck, his chest, his arms. Her soft lips were never still.

Fargo licked a path from her breasts to her navel and rimmed it with the tip of his tongue. She cooed and arched her back. When he licked lower, to her downy thatch, her nails dug into his shoulders. He licked down her right leg to her inner thigh and inhaled the sweet earthy fragrance of her feminine fount. Then, as slowly as a snail, he licked across her thigh, and at the contact, her whole body came up off the ground and she cried out. His mouth found her swollen knob and fastened there.

Utina closed her eyes and moaned long and loud. She tossed her head from side to side. She smacked her lips again and again. Her legs parted wide and she pressed her hands down on the top of his head.

Fargo licked and flicked until his jaw was sore. He drank deep of her nectar, his hands either caressing and kneading her bottom or her breasts or running up and down her sides. She was as ready as any woman had ever been when he rose on his knees and positioned his pole for the plunge into her sheath. He buried himself, and her eyes snapped open and met his.

For long minutes on end Fargo stroked her. The feel of her inner walls contracting around his member was enough to send him soaring toward the brink. She had wrapped her legs firmly around his waist and met his thrusts with matching ardor. Harder and harder he stroked, faster and faster they went.

Then came the moment when the world around them faded and there was only the two of them and their ecstasy and nothing more. The moment when Fargo's whole body pulsed with pleasure.

Utina's own release was an earthquake in miniature. Her head arced back and she called out something in the Ute tongue, and the next second her body bucked and heaved like a mustang gone amok.

His hands on her hips, Fargo let himself go. Potent pleasure engulfed him, until that was all there was, the pleasure and only the pleasure. He rocked and rocked until he was spent and the pleasure began to fade, and with a sigh he collapsed on top of her.

Neither wanted to break the spell so they lay nestled in each other's arms. Fargo felt her fingers curling the short hairs at the back of his neck. She moved them slower and slower until they lay limp, and her heavy breathing told him she had fallen asleep.

Easing onto his shoulder, Fargo succumbed to sleep, himself. He was out for hours. Cold woke him up. It was the middle of the night and the fire had gone out. Grabbing his bedroll, he covered them with his blankets. Her shoulder made a fine pillow, and soon he was asleep again.

Fargo could not say what woke him up the next time. He lay quiet, listening to Utina's heavy breathing, sure it must be close to dawn. Soon Nevava would show up to start him on the hunt. He was debating whether to lie there a while longer or get up and get dressed when the decision was taken from his hands by a piercing scream.

Springing upright, Fargo quickly pulled his pants on and ran to the flap just as a second scream shattered the morning stillness, a scream of sheer fear from somewhere near the stream to the north of the village. He was not the only one who had heard.

Warriors were dashing from tepees, many with no more on than a breechclout. Excited shouts were exchanged. Nevava, armed with a bow and arrow, was leading a rush toward the stream.

Fargo hurried after them. Sunrise was not far off, and the sky had brightened enough to where everyone saw the striped nightmare that appeared on the brow of a low hill with the limp figure of a woman clamped in its viselike jaws.

To a man, the Utes came to a stop.

Lord Sydney dropped his latest victim, raised his huge whiskered head, and unleashed a thunderous roar that silenced every bird in the forest. Fangs bared, his tail whipping from side to side, Sydney was a living embodiment of bestial ferocity. He roared again, a blast that shook the very air. Then he sank his fangs into the woman, turned, and loped off.

Some warriors started after him but Nevava called them back. An angry dispute resulted but ended when the Utes realized Fargo was present.

Nevava came over, declaring, "Your time now, white-eye. Your trail fresh. Get ready."

Fargo didn't argue. Fate had smiled on him and given him a fresh trail to follow. He must set out right away. Conscious of the cold stares from the Utes he passed, he jogged to the tepee.

Utina was outside, fully dressed, her hair still loose over her shoulders. She followed him in and watched as he swiftly donned his clothes and strapped on his empty holster. "Thank you for last night," she signed.

"Be safe," Fargo signed by way of parting. Bending, he removed his spurs and stuck them in his saddlebags. He rolled up his bedroll, placed it beside his saddle, and turned. Utina was still there.

"I have learned much from you, He Who Tracks. I have learned not all whites have bad hearts. I have also learned why there are so many whites." Grinning, she departed.

Fargo had not heard any sounds outside so he was surprised when he pushed the flap open and discovered thirty to forty warriors waiting.

Nevava extended a bow and a quiver full of arrows. "Take these." In his other hand he had a bone-handled knife. "This too."

Another warrior stepped forward to offer him a lance. A third gave him a tomahawk. An older man offered a war club.

Fargo slid the knife under his belt on his right side, the tomahawk under his belt on the left. He slung the quiver across his back and the bow over his right shoulder. He liked the heft to the lance but declined the war club. To himself, aloud, he said, "I wish to hell there was a gun I could use."

"There is," Nevava said, and gestured.

A burly warrior brought a large deer hide pouch

and placed it at Fargo's feet. As Fargo squatted to open it, Nevava explained.

"A dozen winters ago white men attack us. We kill three, they kill five. Red Hawk, father of Walks Fast, take that from dead white. Help you kill ti-ger maybe."

The pouch contained an old Walker Colt, an ungodly big revolver several times as heavy as Fargo's own Colt. This one was one of the early percussion models used in the war with Mexico. Hardly anyone ever used Walkers anymore, not with so many newer and lighter models on the market.

Also in the pouch was a badly damaged box of paper cartridges, lead balls and percussion caps.

Fargo had fired a few percussion firearms so he knew how to load the Walker but he had little confidence in the powder or the caps. Misfires were common in the older models. There was no guarantee the pistol would work when he needed it to.

Done loading, Fargo tucked the Walker under the front of his belt and looked up to find half a dozen arrows trained on his chest. The Utes weren't taking any chances that he might try to fight his way free. He tied the pouch and attached it to his belt at the back, and stood. "I'm obliged for the hog leg."

Nevava was not as unfriendly as he had been the day before. "I am sorry this must be."

"Just take good care of my pinto if I don't make it back." Fargo was almost set. "How about some food to take along?"

At Nevava's command, another pouch was brought, bulging with pemmican and jerky. So was a waterskin. By the time Fargo headed north, he was twenty pounds heavier.

The Utes went with him a short distance, Nevava

in the lead. Twice the tall warrior went to say something but didn't.

At the stream Fargo paused. He scanned the ring of swarthy faces and saw one toward the back that stood out because it was the only face wearing a smile.

Utina touched two fingers to her lips, then held them toward him as if pressing them to his mouth.

"Are you ready?" Nevava asked.

"No. But I don't have any choice, do I?"

Nevava pointed at the hill Lord Sydney had disappeared over. "Begin hunt. And if ti-ger kill you, hope ti-ger kill quick so you not suffer."

"That makes two of us," Skye Fargo said.

17

Lord Sydney's attack on the woman who went to the stream early to fetch water had spelled misfortune for the woman but was a stroke of luck for Fargo. He had a fresh trail to follow. Barely twenty minutes had gone by since Lord Sydney melted into the forest when Fargo came to the brow of the hill and knelt to examine the tiger's pug marks.

A clear blood trail led into the brush. The tiger had dragged the woman as effortlessly as Fargo might drag a child's doll, over a log and through a thicket and on up a gully to a wooded knob midway up a mountain. An ideal spot from which to watch its back trail while it ate.

Based on what Dansay had told him, a tiger's habits were a lot like those of its North American counterpart, the mountain lion. Mountain lions preferred high ground from which they could see without being seen so it made sense tigers did too.

Unlimbering the heavy Walker Colt, Fargo cautiously climbed to the knob. A scarlet smear showed where the tiger had entered the stand. He avoided stepping on the blood as he crept into the trees, pausing after each step to strain his ears for sound. He had gone about thirty feet when he heard the crunch of teeth on bone, followed by an ominous growl that seemed to come from nowhere and everywhere at once. Either the tiger had spotted him or it had caught his scent. He waited, not knowing what it would do. Mountain lions usually ran when a human confronted them, but in that regard Lord Sydney wasn't like his counterparts; the tiger wasn't scared of humans, he sought them out to devour them.

Fargo would have given anything to have his Henry and the Colt. He warily advanced, trying not to make noise even though the tiger probably knew right where he was. He saw more blood, a lot more blood, and then a curled object that he did not recognize until he stood over it. It was the woman's severed left hand, her fingers bent inward. Lord Sydney had bitten clean through her wrist bone as easily as a lumberjack's saw bit through soft pine.

Yet another grisly sight to add to the long string Fargo had seen. He tore his gaze from the hand and moved on, skirting a close cluster of pines. A flesh-hued object lay partially hidden in weeds. Parting them, he frowned. He had found the woman's right leg, or what was left of it after the tiger got done chewing off the flesh on her thigh and calf.

Holding the Walker in both hands, Fargo penetrated deeper. Sweat broke out on his brow and trickled into his eyes but he ignored it. Lord Sydney could be anywhere. Any nook in the undergrowth, any dappled shadow, might erupt at any moment with hundreds of pounds of clawed fury.

At the far end of the stand lay the woman. Her skull had been crushed, half her face was missing, and her intestines were oozing from a cavity in her abdomen. The tiger had left even though it had not finished devouring her. Either it had run off—or it was stalking him.

Fargo figured Lord Sydney was circling him, as Dansay had warned it would. He put his back to a bole so the tiger couldn't get at him from behind and probed the brush for a telltale sign of orange and black. Try though he might, he couldn't spot it. Minutes crawled by, thick with tension. A quarter of an hour, then half an hour, and still Lord Sydney failed to appear.

Of all the carnivores in the wild, few possessed the patience of the big cats. Fargo didn't begin to wonder until a full hour had elapsed. Then, going on past the woman, he soon located pug marks pointing up the mountain.

Lord Sydney had not been stalking him, after all. Evidently tigers were as unpredictable as grizzlies.

The tracks wound through heavy pine and oak forest, in and out of ravines and gorges, always higher, always climbing. The tiger was not in any great hurry, proof it thought it had left him behind.

Fargo kept close watch on his back trail. If Lord Sydney did rush him from ambush, he would have time for one or two shots at the most. He must make each count.

Soon it became obvious Lord Sydney was taking a circuitous route westward. Fargo had an idea he knew where the Bengal tiger was headed; toward the tableland Nevava had pointed out to him. Maybe Lord Sydney had staked it out as his own territory and always returned there after paying the village a visit.

Fargo came to a little stream that fed into the larger stream below, and there, in the soft earth at the water's edge, were tracks left when Lord Sydney had crouched to drink. Fargo assumed the tiger would continue west from there. Instead, Lord Sydney had jumped the stream to the other side and gone up a dry wash to a rocky saddle overlooking a canyon. From there, instead of climbing higher, Lord Sydney had stalked lower, stopping frequently, as the tracks attested.

The tiger's behavior was puzzling. Fargo could make no sense of it until he realized the wind was blowing up out of the canyon, and that Lord Sydney was moving into it, as a cat did when it caught the scent of something that sparked its interest.

A narrow ridge of rock brought Fargo to the canyon floor and the shade of the many trees that lined the canyon wall. Lord Sydney had gone into the thickest of the vegetation, and Fargo had no hankering to follow him in. Instead, he stayed at the edge of the trees and slowly worked his way down the serpentine canyon until the acrid scent of woodsmoke brought him to a stop.

Someone was camped around the next bend.

Fargo figured it had to be Utes. Lord Sydney was stalking them, and they needed to be warned before the tiger struck. He ran toward the bend and was not quite there when he heard the last sound he expected to hear: a man was whistling the tune to a popular song, "Camptown Races."

His first thought was that it might be Richter and Proctor. Slowing, he cautiously moved to where he could see a small fire crackling under the spreading limbs of a giant oak near the far canyon wall. Beside it, merrily chewing on a leg of roast rabbit, was Thaddeus T. Thimbletree. The zebra was tied to a nearby bush, its head hung in exhaustion. Beyond them was the canyon mouth.

Thimbletree's clothes were the worse for wear, his bowler was gone, his leg still bandaged but the bandage was loose and drooped. Of special interest to Fargo were a revolver strapped around Thimbletree's ample waist and a Sharps that lay on the ground beside him. The same Sharps George Hagen had owned, the one Margaret pointed at him that day he stopped at their homestead. Cocking the Walker Colt, Fargo stepped into the open. "Go for a gun and you're a dead man."

Thimbletree looked up. Cheerfully grinning, he declared, "Why, Mr. Fargo! What a delightful surprise. I had imagined I was the only living soul within a hundred miles. Come and share my meal!"

Fargo warily walked toward the fire. The circus owner looked and acted like his old self but this was the same man who had murdered an unarmed family. The same son of a bitch who had shot Margaret. The thought sent raw fury raging through him and he came close to squeezing the trigger then and there, but didn't. "Don't try to draw or go for the Sharps," he warned.

"Why ever would I do that?" Thimbletree merrily responded, and took another hearty bite.

Fargo scanned the trees and thickets lining the canyon wall. "Lord Sydney is somewhere close by. I've been tracking him all morning."

"You don't say?" Thimbletree was not the least perturbed. "Well, if he shows up, we'll invite him to partake, too." He nodded at more rabbit meat sizzling on a trimmed branch used as a spit. "Help yourself."

"No, thanks."

"I'm positively famished." Thimbletree gazed toward the mouth of the canyon. "Marvelous country you have here, Mr. Fargo. Simply marvelous. I must remember to praise it to the king of Greece the next time I'm in Athens. He does so love to hunt, and these mountains are a hunter's heaven." Chortling, Thimbletree waved the rabbit leg. "Why, even I can bring down one of the forest's more fearsome denizens with a lucky shot now and then."

"This looks familiar." Fargo picked up the Sharps.

"I obtained it from those darling settlers, the Hagens. Salt of the earth, those people."

"You *killed* them." As Fargo said it, images of Margaret seared him like a red-hot fireplace poker and he started to lift the Walker to split Thimbletree's skull. Only by a supreme effort of will did he lower it again.

"Nonsense. What an outrageous accusation! I could no more harm them than I could crush a rose in bloom." Thimbletree beamed, chewing lustily.

Fargo's blood boiled in his veins like water in a pot. The Hagens had been kind, decent people. Their cold-blooded murders screamed to be avenged and he was just the one to do it. But as he stared down at Thimbletree a startling truth dawned—Thimbletree wasn't putting on an act. Thimbletree's childlike countenance, his frank and honest gaze, told Fargo that Thimbletree sincerely and truly believed he was innocent of the terrible deed.

There had to be an explanation. Fargo peered closer. He detected no hint of deceit, no sign that Thimbletree was shamming.

"Say, my good fellow, you haven't seen my circus anywhere around, have you?" Thimbletree asked. "I seem to have misplaced it. I remember being camped next to a river but haven't come across a river anywhere. And I really must get back. We have a lot of practicing to do before we arrive in Salt Lake City. Gandolpho and the rest must be in top form for their performances."

"You don't remember shooting him?"

Thimbletree laughed uproariously. "What an absurd notion! I've never shot anyone in my life, and I certainly wouldn't shoot a friend as dear to me as Anthony Gandolpho."

Once again, as amazing as it seemed, Fargo was sure Thimbletree believed what he was saying. Somehow, in some way Fargo could not quite fathom, Thimbletree had erased the awful memories from his mind as a slate was wiped clean of chalk. Fargo had heard that sometimes great shocks had that effect. "Do you remember why you left the circus?"

His brow knitting, Thimbletree scratched his chin, then shook his head. "How strange. No, I can't. The last I recall is sitting around the campfire with you and the twins and Walikali."

Fargo remembered that had been right before Richter and the outlaws appeared.

Thimbletree chuckled. "I daresay everyone will have a great laugh when they hear how I wandered off and became hopelessly lost. Thank goodness you came along when you did or I might well have ended up in Canada."

"Or been eaten by Lord Sydney."

Alarm stiffened Thimbletree. "You weren't jesting when you mentioned he is somewhere close at hand?"

Fargo indicated the thick undergrowth along the right-hand canyon wall. "He's in there right this moment, watching us."

Pushing off the ground, Thimbletree said, "We should leave immediately. A Bengal tiger is a most formidable beast. Get your horse and we'll be off."

"I'm on foot," Fargo revealed, then hefted the Sharps. "But don't worry. This can drop a buffalo or a grizzly. If Lord Sydney shows his whiskers, he's as good as dead."

"I'm afraid I have some rather disturbing news to impart," Thimbletree responded. "You see, for the life of me, I can't remember where I acquired that rifle. But I must not have been thinking clearly at the time because I don't have any ammunition for it. Bizarre, don't you think?"

Fargo checked, and swore. The Sharps was empty, which rendered it worthless except as a club. "How about that six-gun you're wearing?"

Thimbletree drew the revolver. "I don't know where I acquired this, either. It does have two bullets in it, if that's any help."

"Just two?" Fargo took it and checked the cylinder. It was a Remington, a .36 caliber, and while the slugs might drop a man, he doubted they would do more than annoy Lord Sydney.

"What do we do?" Thimbletree asked. "I have no desire to end my days in the bowels of a man-eater."

Fargo's stomach rumbled, reminding him how hungry he was. "I think I'll have some of that rabbit, after all. Finish your meal if you want."

"We can't remain here indefinitely, you know."

"I don't intend to." Facing the other canyon wall, Fargo sat and helped himself to a chunk of hot, succulent meat. He needed time to think, and he might as well fill his belly while he was at it.

Thimbletree sank down across from him. "Tasty fare, is it not?"

Images of the Hagens swirled before his mind's eye and Fargo fought down an impulse to jump up and hit him.

"I'm so happy to see you. I've been having the most terrible headaches the past few days, and at times I can hardly form a coherent thought."

Fargo wondered if the headaches were to blame for Thimbletree's memory loss. "You still spout bigger words than anyone I've ever met."

Thimbletree chortled. "Some things come naturally. I presume my penchant for a grandiose vocabulary is one of them." He paused. "So tell me? How is everyone? Have they missed me?"

To test his reaction, Fargo said, "Juliette sure does. She's worried sick something happened to you."

"Such a sweet woman." Thimbletree smiled. "You would never think it to look at her, covered as she is with all those outlandish tattoos, but she has the disposition of a saint. A kinder soul you will never meet."

Fargo detected no hint that Thimbletree was aware of Juliette's hideous death and the part Thimbletree played in it. He bit into the rabbit meat but suddenly wasn't all that hungry anymore.

"How did Lord Sydney escape, anyhow?" Thimbletree asked.

"Do you really want to know?" Fargo was all set to tell the whole sordid story, to relate every despicable act Thimbletree committed, but he swallowed his resentment and said, "Someone forgot to bar the door to his cage."

Thimbletree clucked irately. "I can't count how many times I've insisted on the utmost diligence in the performance of my staff's duties, but it goes in one ear and out the other. Why, once in Philadelphia, Leo's trainer turned his back for a few minutes and Leo took it into his leonine head to go see the Liberty

Bell. It's amazing how much panic a lion strolling down a city street can cause."

Fargo gave him the Remington. "Hold on to this. You might need it before the day is done."

"Against Lord Sydney? To be honest, I would rather flee than engage a man-eater in violent conflict."

"The tiger isn't your only worry. A Ute village isn't far from here, and they would as soon lift your hair as look at you."

"I saw some Indians a couple of days ago but fortunately they were riding the other way and didn't catch sight of me."

"You also have Judson Richter and Proctor on your heels. They want your chest and they won't rest until they get their hands on it."

"What chest would that be?"

Fargo glanced at him. It had to be some kind of joke. But again Thimbletree wore his sincerity on his sleeve. "The chest full of gold and gems. The chest you would do anything for. Including kill if you had to."

"Don't be preposterous. How many times must I repeat myself? I would never harm so much as a fly. And I'm afraid I can't recall ever owning a chest full of gold and gems. Would to God I did."

"You don't have a chest with you now?"

"Are your ears plugged with wax, my good fellow? All I have are the clothes on my back and my saddle."

Once again Fargo believed Thimbletree was telling the truth. But it begged the question: where *was* the chest with its fabulous hoard? Did Thimbletree lose it? Or bury it somewhere and later forget he ever owned it? They might be able to backtrack and locate the thing, but not until the man-eater was dealt with.

As if Lord Sydney had been waiting for that very cue, from the vegetation across the canyon came a guttural cough.

"My word!" Thimbletree jumped to his feet. "If I've heard that sound once, I've heard it a thousand times. That infernal demon is lying in wait over there for an opportunity to pounce."

An opportunity Fargo was determined not to give him. He rose, saying, "Time to light a shuck. Climb on that zebra of yours and we'll show Lord Sydney he's not as clever as he thinks he is." Gritty talk. To reach the canyon mouth, they must pass the undergrowth the tiger was in. A swift rush and Sydney would be on them.

Thimbletree's fear betrayed him. "Must we leave right this second? Why not wait. Maybe he'll go elsewhere."

Fargo doubted it. And he would rather go now, while it was light out, than try after dark. Selecting a burning brand, he declared, "Let's go."

An impenetrable veil of greens and browns hugged the canyon wall. Not so much as a bird stirred anywhere. Fargo swore he could feel Lord Sydney's eyes boring into them but it could just as well be his own nerves. He had left the useless Sharps by the fire and held the Walker Colt in a two-handed grip, the hammer cocked, his forefinger around the trigger.

The zebra's small hooves clinked on stones like the striking of a flint on steel. Fargo stayed slightly in front of it so that the man-eater must get past him to reach Thimbletree. Here he was, risking his life to protect a man he would not mind seeing dead in the dust. No one could ever say fate didn't have a sense of humor.

"I remember Dansay mentioning that tigers don't

like loud noise," Thimbletree remarked. "Maybe we can drive it off." He commenced yelling and whopping gibberish.

Fargo turned to tell Thimbletree to be quiet, when out of the corner of his eye he saw a flash of orange deep in the brush, moving away from them, not toward them. "Hurry out of the canyon," he directed. "I'll cover you."

The zebra didn't move. Fargo glanced back and saw Thimbletree with his mouth hanging open wide enough to catch flies, staring at the canyon entrance. He shifted toward it, and swore.

Two men on horseback blocked their escape. The riders and mounts were caked with dust and haggard with fatigue, but the men were grinning. They also had their rifles leveled.

"Who says prayers aren't answered?" Judson Richter said.

Proctor laughed. "Here we were, trailin' the fat one, and we find him with the one hombre in this world we most want to kill."

Thimbletree found his voice. "Where did you two gentlemen come from?"

Richter winked at Proctor. "Did you hear that? 'Gentlemen,' he calls us." Richter leaned on his saddle horn. "We've been after you for days, old man. Some Utes delayed us but we gave them the slip and circled around to pick up your trail."

"And here we are," Proctor gloated. "About to become two of the richest 'gentlemen' this side of the Divide."

Fargo didn't try to use the cumbersome Walker. He would be dead before he raised it halfway. "There's something you should know. He doesn't have the chest anymore."

"I thought you told me it was with the circus?" Proctor said. "If they don't have it and he doesn't have it, who in hell does?"

"We'll get to that soon enough," Judson Richter interjected, and took aim at Fargo. "Right now I want you to drop that hand cannon, mister. And the old man to shuck his six-shooter. Need I say to do it a mite slow?"

Only when the guns were on the ground did Richter and Proctor knee their horses closer. Richter looked Fargo up and down, and smirked. "What are you up to? Going Injun? You're totin' more redskin weapons than a damned war party."

"The Utes caught me," Fargo said.

"And you got away?" Richter leaped to the wrong conclusion. "That's right accommodatin' of you. Now I don't have to hunt you up after we're done with Thaddeus, here." His tone hardened. "Shed the bow and such. Then I want you and keg belly over by that fire I see yonder."

The skin on Fargo's back crawled as he disarmed. He imagined Lord Sydney crouched nearby, watching all that was going on. His hands in the air, he was marched at gunpoint over to the oak. Thimbletree was told to dismount and stood wringing his pudgy hands.

"Now then." Judson Richter had swung down but Proctor stayed on his horse. "Tell me again about not havin' the chest."

"What chest is this everyone keeps mentioning?" Thimbletree said. "And why is it so important?"

Richter jabbed him with the Spencer. "It won't work, old man. Playin' dumb won't stop us from whittlin' on you until you fess up where it's at. We've gone through too much to give up now."

"I honestly don't—" Thimbletree said, but got no further.

Judson Richter smashed the stock of his rifle into Thimbletree's face and Thimbletree dropped where he stood. The blow split his cheek and his upper lip, and blood flowed profusely.

"I'm not in the mood, old man, for more of your games. Start talkin' or start sufferin'."

Fargo felt little sympathy for Thimbletree but that didn't stop him from saying, "He's lost part of his memory. He doesn't remember anything after you and your men showed up at his camp until a day or so ago."

"Is that what he told you? And you believed him?" Richter laughed. "Hell, you're more gullible than my grandmother, and she was a Quaker." He jabbed Thimbletree with his toe. "Ready to talk?"

"If I knew, don't you think I would tell you and spare myself more pain?" Thimbletree placed both hands to his temples. "Please! You must listen! I've been having the most excruciating headaches."

"Is that a fact?" Richter said, and kicked Thimbletree in the gut. "My patience is wearin' thin, old man."

Fargo couldn't keep quiet. "What if he's telling the truth?"

"For an hombre who is supposed to be so savvy, you're as dumb as a stump." Richter kicked Thimbletree again. "Doesn't he know what you did for a livin' before you took up the circus life?"

"What are you talking about?" Fargo asked.

Judson Richter was enjoying himself. "This sack of lies was an actor. That's right. He made his livin' by pretendin' to be other people. Just as he's pretendin' not to know where his damn chest is." Richter trained the Spencer on Thimbletree. "I am plumb talked out, you old buzzard. Spill or bleed."

18

Skye Fargo had looked into Thimbletree's eyes and believed he was telling the truth when he claimed he couldn't remember anything that had happened. He still believed it when Richter and Proctor staked Thimbletree out spread-eagle. He believed it when Richter stood over Thimbletree and threatened to cut off Thimbletree's fingers one by one unless he fessed up. He believed it when Richter cut off the little finger on Thimbletree's left hand and Thimbletree howled and shrieked and thrashed.

Then Richter bent and gripped the bloody hand and announced, "One finger down, nine to go. And after them, I start on your toes." He lowered the bloody blade.

"Wait! Wait!" Thimbletree screeched. "I'll tell you! I'll tell you whatever you want to know! But for God's sake, don't cut off another one!"

"You were lyin' the whole time about losin' your memory, weren't you?" Judson Richter asked.

Thimbletree mutely nodded.

"Hear that?" Richter taunted Fargo. "I told you, didn't I? Just because I steal and kill doesn't mean I'm stupid. What's your excuse?"

Fargo had none. His instincts had let him down. He

prided himself on being able to read people as well as he read sign, but Thimbletree had hoodwinked him, and hoodwinked him good.

"Look at you," Richter said. "You look like you just swallowed horse piss." He laughed, and Proctor joined in.

Fargo was mad. Mad at himself for being so stupid. Mad at Judson Richter for rubbing his nose in it. But most of all, mad at Thimbletree. No one would suspect it to look at him, at that smiling, open face, that under the surface lurked a sidewinder as vicious as Richter, and far craftier.

Judson Richter gouged the tip of his knife into Thimbletree's chin. "So where's the chest?"

"In the grass behind the oak tree."

"You had better not be lyin' to me, you old coot, or so help me—" Richter ran behind the oak and cast from side to side. "Where? I don't see it?" Suddenly his face lit up like a lamp and he bent down, his hands outstretched. "Well, what do we have here?"

Proctor was giddy with glee. "Why, that thing must be worth a king's ransom all by its lonesome! Can you imagine what must be inside?"

Holding it in front of him with the reverence a man of the cloth might hold the Holy Grail, Judson Richter set the chest down, and hunkered. He undid the clasp and slowly raised the lid.

"Land sakes, Jud!" Proctor exclaimed. "Tell me I'm seein' what I think I'm seein'."

"You're seein' it," Richter confirmed, in as much awe as his friend. Dipping a hand in, he cupped a handful of coins and gems. "There's enough here to make a hundred men rich." He let them trickle through his fingers, then glanced at Thimbletree. "Why do you bother runnin' that stupid circus when you could be livin' high on the hog in a mansion somewhere?''

Thimbletree had tears in his eyes. "I wanted more. Another tour of Europe and Asia and think of how much I could have."

"You're an idiot, old man," Richter said. "You don't have the sense to quit when you're ahead."

Proctor bent down over the chest. "I want to touch them, too." Overcome by greed, he had taken his eyes, and his rifle, off Fargo.

"Let's take care of these two first," Richter said, and went to close the lid.

"Don't you dare," Proctor objected. "You're actin' like it's yours and not ours.We have a deal, remember? A fifty-fifty split."

"I haven't forgotten."

Neither noticed Fargo until he was on top of them. He slammed into Proctor, knocking Proctor, in turn, into Richter, and all three of them tumbled to the ground. He was the first one up. He landed a solid uppercut to Proctor's jaw as Proctor scrambled to his feet and it flattened the outlaw like a board, right on top of his partner.

Judson Richter was cursing like a madman. He had drawn his revolver but pinned as he was, he couldn't get a clear shot. "Get off me, you damned jackass!"

Proctor tried. Groggy from the punch, he got one hand under him.

Fargo drew back his right leg and kicked Proctor in the jaw. Down the gunman went, out cold. Pouncing on Richter's right arm, Fargo trapped it with his knee. Another moment, and he would wrest the revolver from the other scout's grasp. Then he heard Thimbletree screech his name and add something about the tiger.

242

Glancing over his shoulder, Fargo froze.

Lord Sydney was slinking toward them. The tiger was twenty feet beyond the horses and the zebra but he wasn't looking at them. Lord Sydney was staring at Thimbletree.

Richter cursed and tried to push Proctor off to free his trapped arm. Suddenly raising his head, he too, froze, blurting, "Where the hell did that thing come from?"

Ears laid back, his fangs bared, Lord Sydney halted.

"In God's name let me loose!" Thimbletree bawled, frantically tugging at the stakes to which his wrists were tied.

Fargo wasn't about to make any sudden moves with the man-killer so close. Proctor's rifle was a few yards away but it might as well be on the moon. He had seen how fast the tiger could move.

Lord Sydney started forward again, his body low to the ground, his muscles rippling under his sleek hide.

"Help me!" Thimbletree wailed.

One of the horses realized the tiger was there, whinnied, and bolted. The other horse and the zebra were quick to do the same. Lord Sydney let them go. He was only interested in Thimbletree.

That changed, though, when Proctor abruptly rolled off of Richter and stood, his back to the tiger. Drawing his revolver, he pointed it at Fargo, and declared, "I've got you now, you bastard!" He was unaware Lord Sydney was there but he didn't stay unaware long.

Lord Sydney roared and charged.

Proctor wheeled and turned to stone. He had a heartbeat or two in which to shoot but he squandered them. The man-eater flashed past and a swipe of a powerful forepaw sent him reeling.

Fargo was in motion the instant the tiger sprang. He didn't try for the rifle. It would be suicide. Unarmed, he was easy prey, and since he didn't believe in throwing his life away, he did the only thing he could. He whirled and raced to the oak. He thought he heard the tiger after him. A low limb offered salvation, and vaulting upward, he caught hold and swung up.

Proctor was on his side in the dirt, unmoving, scarlet rivulets trickling from claw marks in his cheek and chin.

Judson Richter was nowhere to be seen.

As for Lord Sydney, he was straddling Thaddeus T. Thimbletree. Snarling savagely, his tail lashing, he lowered his great head.

Thimbletree was panic-stricken. All he could do was gape at the bristling maw so close above him. "Please!" he mewed. "Please!"

Incredibly, instead of biting him, Lord Sydney licked Thimbletree's face. Fargo remembered how Leo had licked Dacia, but this wasn't the affectionate act of a tame animal. Dansay had told him that maneaters sometimes licked the skin off their victims, and that was exactly what Lord Sydney was doing. Again and again and again his sandpaper tongue darted out, again and again and again Thimbletree shrieked and cried, "It hurts! Stop! It hurts!"

Lord Sydney licked until Thimbletree's face was a wet, red mess, devoid of hair and skin. Then, like a kitten lapping milk, the tiger lapped the blood up, his eyes half shut in contentment.

Fargo heard a new sound that took a few seconds to register. Sydney was purring! It occurred to him that if he were going to slip away, he should do so now, while the man-eater was distracted.

Grabbing another limb, Fargo climbed around the

trunk to the far side of the tree. A glance assured him the tiger had no interest in him but that might change once he was on the ground. It was a chance he had to take. Thimbletree was blubbering and weeping loud enough to drown out what little noise Fargo made as he slowly lowered himself down. He made sure to stay close to the trunk.

The lapping and the purring and the blubbering went on unabated. Fargo peeked past the bole and Thimbletree spotted him.

"Help me! Please! You can't let me die like this!"

Yes, Fargo could. All he had to do was to think of Margaret. He turned to slip away.

"Wait!" Thimbletree screamed. Once more he strained against his bounds but he was too old and too weak to do more than anger Lord Sydney. The tiger stopped purring and growled.

Crouching, Fargo carefully backed from the oak, placing one foot behind the other.

"Save me!" Thimbletree pleaded. "You can have my gold! Do you hear? I want to live! I want to live!"

Fargo had gone far enough that he felt safe in circling toward the canyon mouth. To reach it he had to cross an open space, and when he was halfway across he glanced back.

Thimbletree was sobbing hysterically, his face a liquid red bubble, his legs jerking like those of a frog nailed to a board. "Please!" he screamed. "Please! Please! Please! Please!"

Snarling, Lord Sydney cuffed him and Thimbletree's cries died. With a loud crunch of teeth on bone, the tiger sheared his fangs into Thimbletree's shoulder.

To Fargo's right lay the Ute weapons given to him by Nevava and the other warriors. He looked at them and looked away and took another step, and stopped.

Fifteen more yards and he would reach the canyon mouth. Fifteen more yards and he would be safe.

Another bone crunched as Fargo ran to the pile and slung the quiver over his back. He reclaimed the knife, the tomahawk, the lance, the Walker Colt. Nocking an arrow to the ash bow, he walked toward the man-eater.

Lord Sydney had bitten Thimbletree's right arm clean off and a pool of blood was rapidly forming. Now the tiger was clawing through Thimbletree's jacket and shirt to get at the soft flesh underneath. Incredibly, Thimbletree was still alive, still crying and mumbling incoherently and trembling.

Placing the lance at his feet, Fargo planted himself, pulled the sinew string back to his right cheek, and sighted along the arrow, centering the barbed tip just behind the tiger's right front leg, trying for the heart or a lung. He was using the bow instead of the Walker Colt because he wasn't one hundred percent sure the Colt would fire. There was a moment when he almost changed his mind, when the folly of what he was attempting overrode his resolve. Then he thought of Juliette, and the Ute children, and he drew the string back an extra inch, steadied his arms, and let fly.

Lord Sydney's roar of pain shook the canyon walls. The tiger leaped straight into the air and came down with his paws spread wide. Twisting, Sydney bit at the feathered end of the shaft jutting from his ribs. When Sydney found he couldn't reach it, he voiced a series of roars, each more ferocious than the last.

Fargo had a second arrow nocked. The string twanged, the arrow flew true. This time the man-eater whirled and saw him and came at him like a bull gone berserk. He reached behind him, plucked a third arrow, notched it to the string, pulled the string back.

Lord Sydney was only twenty feet away when the shaft streaked from the bow. The shaft caught the great cat full in the chest and Sydney snapped around as if he had been jerked on the end of a rope. But in a twinkling he hurtled forward again.

Stooping, Fargo exchanged the bow for the lance. He barely got it as high as his hips when the tiger reached him. Lord Sydney tried to stop but had gained too much speed and it was hard to say which of them was more surprised when the man-eater ran onto the head of the lance, impaling himself and nearly bowling Fargo over.

Roaring hideously, Lord Sydney sprang back a dozen feet. The lance slipped from his body, leaving a gaping wound that poured blood. But the tiger did not appear the least bit fazed. Crouching, it tensed to spring.

Fargo braced the lance with both hands but he didn't wait for the tiger to charge him. *He* charged *it.* He thought Sydney would leap to one side and he was ready to bury the lance in the man-eater's body but the wily cat leaped into the air above the lance just as the lance was about to spear into him, twisted in midleap, and came down on Fargo's left, so close they almost brushed one another.

For a few moments they were eye to eye. Fargo was sure Lord Sydney would spring and tear him to pieces before he could stab with the lance. But once again the tiger proved how unpredictable the breed was by turning and racing for the trees, the feathered tips in Sydney's side bobbing up and down with each long, loping stride.

Dropping the lance, Fargo drew the Walker Colt, thumbing back the hammer as it cleared his belt. He aimed at the tiger's rippling shoulders and stroked the trigger but the only sound was a *click*. As he had suspected, the ammunition had gone unused for too long and the caps or the powder or both were defective. Even so, he cocked it again and squeezed the trigger, more out of frustration than the belief it would go off, and much to his surprise, it did. The Walker boomed like a cannon, its recoil as strong as the kick of a Missouri mule. He saw the slug raise a puff of dust a few feet to the right of the man-killer.

The next moment Lord Sydney reached the trees, and disappeared.

All Fargo had succeeded in doing was wounding him. Now the tiger was twice as dangerous. Fargo had to go after him before Sydney got too far, but not without a gun. The last he had seen of Proctor's rifle it was over near the fire, so that was where he bent his steps.

Proctor was still unconscious.

Thimbletree was shaking like an aspen leaf, the stump where his arm had been a jagged ruin. His face was worse, a hideous abomination leaking blood like a sieve. As Fargo's shadow fell across him, Thimbletree's eyes swiveled and a mouth without lips croaked sibilant sounds.

"I can't understand you," Fargo said, looking for the rifle. It wasn't where he remembered it being.

"Do it," Thimbletree said clearly.

"Do what?" Fargo noticed that Proctor's pearl-handled Colt was also missing.

"Finish me off."

Fargo stared at the bloody bubble. "No."

"You owe it to me. A favor from one human being to another human being."

"I don't owe you a damn thing," Fargo responded. He had been played for a fool for the last time. "You brought this on yourself. I hope you take days to die, and I hope you suffer like hell every damn minute."

"Like Juliette suffered when Lord Sydney tore her apart?" Thimbletree goaded.

"Go to hell."

"Like the girl Margaret must have suffered after I shot her in the barn and left her to die?"

Fargo's whole body quivered with rage. "For that you can lie there until you rot."

"I know you, Trailsman. I know you're a hellion but I also know you're a decent man at heart. Put me out of my misery or you'll never be able to live with yourself."

Fargo came close to stomping on Thimbletree's face until it spilt like a rotten pear. "Watch me," he said bitterly.

The mouth without lips smiled. "You don't deceive me. Unlike Richter, unlike me, you have limits. Lines you will not cross. Things you will never do."

"So?" Fargo was tired of arguing.

"You would never let a woman be ripped apart. You would never harm a child. You're too decent. I never thought I would, either, until something snapped deep inside of me. I'm not the man you first met. I'm his evil reflection."

"You're full of shit."

"I'm getting to you, aren't I? You realize that each of us has that same darkness deep inside. The only difference between us is that you've never let that darkness out. Now's your chance. For a few fleeting moments I want you to let loose your darkest desires. Maim me. Bleed me. Do me in."

"You're loco," Fargo said in disgust.

"You want to. You know you do. I saw it in your face when you surprised me at the fire. Why do you think I pretended to lose my memory? I could feel your hatred, feel your hunger to kill me."

Fargo turned to where the chest had been, but it was gone, too. He faced the weeds flanking the oak and immediately found it, cradled in the left arm of Judson Richter. In Richter's other hand, leveled at his stomach, was Proctor's rifle. "I thought you'd be long gone by now."

"And miss the heart-to-heart you two lunkheads were havin'? Not on your life." Richter's grin was as sadistic as ever. "I seem to recollect tellin' you to get rid of that hand cannon and the rest."

The Walker Colt, the knife, and the tomahawk made a pile at Fargo's feet.

"That's better." Judson Richter strolled toward him. "What's that old sayin'? Something about the third time is the charm?"

Fargo tensed to make a try for the Walker.

"Well, hoss, in case you can't count, this is the third time I've gotten the drop on you. And this time will be the last."

19

"Go ahead and pull the trigger," Fargo said. "Bring the Utes down on your head."

"There aren't any Utes on our trail this time. It's just you and me and faceless there."

"Maybe the Utes aren't still after you but they're still after me," Fargo bent the truth. "So shoot. I like the notion of your scalp hanging in a Ute lodge."

"You're bluffing," Richter said, but he glanced up the canyon and toward the canyon mouth.

"I only bluff at poker."

Judson Richter mulled that a bit. "Back up until I tell you to stop." To accent his demand he thumbed back the rifle's hammer.

Fargo took one step back after another until he had gone nearly ten feet.

"That's far enough." Richter stepped to the pile of Ute weapons, set down the chest, and picked up the tomahawk. Slashing the air, he sidled over to Thimbletree. "So did I hear right, old man? You want to be put out of your misery?"

"More than anything in the world," Thimbletree said. "You'll do that for me, Jud?"

"That's the first time you've ever called me by my first name," Richter said, and grinned. "I reckon it's hard to look down your nose at someone when you're flat on your back."

"Please, just do it and get it over with," Thimbletree urged. "Can't you see how much torment I'm in?"

"If you ask me, you're not in anywhere near enough." And with that, Judson Richter raised the tomahawk overhead and buried it in Thimbletree's groin.

A howl tore from the circus owner's throat and echoed off the high canyon walls. Thimbletree broke into convulsions and gibbered obscenely.

Chuckling, Richter left the tomahawk buried where it was and asked, "How much torment are you in now?"

It was doubtful Thimbletree heard. His eyes were rolling in his sockets and pink froth spewed from his mouth.

Richter returned to the pile. Covering Fargo, he tucked at the knees and wrapped his hand around the hilt of the knife.

"You're as low as they come," Fargo said.

"And damn proud of it." Richter nodded at the pathetic husk bound to the stakes. "You're just jealous because I did what you wanted to do but couldn't." Admiring the knife's long blade, he walked to where Proctor still lay.

"Him, too?"

"It's his own fault for being stupid enough to think I was willin' to share. If I didn't do it now, I'd do it later."

"He trusted you."

"I never trust anyone except the gent I see when I look in a mirror. He'd have been smart to do the same." Squatting, he held the blade to Proctor's throat. "One time I did a squaw this way. Damn near cut her head off by mistake." His hand moved and a red geyser spurted.

Proctor never moved, never made a sound.

Throwing the knife into the grass, Judson Richter retrieved the chest. "Now it's just you and me."

"If you expect me to be as easy as them, you're mistaken," Fargo promised him.

"Oh, I don't doubt for a minute you'd force me to shoot you out of sheer spite just so the Utes might hear," Richter said. "But I've got me a better idea."

Fargo waited.

"Catch," Richter said, and tossed the chest.

Taken off guard, Fargo almost dropped it. He shook it so the coins clinked and and commented, "Awful generous of you."

"Generous, hell. I need my hands free." Richter gripped the Spencer. "And with the horses gone, you're my beast of burden until we find them. Head out of the canyon. I'll be right behind you."

Fargo glanced at Thimbletree. His eyes had stopped rolling in his head and he had stopped shaking and was gazing at them in abject horror, his face seamed in agony. Somehow he was able to speak. "Surely you won't leave me in this condition."

"Surely we will," Richter said. "I figure it'll take you a good two to three days to die providin' that tiger doesn't get hungry. Be seein' you, old man." He touched his hat brim, and motioned.

Fargo never looked back, even when Thimbletree begged and wept.

"Did you ever hear such carryin' on?" Judson Richter remarked. "You won't hear me bawl like a baby when my time comes."

The horses and the zebra had fled into the woods below. Fargo hiked slowly until Richter snapped at him to pick up the pace. He racked his brain for a way to turn the tables but the other scout hung back, well out of reach.

Richter was in fine spirits. "Funny how life is sometimes. Nothin' worked out quite like I planned but I got what I wanted anyhow. And that's what counts."

"The circus people will report what you did when they reach Denver."

"Let them. I'm headin' east. I'll give myself a new name and start a new life." Richter paused. "I've given it a lot of thought and I'm going to call myself Arthur Hamilton. It has a fancy shine that will make folks sit up and take notice."

"A pig in a suit is still a pig."

Judson Richter chuckled. "You're tryin' to get me mad so I'll do something stupid and you can take the rifle from me. Keep at it and maybe it'll work."

Fargo constantly scoured the ground for a rock, a limb, anything. To keep Richter talking, he shook the chest so it jingled, then commented, "Without this money, the circus will go out of business."

"Hell, they're out of business anyway with the old skinflint dead. Not that I care one way or the other. I learned a long time ago that the only way to get ahead in this world is to take what you can and to hell with everyone else. It's coyote eat coyote, and me, I'm the trickiest coyote around."

Glancing over his shoulder to respond, Fargo glimpsed a moving patch of reddish-orange a hundred yards behind them. He did not let on that he had seen it. "Sooner or later what we do catches up to us."

Judson Richter snorted. "Listen to you. I swear, you should have been a preacher, the way you carry on. Our misdeeds only catch up with us if we're stupid enough to let them."

"We'll never think alike, you and I. I don't kill unless I have to."

"I never took you for the squeamish type," Richter baited him. "To me, killin' has always come as natural as breathin'. I never think about it. I just do it."

"Sort of like that tiger back there," Fargo said.

"Exactly. A tiger, a griz, a cougar, it's all the same to them. They kill because they have to, and that's that."

"Animals don't know any better." Fargo looked at Richter, or gave that impression, because he was really staring into the woods behind them. He didn't see Lord Sydney but he was sure the man-eater was still back there.

"And I should because I'm human and I'm supposed to have a conscience?" Richter sneered. "I've heard that silliness before. But the thing you don't seem to savvy is that not everyone thinks like you do. Some of us don't have a conscience and don't ever want one. We like ourselves just as we are."

In his wanderings Fargo had met a lot of men who thought no more of snuffing out a life than they did squashing a bug. "I savvy all right." It boiled down to choice. They were killers because they had chosen to be. Not that he could ever convince Richter. "I'm glad I'm not like you."

"You're a fine one to criticize," Richter said. "I've heard the stories about the men you've gunned down, the gals you've bedded. So don't be lookin' down your nose at me when you're no better."

Fargo had to keep him talking so he wouldn't realize the tiger was after them. "Sure I've killed, but not for the reasons you do."

"Killin' is killin'. Is a lawman who kills twenty badmen any better than a badman who has only killed five people?"

"You have a strange way of looking at things." Fargo wanted to glance back but it might arouse Richter's suspicions.

"No two people ever see things the same. What's important is how *I* see them, and I see myself wallowin' in luxury the rest of my days and you pushin' up tumbleweeds."

Further down, the forest thinned at the border of a high-country meadow, and Fargo spied another striped animal, the zebra, in the company of the two horses that ran off, grazing in the tall grass. Richter saw them, too.

"Well, lookee there. You're about to outlive your usefulness, and you know what that means."

Fargo passed a cluster of rocks but they weren't close enough to grab without taking a slug.

"Yes, sir," Richter said. "I'm going to enjoy buckin' you out in gore. The great Trailsman. The best scout alive. Able to track anyone or anything, anywhere anytime. I've always thought your reputation was a lot of hot air."

"Put down that rifle and we'll put it to the test."

"Like hell. I wasn't born in a turnip patch. I won't give you any more of a break than I'd give that tiger. One shot through the brain and your reputation dies with you."

The zebra had raised its head and was staring in their direction. Within moments the horses followed suit. The breeze was blowing toward them, and they were testing it with their nostrils.

The stock of Fargo's Henry jutted from one end of the bedroll on Proctor's mount. Fargo imagined his Colt and the Toothpick were rolled up inside, as well. If only he could get his hands on them, he thought.

But when he neared the tree line, all three animals snorted and wheeled and raced east.

"What the hell?" Judson Richter fumed. "Go after them! We can't let them get away."

The muzzle of Richter's rifle jammed into Fargo's spine so hard, he nearly fell. His first instinct was to whirl and cram the barrel down Richter's throat but he jogged after the horses. Richter was hollering for the animals to stop but they weren't about to listen. Unknown to Richter, the animals weren't fleeing because of them. They were running off because they had caught scent of the tiger.

"That's far enough," Judson Richter declared when they were almost to the other side of the meadow. "Damn stupid critters! What got into them?"

Fargo didn't answer.

"Usually my horse doesn't act up like that." Richter uttered a few choice cuss words. "Lucky for you though. You get to go on totin' that chest a while yet."

Little else was said over the course of the next hour as they hiked steadily lower through dense timber. The horses had galloped quite a distance before they slowed to a walk and were a mile or more ahead. Overtaking them before nightfall was out of the question, a fact that soured Richter's mood more than it already was. "I swear," he grumbled at one point, "if things ever went right, the shock would kill me. I don't much like the notion of havin' to keep an eye on you all night."

Fargo didn't mind at all. The longer they were together, the better the prospect of his gaining the upper hand.

"No, sir, I don't like it at all," Richter went on. He added ominously, "Maybe I'll have to carry the chest myself after a while."

Now and then Fargo felt the warmth of the sun on his back and shoulders as he threaded through the tall pines, but for the most part he walked in shadow and in silence, his footsteps muffled by the carpet of pine needles. Since he wouldn't put it past Richter to shoot him in the back, he kept one eye on him as much as he could.

The renegade was deep in thought, but what he was thinking about was anyone's guess. "This is far enough," he suddenly announced.

Fargo turned, the chest at his waist, the clasp facing him. "It's early yet to be stopping."

"Who said we were?" Richter reponded. "We're takin' a short rest, is all." He leaned against a tree and gestured at a log. "Take a seat, why don't you?"

Fargo preferred to stand but the rifle trained on his midriff discouraged debate. Sinking down, he contrived to hold the chest between his legs. "So you've finally decided to get it over with."

Richter grinned. "Nobody lives forever."

"That goes for you, too." Fargo pried the clasp open with his thumbnail, then cracked the lid open.

"Which one of us has his finger on the trigger and which one of us is sittin' there like a duck in a shootin' gallery?" Judson Richter gave voice to a vicious laugh. "Seems to me you've got it backwards."

"I never thought I'd end my days shot by a sack of scum too yellow to fight me man to man."

"Quick or slow? That's the question. Keep insultin' me and it sure as hell won't be quick."

Off in the pines a four-legged shadow materialized out of nothingness. Moving as silently as a ghost and avoiding stray sunbeams, the man-eater crept toward them.

"What if the Utes hear?" Fargo stalled.

"That dog won't hunt this time around. We've gone far enough I can risk it." Richter smiled. "Want me to let you in on a little secret? I've wanted to blow out your wick since the day we met. There's something about you that's always rubbed me wrong."

"Maybe it's because I take more baths than you," Fargo said.

Lord Sydney's hellish eyes were fixed on Judson Richter's back. Whenever Richter moved his head, however slightly, the tiger froze.

"Slow it is, then," Richter declared. "I'll start with your arms and legs, and once you're down, the crotch and the knees and the throat."

A few seconds more were all Fargo needed. "Strange, isn't it."

About to take a bead, Richter paused. "What is?"

Fargo saw the tiger crouch, saw the long tail stiffen and the ears lay back. "When we get up in the morning we never know if we'll still be alive at the end of the day."

"We all die sometime. You're lucky to have lasted as long as you have, as stupid as you are."

"I wasn't talking about me," Fargo said, and threw himself behind the log just as Lord Sydney roared and sprang.

Judson Richter spun, but he wasn't quite all the way around when the Bengal tiger smashed into him and bore him to the earth, pinning the Spencer under him. Then, as if venting pent-up rage, Lord Sydney tore into Richter in a berserk fury, ripping and rending and shredding, clawing through clothes and flesh, opening Richter up clear down to the bone, and in the process scattering ruptured chunks of internal organs every which way.

Fargo didn't stay to witness Richter's final few moments. On his hands and knees he crawled past a tree, then rose and ran. He looked back often to see if the man-eater was on his trail.

Fargo's sole hope was to get to the horses and get his hands on the Henry. But they were so far ahead it would take hours, hours his next glance showed he didn't have.

Lord Sydney was after him. The tiger was moving at a walk, as if confident it had all the time in the world.

Fargo ran flat out but he was only fooling himself. He flew past a boulder and under a white oak, and abruptly stopped. He had an idea, a crazy idea. Tearing off his hat, he glanced into the tree and moved to where the branches were thinnest. He placed his hat on the ground, ran to the lowest limb, and climbed with an urgency born of self-preservation. He climbed until he was over sixty feet above the ground and positioned himself on a limb so he was directly above his hat.

Seconds later Lord Sydney padded around the boulder and came to within a few yards of the oak. Halting, he stared at the hat.

Fargo didn't twitch, didn't hardly breathe. Dansay had told him tigers never looked up, but there was always a first time for everything.

The man-eater was sniffing the air. Bristling suspiciously, he stalked closer to the hat but not close enough.

Come on! Fargo thought. Just another couple of feet.

Lord Sydney looked right, he looked left. He padded to the hat and crouched and sniffed it.

Tucking his knees to his chest, Fargo let go. He narrowly missed two branches and then he was falling free. Straightening his legs, he locked his arms at his sides. Focused on the tiger's neck, he fell faster and faster. The tree became a blur. Instants before impact, the man-eater either sensed him or heard the rush of wind and glanced up.

It was as brutal as Fargo imagined it would be. His boots slammed into Lord Sydney's spine with a sharp *crack*. Then he was tumbling and the lower half of his body was pulsing with pain, and in his wild spill he struck something hard, another tree or a boulder, and the world spun and sparkled and he came close to passing out. Gradually the fireflies faded and the sky and the earth assumed their rightful places, and he looked toward the white oak and saw Lord Sydney on his stomach, his head bent at an unnatural angle.

"Damn," Fargo said aloud. "It worked."

He overtook the horses and the zebra shortly before sunset but only because they had stopped at a stream and were too tired to run off. The next morning he rode to the white oak. None of the animals would go anywhere near the tiger so he tied them to a pine and drew his Toothpick and set to work. It took over an hour to sever the head and when he was done, his arms were caked with blood and gore. He wrapped the trophy in a blanket and tied it on the least skittish of the horses.

Nothing had changed at the canyon. Thimbletree was alive but he did not seem to hear when Fargo rode up. He lay staring blankly at the sky and every so often tittering like the madman he had become.

Fargo gathered up the Ute weapons and the guns and left. He arrived at Nevava's village about midday and was perplexed to find it deserted. Drawing rein in the center of a circle, he shouted to bring the Utes from their tepees, but no one appeared.

Something else did, though. Something huge and

gray, trumpeting her pleasure. From on top of the elephant Walikali grinned down at him. "Greetings, bwana. Tembo has been so worried, I could not keep her from searching for you. We came to this place a while ago and all the people ran off."

"I wonder why," Fargo said as Tembo ran her trunk along his neck and down his back.

"Isn't that your horse hobbled over there?" Walikali asked, pointing at a lodge across the way.

Fargo galloped over. It was the lodge he had stayed in. His saddle and belongings were where he had left them, and as he saddled up, Walikali relayed the latest.

"The circus has arrived at the cabin and everyone awaits your return with great anticipation. We have little money and fear we will be stranded if Thaddeus does not come back. Your advice will be most welcome."

"Don't worry. You'll all be able to afford passage home," Fargo promised, imagining the looks on their faces when they saw the contents of the chest. Minus the five hundred dollars Thimbletree had offered him as payment for his tracking skills. As he recollected, Saint Louis was hosting a high-stakes poker game in a month or so. He aimed to sit in.

"Miss Dacia and Miss Cyrena asked me to say they are more anxious than anyone to see you again. They said you would understand why."

Skye Fargo smiled. He had a lot to look forward to.

No other series has this much historical action!

THE TRAILSMAN

Available wherever books are sold, or
to order call: 1-800-788-6262

SIGNET BOOKS

"A writer in the tradition of Louis L'Amour and
Zane Grey!" —*Huntsville Times*

National Bestselling Author
RALPH COMPTON